AF787631

STAR WARS™

THE HIGH REPUBLIC

SURVIVORS OF THE STORMWALL

TITAN MAGAZINES

STAR WARS

THE HIGH REPUBLIC

SURVIVORS OF THE STORMWALL

Adventures within the Occlusion Zone...

This volume features original fiction set during Phase III of *The High Republic*, chronicling the ongoing battle against the Nihil centuries prior to the fall and purge of the Jedi Order.

Following the destruction of Starlight Beacon and the expansion of Marchion Ro's galaxy-splitting Stormwall, the crew of the *Aurie*, a lone Republic Longbeam, find themselves lost in the Occlusion Zone. Meanwhile, a Jedi Padawan searches for a route through the impenetrable barrier.

Also included is a detailed summary of Phase III stories, and a discussion regarding the creation and legacy of the ambitious publishing initiative with authors Zoraida Córdova, Tessa Gratton, Lydia Kang, George Mann, Daniel José Older, Cavan Scott, Charles Soule, and Lucasfilm Publishing creative director, Michael Siglain.

Editor Christopher Cooper
Designers Dan Bura & David Colderley
Group Editor Jake Devine
Editorial Assistant Holly Smith
Art Director Oz Browne

TITAN EDITORIAL
Senior Creative Editor David Manley-Leach
Lead Creative Editor Phoebe Hedges
Editors Jonathan Wilkins & Louis Yamani
Assistant Editor Ibraheem Kazi
Designer Matt Bookman
Production Manager Jackie Flook
Production Controllers Kelly Fenlon & Caterina Falqui
Publicity Manager Will O'Mullane
Publicists Julia Oprzondek & Erina Shaughnessy
Direct Market Sales Coordinator Bryce Walker
Marketing and Advertisement Assistant Lauren Noding

Digital & Marketing Manager Jo Teather
Sales and Circulation Manager Steve Tothill
Head of Rights Iga Kaminska
Rights Executive Mary-Beth Prindezi
Head of Creative & Business Development Ducan Baizley
Publishing Directors Ricky Claydon & John Dziewiatkowski
Executive Vice President Andrew Sumner
Publishers Vivian Cheung & Nick Landau

DISTRIBUTION
U.S. Distribution: Penguin Random House
U.K. Distribution: MacMillan Distribution
Direct Sales Market: Lunar Distribution
General Inquiries: customerservice@titanpublishingusa.com

First edition: August 2026

Star Wars: The High Republic: Survivors of the Stormwall is published by Titan Magazines, a division of Titan Publishing Group Limited, 144 Southwark Street, London, SE1 0UP
Printed in China.
For sale in the U.S., Canada, U.K., and Eire

ISBN: 9781806184026

A CIP catalogue record for this title is available from the British Library.

10 9 8 7 6 5 4 3 2 1

Cover illustrations:
"Longbeam" Concept art by James Clyne

LUCASFILM EDITORIAL
Senior Editor Brett Rector
Creative Director Michael Siglain
Art Director Troy Alders
Story Group Leland Chee, Pablo Hidalgo, Matt Martin, Emily Shkoukani, and Kate Izquiero
Creative Art Manager Phil Szostak
Asset Group Chris Argyropoulos, Allison Bird, Jackey Cabrera, Elinor De La Torre, Gabrielle Levenson, Nick Miano, Bryce Pinkos, Sarah Williams
Special Thanks: Ryan Jalernpan, Kevin Pearl and Eugene Paraszczuk

TITAN MAGAZINES

DISNEY · LUCASFILM

Illustration by Jake Lunt Davies

Illustration by Jake Lunt Davies

STAR WARS THE HIGH REPUBLIC

CONTENTS

STAR WARS

THE HIGH REPUBLIC

CHRONICLES OF CORELLIA

"Heir Apparent"

By Alyssa Wong

The walls of the abandoned, derelict apartment building reeked of old, stale smoke. As Krix Kamerat climbed the fire-damaged stairs, the scent grew stronger with every ascending floor. By the time he reached the highest level, five stories up, the smell was thick enough to choke on.

What was left of the structure was scorched and peeling away in chunks. Pieces of the collapsed roof littered the stairs and filthy floor. Krix picked his way around them, heading for the last apartment down the hall. He ignored the CONDEMNED BY ORDER OF CORONET CITY notice scrawled on the door and sauntered inside.

A single lantern lit the tiny, makeshift interrogation room, its faulty power cell buzzing and flickering like glowflies trapped in a bottle. Fist-sized noise-dampening devices were placed in each corner of the room. A section of the floor by the far wall had caved in, creating a vast, yawning pit that stretched all the way down to the ground level, five stories below. A Togruta man wearing Nihil gear, a patchwork of scavenged metal and leather armor, sat in a broken chair at the center of the apartment. He wasn't cuffed or bound to it.

He didn't need to be.

A teenage Lucem boy in dark clothing sat on a crate across from him, leaning close to the man and cradling the Nihil's face in his hands. He was slim and unassuming, slightly younger than Krix, and his pale, semi-translucent skin—even paler than Krix's human skin—glimmered with strange, blue-tinted iridescence. A silver-hilted lightsaber hung from his belt. A Nihil gas mask rested on his other hip. His white hair was tucked behind his ear, exposing his face. He gazed directly into the Togruta's eyes as the man twisted and sobbed.

The Nihil was a large, bulky man with a powerful build and long white-and-blue-striped lekku. But his orange skin was ashen and sickly. Sweat poured down his face, staining his shirt, and his expression was wild with terror.

"It's alright," the Lucem boy said softly. "Just tell me what I want to know and this can end."

"He won't be telling you anything like that, Ruu," Krix said, leaning against the door frame. He couldn't keep the sneer off his face. "Look at him. He's barely conscious."

Ruu's gaze flickered toward Krix, and for a dizzying, sickening moment, Krix saw what the Togruta saw: Ruu's eyes were an endless black expanse, like the cold void of space. His myriad white pupils clustered and stretched into horrible holes; they seemed to ooze beyond the confines of his lower eyelids,

A single lantern lit the tiny, makeshift interrogation room, its faulty power cell buzzing and flickering.

dripping down his cheeks like molten wax and warping the air around his face. A wave of instinctive horror, disgust, and vertigo hit Krix, and his stomach lurched violently—

And then Ruu blinked and his eyes were normal again. His white pupils were small, speckling his black sclera like stars. "Where have you been?" he asked flatly. "You're late."

"Late's a matter of opinion," Krix said. He wiped his sweaty palms discreetly on his trousers. *Those karking Lucem eye tricks.* "I walked the building's perimeter. No one else is around."

"People think this area of Coronet City is haunted," Ruu said. He rarely spoke without his boss, Crash Ongwa, or her girlfriend, Svi'no Atchapat, present, but when he did, his voice was quiet and deliberate, as if every word cost him. "A deadly fire swept through the neighborhood a few years ago. Folks say that if you listen at night, you can still hear ghosts crying."

That was why they had chosen to hold the interrogation here. Even if the noise dampeners failed, no one would think twice about strange sounds coming from the building.

"I still can't believe your boss signed off on this operation," Krix said, walking toward Ruu. The burned, rotted floorboards creaked uneasily with each step. "It's a little brutal for her taste, isn't it? I didn't think she had it in her." He smirked. "But then you never thought she'd make you work with a Nihil, did you?"

Ruu's hand twitched toward the lightsaber on his belt.

Like many Jedi Padawans, Ruu had lost his master in a battle against the Nihil. *One less Force-using abomination in the world,* Krix thought with satisfaction. It was a shame Ruu hadn't died, too. But if his master was anything like the Jedi who had stolen away Krix's beloved Zeen—

Well. That Jedi had gotten what she deserved.

"You're very lucky," Ruu said. He rose to his feet, unfolding with lethal grace. Standing face-to-face, he was a hair taller than Krix, though not as broad in the shoulders. His voice was as soft as ever. "Crash asked me not to kill you as a favor. That's the only reason you're still breathing."

"You're always so obedient to her," Krix mocked. "Some Jedi lessons are hard to shake, huh?" He nodded at the Nihil man in the chair. "Let's not get distracted and forget why we're here. You've had your chance. It's my turn."

Krix dragged another discarded chair over, flipping it backward and setting it in front of the shivering prisoner. He sat and rested his elbows on the top rail. "Hello, Haakon Pav," Krix said pleasantly. "Do you know who I am?"

"Make him stop," Haakon muttered over and over, his breath short with panic. "Make him stop, make him stop, make him stop." His eyes were glassy and he didn't seem to register Krix's presence. ►

Krix felt a spike of fury–how *dare* this insignificant man ignore him?–and slammed the metal toe of his boot into the Togruta's leg. There was a *krak*! and the man screamed. The pain seemed to clear his head, though, and his awareness slowly returned. "Who... where am I?"

"Not important," Krix replied, flicking a bit of ash from his chair. "I'll ask again. Do you remember me, Haakon?"

Haakon struggled to find an answer, searching Krix's face for clues: hard green eyes, freckled skin, blond hair shaved on the sides. It clicked when he spotted the long scar running up Krix's cheek. "No, it can't be. But... you're dead," Haakon gasped. Krix hummed nonchalantly. "*Commander Krix Kamerat?*"

"That's right. I'm Krix Kamerat, Marchion Ro's chosen son and right-hand man." Krix smiled, bright and cruel. He flicked out his knife. "And you are going to tell me everything I want to hear."

Three days prior, a package arrived for Krix. It was a rectangular metal crate, neatly addressed and delivered to the doorstep of Crash's shipyard hideout. It reeked in the Corellian heat, a sickly, spoiled smell that clung to everything around it.

Krix clenched his fists and glared down at the crate. He didn't open it. Neither did Crash, who was perched on a nearby pile of cargo. They both knew what was inside.

"So much for your Nihil contacts," Crash drawled, flipping her close-cropped pink hair out of her face. She was a short young human woman in a white tank top and flight suit overalls. There was a clever, piercing gleam in her dark brown eyes, drawing attention away from the sleepless shadows under them. "All of your assassins have been second-rate. Guess you don't have as much clout as you thought you did."

"Of course I do," Krix hissed. Anger boiled under his skin. Crash always thought she was so *smart*. She ran a personal security company in Coronet City and thought that made her important, instead of a jumped-up little scurrier. She never gave him the respect he deserved. One day, he would enjoy making her pay for that. "The only reason you're even here is because of my connections–"

"No, the only reason *you're* here is because of your connections," Crash said flatly. "We broke you out of that Republic prison because you promised us Marchion Ro's head. So far, all of your grandstanding has gotten us nothing but four dead Nihil assassins in boxes. If you can't deliver, we can always put you right back where we found you."

Krix had no desire to return to the prison where he'd languished after Starlight Beacon, the space station that represented the Republic and Jedi's shining hopes, was blown from the sky in a brilliant Nihil tactical assault. Krix had been aboard the doomed vessel at the time, cleverly escaping the Jedi and playing a key part in destroying the station.

That was how he preferred to remember it. The truth was smaller than that–the indignity of being captured by Zeen and the Jedi, being trapped in a cell aboard Starlight, and a desperate escape–but Krix had no use for the truth. He carefully sanded down its edges and tucked it away in his head, building something better and grander in its place. *The Legend of Krix Kamerat.* Hero of the Nihil, scourge of the Jedi, the renegade who single-handedly sent Starlight Beacon crashing down into the sea. Marchion Ro's trusted right-hand man. His chosen son. His heir.

He repeated these things to himself and to anyone who would listen, knowing that repetition cemented words into reality. Anyone could create it. But Krix wasn't just anyone–he was *special*.

After Starlight, Krix remembered waking up twice: first, on the shore of Eiram, a brief moment of lucidity before being knocked unconscious, and then again in a Republic prison. He bided his time, certain that Marchion would send his Nihil to liberate him at any moment. But weeks stretched to months with no rescue in sight. It didn't make sense. Marchion had elevated him within the Nihil, so why hadn't he swooped in to take back his most loyal soldier? The thought chewed away at him.

By the time Crash had appeared, Krix's time in isolation had stoked his fury into obsession with Marchion's treachery and a desire for revenge. If she was wise, she would have killed him. Luckily, Crash was a fool. She thought he was one, too, and it was a part he was willing to play in order to manipulate her. Krix was happy to give her what she wanted–what they both wanted: the chance to murder Marchion Ro.

Of course, it ended up being more difficult in practice.

"Ruu," Crash said to the shadow behind her. The Lucem angled his head toward her, never taking his eyes off Krix. "Check the box?"

Ruu moved silently toward the crate. As he passed, their shoulders almost brushing, Krix felt a reflexive shudder of hatred. Every Jedi reminded him of Zeen, the Mikkian girl he'd grown up with, and her cruel betrayal. The way she hid her own Force affinity from him and joined the Jedi, discarding the values they had grown up with on Trymant IV. Discarding him.

Ruu crouched and opened the crate, peering inside. "They're in pieces," he said, his voice barely audible above the steady hum of machinery. "Just like the others. But...." He drew his lightsaber. The blue blade crackled to life, and with one swift motion, he sliced the crate's lid off. The heavy metal slab clanged to the ground. Ruu flipped it over with his boot, revealing a set of markings painted on its underside. "There's a message."

That got Crash's attention. She joined them, scanning the writing with her clever, sharp gaze. As she read, her shoulders tensed. "It's a message for you," she said, angling her chin at Krix. "From Marchion."

The message was brief, in the Eye's distinctive handwriting. Krix drew near, eagerly drinking in the words of his former mentor–the man he had spent the past several weeks trying

By the time Crash had appeared, Krix's time in isolation had stoked his fury into obsession with Marchion's treachery and a desire for revenge. If she was wise, she would have killed him.

to kill. But when he read them, his mouth flooded with hot, bitter rage.

I expected more from you, Krix.

Krix snarled, grabbing the lid and hurling it across the cargo hold. "That druk-eating karker!" He whirled on Crash and Ruu, looking for a target for his rage. "He knows where I am! That I'm the mastermind of this plan! I've sent Nihil from his inner circle to kill him, and he didn't even bother to send one back!"

"Technically he did send one back," Ruu muttered. He extended his arm toward the crate lid, using the Force to lift and drag it toward him. The lid settled back over the crate as if by its own will, sealing it shut. *Unnatural.* "Marchion's aware of what we're doing. He just doesn't care. You're not worth his time."

"Shut up," Krix growled. The stench of decay was seeping into his skin. He wanted to wrap his fingers around Ruu's neck and squeeze. The impulse itched behind his teeth. "You trash are below his notice, but I'm nothing like you. Maybe you don't understand it because Jedi are too weak to form bonds." He punctuated his words with a sneer. "You'll never understand what it's like to have a family."

Ruu went unnaturally still. His dark eyes glinted behind his pale ▸

hair. "If Marchion considered you family, he wouldn't have thrown you away and left you to rot," he said, his voice laced with contempt. "You keep calling yourself his son, but it sounds like you're barely an afterthought to him."

Krix lunged for his throat. His knuckles connected with Ruu's jaw, knocking the Lucem to the ground. Krix hit him again, each impact giving him a flash of white-hot, furious satisfaction. Then Ruu punched him in the stomach, knocking the breath from his lungs. Something wrapped around Krix's ribs, squeezing like a giant, invisible hand. Krix wheezed, his hands scrabbling at nothing as he was lifted into the air.

Ruu lay on his back, propped up on one elbow. His other hand was extended toward Krix, palm open. He curled his fingers, slowly and deliberately, and the pressure around Krix's ribs intensified. Ruu's lip was split and smeared with blue blood, and there was no mercy on his face.

"Enough!" Crash shouted. She stepped between them, grabbing Ruu's shoulder. "Put him down, Ruu!"

Awareness flooded back into Ruu's expression. The invisible pressure immediately vanished. Krix fell to the floor, gasping for air. Ruu pulled his hand back, his eyes darting toward it like he was holding a venomous snake. "Crash, I–I don't know what...." His voice trailed off. "Sorry."

"Get ahold of yourself," Crash said, keeping her voice low. Krix heard it anyway. "He's riling you up on purpose. You're better than this." Ruu nodded, gaze fixed on the ground. Crash turned toward Krix, jabbing a finger at him. "And you! I know what you're doing. If you keep antagonizing my crew, I'll kick you out of an airlock myself."

Awareness flooded back into Ruu's expression. The invisible pressure immediately vanished. Krix fell to the floor, gasping for air.

It grated on Krix, but he managed a smile that almost looked sincere. "Noted," he said.

Crash dragged her hand down her face. "This plan clearly isn't working. We'll have to find a different way to get to Marchion. The Stormwall has sealed off Republic space and trapped planets in Nihil territory behind its impenetrable borders. Only the Nihil can travel back and forth, finding a way across it is almost impossible. Corellia's on the outside and we can't reach Marchion when he passes through." She shook her head. "Krix, your Nihil contacts were already on the other side of the Stormwall, which is why we went with your plan in the first place. But even when your assassins made it onto Marchion's flagship, the Gaze Electric, well...."

They all looked at the crate.

My plan was perfect! Krix wanted to scream. *It only failed because other people were incompetent!* The assassins had been his former Nihil underlings. If they were alive, he'd kill them again for failing him.

He took a deep breath and collected himself. "You know what they say. If you want a job done right...."

"You do it yourself," Crash finished, regarding him like he was a particularly slow droid. "That is what we're trying to do here."

"No, we've been sending proxies. To kill Marchion, *we* need to go to the *Gaze Electric.*" Krix spread his arms gleefully. "The Stormwall is your biggest barrier. But if we can get the coordinates, then it stops being a problem."

He'd baited the hook, and Crash bit. "We could cross it any time we wanted," she realized. "Anyone from the Republic could." It was an opportunity too good to pass up and they both knew it. Still, she cocked her head suspiciously. "Where exactly do you plan to get this information?"

"I've been out of the game for a year," Krix admitted. "But one of my former Nihil rivals is stationed aboard the *Gaze Electric.*" Possibly Krix's last living Nihil contact aboard Marchion's ship, but one would be enough. "His name is Haakon Pav. Tall Togruta, loves sabacc almost as much as he loves betting on underground fights in Coronet City. I didn't try to recruit him for our previous mission because he hates me and he'd never make it past Marchion's bodyguard, but we don't need him to fight." He grinned unpleasantly. "In fact, it's better if he doesn't."

"You really think this guy knows the Stormwall coordinates?"

"That data is logged aboard the *Gaze Electric*. Haakon knows. If he claims he doesn't, we'll help him remember." Krix caught the way Crash and Ruu exchanged trepidatious glances. "It won't be pretty," he warned. "But do you want the coordinates or not?"

Crash hesitated. Ruu shook his head, barely. "Crash.... we've done a lot of things and hunted down a lot of Nihil, but this is different. If we go through with this, you're…"

"Do it," she told Krix, setting her shoulders. "And Ruu, I'm sending you too. I wouldn't trust Krix with a grocery list, much less info this important. Keep him in line, okay?"

Ruu clearly had reservations. That was happening more often, Krix noted; he trusted Crash with his life, but Crash's decision to rescue Krix had driven a wedge between them. It was a point of contention that they never settled. Their friendship was slowly fracturing under the weight of their disagreements. It was delightful to see, and Krix slyly aimed his jabs at its fissures, cracking it open further at every opportunity. Would today be the day they fell apart?

But no. Ruu did what he was told, as always. He nodded, wiping the smear of blood from his face.

"Great!" Krix said cheerfully, sliding his fool's mask back into place. He turned away with a lazy wave. "Glad that that's settled. Haakon should be in town to gamble away his credits in three days; he's not creative, but he's consistent. We'll snatch him then."

Krix disappeared back into the hideout, abandoning the crate and leaving the mess for the others to clean up.

It was laughably easy to lure Haakon back to Coronet City. It was even easier to lure him to the back room of his favorite casino. He wasn't expecting the needle that bit into his side, injecting him with a powerful sedative. The big man's knees buckled and his eyes rolled up. He never hit the ground; two pairs of arms caught him before he collapsed on the ugly, gaudy carpet.

They'd had three days to plan. And now that they had him, they had the perfect place to take him.

"Coordinates to pass through the Stormwall?" panted Haakon. He looked feverish, slumped and straining to hold himself up in his chair. The first few times Krix had cut him, he'd tried to lurch out of the chair to attack him, but Ruu hadn't let him. He had kept him pinned to his seat with the Force until Haakon finally stopped struggling. Now the eerie Lucem slowly circled both Nihil, dipping in and out of the lantern light. "Why do you want those?"

"Because I do," Krix said. He didn't need to explain himself to Haakon. The man was a flea, insignificant. He wouldn't make it out of this room anyway. "I'll keep asking you as many times as I need to. The faster you tell me, the faster we can be done."

There was a glimmer of their old enmity in Haakon's sneer. "Shouldn't you know a path already, if you're Marchion's right-hand man?" he asked. "Or maybe…" The man was piecing together a thought with startling lucidity. He wet his lips and smirked. "He doesn't know you're alive, does he?"

The back of Krix's neck heated. "I've been undercover," he snapped.

"On a special mission from Marchion himself. You wouldn't know about it."

"I don't think it exists," Haakon said. His smile stretched too wide. He was gloating. "Marchion has a new inner circle. His Ministers. His chosen ones. But you're not among them, because he cast you aside like yesterday's trash."

Krix lashed out, slicing at Haakon. "That's not true!" he snarled. The words cut deep, baring his greatest fear: that he was replaceable. Zeen had replaced him in her affections with a Jedi girl, Lula Talisola; now Marchion had replaced him with his Ministers, giving away the position that should be rightfully his. "You don't know anything!"

The situation was spinning out of control. No matter how many shallow gashes Krix made, Haakon kept laughing at him until the apartment echoed.

But Haakon's laughter dried up when a pair of pale hands rested softly on the back of his chair. Ruu stood behind him, leaning over the Nihil so he could look down into Haakon's face. "I would like to know the path," he said. His tone could be mistaken for gentleness. Krix knew better.

Ruu tilted the man's face up as Haakon began to shake. "Won't you tell me?"

This is my interrogation! Krix thought furiously, glaring at Ruu. *My operation, my intel!* He reached out and squeezed Haakon's arm, digging his fingers into one of the uglier cuts. Haakon screamed, breaking eye contact with Ruu, his attention snapping back to Krix. There, that was better.

Ruu's attention was on him, too, his bizarre black eyes filled with cold, cold stars.

"Stop wasting my time, you little worm," Krix hissed. In that moment, he wasn't sure which of them he was speaking to. "Give me what I deserve."

Every night, Krix's thoughts turned to Zeen. His Zeen. She haunted him like the most welcome ghost. He could conjure up her luminous pink skin, her playful Mikkian head tendrils tipped with purple, her sparkling brown eyes like fine-cut amber. They had been raised under the care of the Elders of the Path. The Elders didn't believe in families, but he and Zeen had always had each other. She was his past, present, and future. Falling in love with her had been natural.

And Zeen loved him, too. Of course she did. How could she not?

The last time he'd seen her, in that cell aboard Starlight Beacon, she told him he meant nothing to her.

Krix knew better. Zeen was in denial, seduced away by that young Jedi. The Force had corrupted her and twisted her into someone he didn't recognize. She refused to see reason. Instead of abandoning the Force as was good and right, Zeen turned to the Jedi and their poisonous teachings.

She deserved to die for rejecting him. But he was merciful. With Lula gone, Zeen would fall weeping into his arms. He imagined their reunion: her beautiful eyes filled with tears as she clung to him. "I was wrong," she would sob. "Of course I love you, and only you. I'm sorry about everything. I'll never use the Force again."

(The reality of Zeen didn't bear thinking about. In his dreams, she was perfect.)

Yes, Krix thought. His triumph was assured. His enemies would perish at his hand: Lula, who had gone down in flames with Starlight Beacon; Crash, who would choke on her mocking words; Ruu, who would be a pleasure to kill; Marchion's Ministers, who had supplanted him and would be supplanted in turn. Their scorn would burn to ash with their bodies. Marchion would acknowledge Krix's ambition and cunning, embrace him, and welcome him back into the fold. Zeen would look at Krix adoringly again, and the warm weight of Marchion Ro's approval would settle across his shoulders as he ascended to his rightful place. His most trusted Minister. The future chancellor, even.

"I'm proud of you," Marchion would say, and the world would realign into the shape that Krix knew it should be.

And if he couldn't have that, he would kill them. If Marchion turned away from him again, Krix would step over his corpse. If Zeen refused to live in his perfect world, then he would cast her aside.

The Stormwall coordinates were only the first step toward his destiny. The galaxy awaited, ready to be remade in his image. It was only a matter of time before it all belonged to him.

In the end, they got what they needed.

"That was pleasant," Krix said, wiping his blade clean on the knee of Haakon's trousers. The Togruta breathed shallowly, clinging to consciousness. It was almost impressive. "I'd say *'Let's do this again,'* but there won't be a next time for you."

Krix was familiar with the way that fear sparked into adrenaline, so he was ready when Haakon made one last, desperate lunge for him. But the man stopped, frozen in midair.

Ruu held his hand out with his fingers slightly bent, his face serene, almost blank. His split lip had torn open again. The lenses of the gas mask on his belt glinted. Krix had seen him cut down Nihil before during missions with Crash, but only and always wearing that mask. He wondered if this was what Ruu looked like when he killed.

Haakon twisted in the air, caught by the Force. Ruu moved his arm and Haakon moved with it until the Nihil was dangling over the giant, yawning pit in the floor. Haakon kicked desperately, babbling in terror until his words no longer made sense. His gaze caught on the silver-hilted lightsaber at Ruu's waist. "You're a Jedi?!" the man gasped. "You–you wouldn't drop me! You're better than this!"

Ruu considered him, head cocked slightly to one side. "No," he said, his quiet voice cutting deeper than Krix could with his blade. "The Jedi are better than me."

And he let go.

The Nihil plummeted, screaming, into the pit. Ruu was already moving before they heard the man hit the ground five stories below, stepping away and using the Force to gather the noise-dampeners in a floating cluster. He dropped them one by one into a bag by the door.

Krix clicked off the lantern and tucked it under his arm. The glass was still hot. "What are you going to tell Crash about what happened tonight?" he asked.

Ruu paused. "We got the coordinates," he said at last, scooping up the bag. When he glanced at Krix, there was barely anything recognizable left of the Jedi he once was. Instead, Krix recognized someone else: the person who had almost crushed his ribs with the Force, who would have kept squeezing if no one had interfered. "And he was just a Nihil. She doesn't need to know anything else."

Looking into Ruu's lightless eyes, Krix knew he'd already won.

"Come on, then," Krix said, hitting the button by the door and letting it slide open with a heavy *thunk*. He didn't bother hiding his savage, triumphant grin. The mask wasn't necessary anymore. "Let's go deliver the good news."

The night was quiet. No insects sang; no windows were lit. A lone streetlamp stood watch at the corner, casting a murky halo into the gloom. As two young men left the apartment building behind, their shadows stretched onward until they merged with the dark.

Krix clicked off the lantern and tucked it under his arm. The glass was still hot. "What are you going to tell Crash about what happened tonight?"

STAR WARS

THE HIGH REPUBLIC

CHRONICLES OF CORELLIA

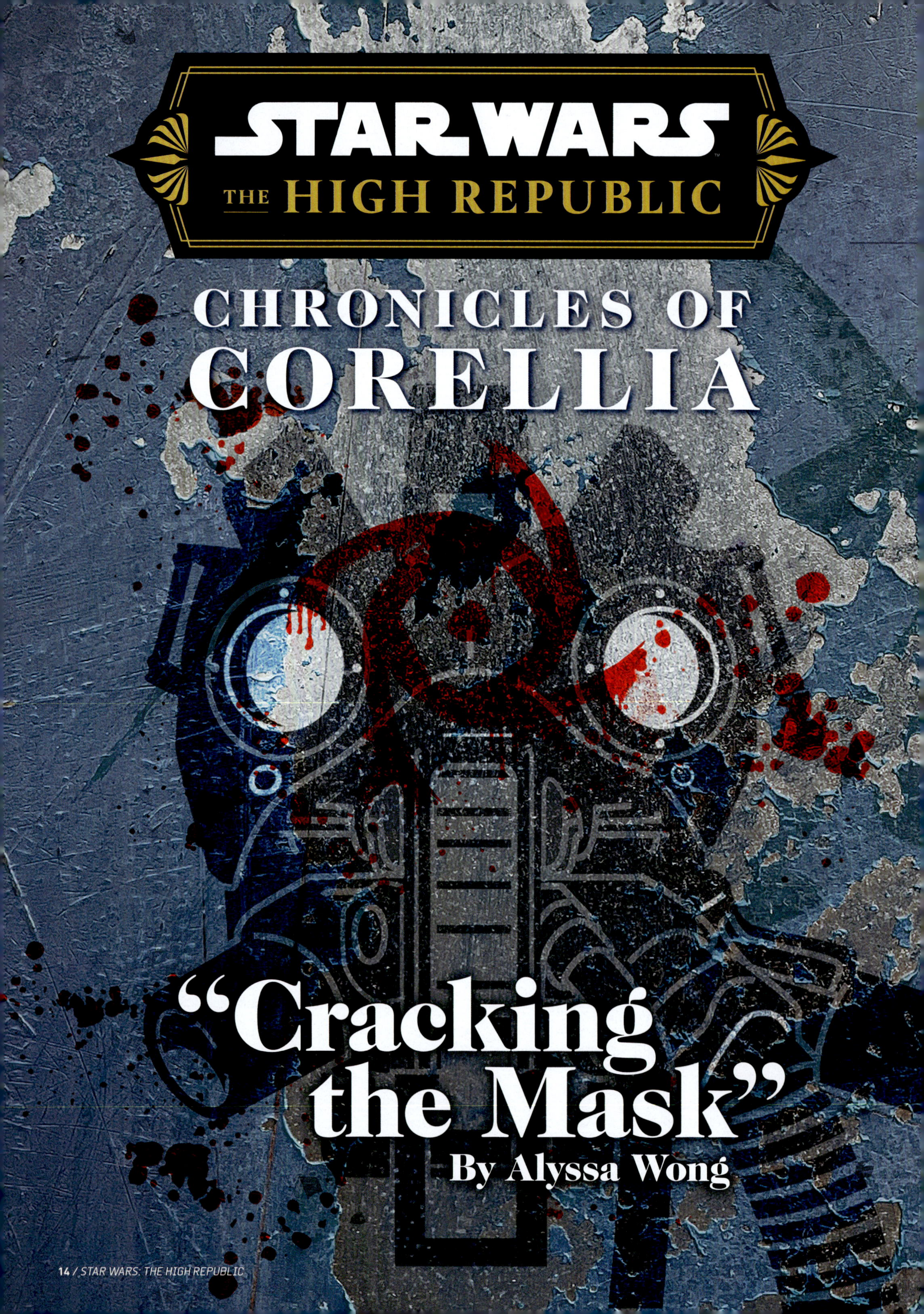

"Cracking the Mask"

By Alyssa Wong

Previously, in a galaxy far, far away....

Krix Kamerat and former Jedi Padawan Ruu came to blows during a mission to Corellia to secure coordinates from a Nihil prisoner, allowing safe passage through the Stormwall. Now, Ruu has been chosen for another mission, one that will make use of his unique and deadly skills.

Meanwhile, Driggit Parse has fallen in with the Nihil, but she has plans of her own.

Driggit Parse turned fifteen aboard a Nihil warship, deep in the heart of the Occlusion Zone. She didn't tell anyone. Instead, she curled up in the repurposed storeroom she had made her home, listening with her eyes closed to the little portable radio in her arms. She tucked her nose into her rust-colored scarf and pressed her headset close over her ears, letting the crackle of a familiar comms frequency seep into her heart.

"This is the Scarlet Skull broadcasting live from Valo!" Driggit knew his voice as well as she knew her own. After a decade of inseparable friendship, it was impossible to forget how Gavi sounded. How his voice brightened with passionate excitement when he talked about the Force, the slight whistle between his oversized front teeth when he laughed too loud. The persona of the Scarlet Skull, freedom fighter of Valo, couldn't hide those tells. "Thanks to our subterfuge, the Nihil still believe Lonisa City and the rest of the planet is under their control. But we've driven off the occupying enemy forces and taken back our home!"

With her eyes shut, Driggit could pretend he was sitting on the other end of her makeshift bed, his Jedi youngling robes pooled around him. Even though they weren't related by blood, Gavi and Driggit bore a strong resemblance to each other: they shared the same short, slight build, sandy-blonde hair, apocalypse of freckles, and light brown eyes. *Fake twins.* They'd spent years swapping places and outfits, mimicking each other's mannerisms, fooling whoever they could. But there were some gaps they couldn't bridge. Gavi was a Jedi, and Driggit was just a girl from Lonisa City. His impersonations of her couldn't mask the truth of him: he was protective and sweet, kind and fierce, powerful in the Force.

He was special, and she adored him for it. Her best friend, her favorite person, the epitome of everything a Jedi should be. Because she believed in him, she could believe in a future.

And then she had tried to kill him.

Driggit had already sacrificed everything else to protect Valo. Her innocence, her conscience, her faith. What was one more person? *Even if that person was Gavi?*

Gavi lay on the Innovator's *cold metal floor, fighting for breath and paralyzed by fear, affected by a nearby Nameless' Force-sapping aura. Driggit, now a Nihil, crouched over him, gripping her vibroblade as hard as she could to hide her trembling fingers. The knife's point hovered over Gavi's chest.*

He couldn't move, but he stared up at Driggit with betrayal in his eyes.

Don't look at me, she wanted to scream. Not like that, not ever again. Don't look at me like you know me. Don't look at me like you still believe in me. Don't look at me like you and the other Jedi didn't betray Lonisa City first by abandoning us to the Nihil.

Don't look at me like what I've become isn't your fault.

When the Nihil had taken over Lonisa City a year prior, they had taken everything, including Driggit. She bargained away her freedom to protect her family. The Jedi wouldn't protect them; instead, they had fled from the Nameless with their Padawans and younglings, leaving the Valoans to fend for themselves. Gavi and their mutual friends Kildo and Tep Tep hadn't even said goodbye, just vanished into the night without a word.

That evening, as her city burned, Driggit learned that the only future she could believe in was the one she created herself.

"You can live with yourself knowing that you did this to us?" Gavi whispered.

Driggit had already sacrificed everything else to protect Valo. Her innocence, her conscience, her faith. What was one more person?

Even if that person was Gavi?

"As long as the Scarlet Skulls are around, the Nihil are never going to leave Valo," she told him, bending close enough to say goodbye. Her crushing grief and hatred for the Nihil had seared a hole in her heart, and it was about to swallow up the last sliver of hope she'd kept for herself. "And I want these people off my planet."

Driggit brought the knife down.

The radio crackled again, Gavi's voice pulling her back to the present. He was alive.

He was *alive.*

And according to his broadcast, Lonisa City was safe. Driggit breathed, her chest loosening. That was everything she'd wanted.

Driggit curled tighter around her radio, burying her whole face in her scarf. She wore it every day, and behind the scorched scent of smoke and stale, recycled ship air, the fabric still smelled faintly like home. The floral perfume her mom used, the incense from the Jedi temple where Gavi had woven the scarf for her birthday long, long ago.

Don't think about him.

She'd left Lonisa City knowing that she couldn't ever return, and that if Gavi survived, she'd never be able to make things right between them again. That choice had ripped her to pieces. But Driggit knew she would do anything and become anything to destroy the Nihil, even if it destroyed ►

her in the process. Gavi was just a reminder of what she had lost. What was it the Jedi at the Valo temple always said? *"Let go of what burdens you. Feel the Force in everything around you, and release your attachments."*

It was wise advice. But Driggit was not a Jedi, never would be, and she held tight to Gavi's words over the radio. "Resistance isn't just possible–it's necessary," Gavi announced. "If we stop fighting, if we stop speaking out, then the Nihil win. So don't forget! Your voice is important. We are all Valo, and together, we can defeat them.

"And..." his voice trailed off. The veneer of the Scarlet Skull fell away, leaving only the boy. "And if you're out there, listening... happy birthday. Wherever in the galaxy you are."

Gavi cleared his throat, sliding back into the Scarlet Skull's voice. "Scarlet Skull, out!"

The broadcast cut out just as the door to Driggit's room slid open. The Warden, commander of the Nihil forces on Eriadu, filled the doorway. He was a huge alien man with tawny-colored fur, a mouth full of circular rows of teeth, and claw-tipped fingers. He wore cruelty like he owned it. "There you are, Driggit," he said. His voice was low and grating, with a strange, rumbling purr at its core. His eyes fell upon her radio. "Listening to anything interesting?"

Driggit slipped off her headset, subtly flicking the radio dials to a random frequency. "Nothing new from Eriadu," she said. "I've been scanning local broadcasts to pick up information, but no luck. What do you need, boss?"

The Warden glanced around the storeroom, which was scattered with blankets, tools, and an assortment of scavenged items. "We have beds aboard the ship," he said. The *Star Hopper* had been a Jedi educational vessel, equipped with dorms for Padawans and teachers.

"I don't like people watching me sleep," Driggit retorted. She shoved the radio under her pillow. "So what is it?"

"Come with me, little lieutenant," was all he said. The Warden led her to his war room, a converted Jedi classroom now covered in maps and diagrams knife-scored into the walls. His other lieutenants awaited them, eyes sliding judgmentally over her. They were adults, seasoned marauders, and Driggit knew

The broadcast cut out just as the door to Driggit's room slid open. The Warden, commander of the Nihil forces on Eriadu, filled the doorway. "There you are, Driggit," he said. "Listening to anything interesting?"

what they saw when they looked at her: a child, fangless and soft, with the Warden's inexplicable favor.

She didn't mind. In fact, she counted on that impression. Their envy made them weak.

"Now," the Warden said, activating the holoprojector at the central table. A blue hologram of a space station appeared in the air in front of him. "I've heard that another Nihil faction led by Grend Semant has stumbled upon quite the find. They've taken over Frander's hidden depot, a workshop run by a genius Lasat shipbuilder. He's developing a special project that could change the face of aerial battles... and could secure our control of Eriadu." He pointed a claw at the holo. The face of a purple-skinned, six-horned Theelin with bright red hair, a set of wicked scars across his face, and one tattered ear appeared next to the station. "Grend Semant does not share. Neither do I. I want the ship he's having Frander build. Who of you will get it for me?"

The discussion devolved into a shouted argument, but Driggit cut through it by sinking her vibroblade into the tabletop. "Send me," she said, cold and quiet. "I'm the right choice."

"Can you even see over the controls to pilot a ship?" one of the others sneered.

"Anyone can steal a ship," she replied, bored. It was an affect she'd learned from a former companion, an arrogant teenage Umbaran scientist named Niv Drendow Apruk. During their time together, Driggit had carefully cultivated his trust and dependence on her, studied him like one of his own experiments, and coaxed a wealth of confidential information about the Nihil out of him. They'd been separated before she could learn everything, but that boy did love to talk. Slipping his mannerisms on like a coat was easy. "There's something much more valuable on that station."

The other lieutenants muttered, but the Warden looked pleased. "Oh?"

Driggit grinned. This time, it was the Warden's expression mirrored back at him. "I'm going to get you the schematics."

The Force was a storm. It hadn't always been for Ruu; throughout his whole life, its presence felt like the weather–sometimes bright and warm like the sun on his skin, sometimes guiding him like a playful wind. It was alive, almost tangible. Ruu was quiet, painfully shy, and bad with people, but the Force never judged him for it. It didn't care that he struggled with words, both spoken and read, and that linking letters together was so stressful it sometimes felt impossible. The Force was with him, as it was with every Jedi at the Corellian temple, and with everything in the entire galaxy. It was as dependable as the muggy Coronet City heat and the rainstorms that followed. As a youngling and Padawan, Ruu would lie on the temple floor and let the Force settle over him like humidity, or wander the city with his master, Conithr, following the Force as it flowed and soared like thermals.

But these days, the Force never settled. It boiled in him, like dark heavy clouds rolling across the sky. It was the promise of thunder and violent monsoons. No peace, no rest, only inevitable, powerful movement.

During moments like these, Ruu wished he could ask Master Conithr for advice. But she was gone, having sacrificed herself to win a battle against the Nihil a year ago, and he was alone with no answers and no guidance, no longer a Jedi at all. What he had instead was a growing headache as he argued with Crash Ongwa.

"It has to be you," Crash told him. The short human young woman looked as ragged as Ruu felt, but her dark-brown eyes were steely with conviction. She wore a sleeveless shirt under an old set of flight suit overalls, and her arms were folded over her chest. "Everyone else in this crew is easily recognizable. Yes, you're the only Lucem on the team, but you wear a Nihil mask on missions, so no one's seen your face."

"Yeah, but they all pretty much wear masks ," Ruu argued. His voice was quiet but heated. They'd been going around in circles for nearly an hour. The rest of Crash's Corellia-based personal protection company had slowly filtered out of the main room of their new Eriadu City base. "Infiltrating a Nihil squad–pretending to be one of them–"

The idea of it made the Force churn within him.

"I know it would be difficult for you," Crash said, gentling her voice. *She didn't know at all*, Ruu thought. If she did, she wouldn't be asking him to do it. "But I need someone who can get the job done, rescue Frander, and do a lot of damage if the situation calls for it."

You need a killer, Ruu thought, sick. The worst part was that she wasn't wrong.

"You're my best choice for this infiltration and rescue mission. You're my only choice." Crash scrubbed her hand through her cropped pink hair. She looked apologetic and pained. "If there was any other way, or anyone else I could send, I would. We have access codes to cross the Stormwall thanks to *Krix Kamerat*," she spat the former Nihil commander's name, "but I don't know how long they'll be active."

"And you trust his information? The last time you trusted Krix, he moved the Stormwall over Eriadu!" Ruu snapped. "Everyone on this planet is trapped in Nihil Space now!"

"I know that!" Crash shouted back. There were deep lines under her eyes that hadn't been there a year ago, worn into her skin by guilt. "I know I karked up, okay? But look, you worked with him to get that intel. I don't trust him, but I trust you."

Krix Kamerat. Ruu had never told Crash the details of how he and Krix had extracted those access codes from a Nihil prisoner. Now Krix was gone, thank the Force, and Ruu alone carried the secret of that awful interrogation. What scared Ruu the most about the memory of that night wasn't how he had killed the Nihil prisoner, lifting him into the air with the Force and dropping him five stories to his death–it was the way Ruu had felt no guilt or sympathy, just cold satisfaction.

It had felt *right*.

"I don't like who this is turning me into," he whispered.

Crash hesitated, then moved forward and wrapped him in a hug. She was so confident and strident that it was easy to forget she was only nineteen, a few years older than him. "I know," she said, almost as quiet. "I'm sorry."

They both knew it didn't matter.

I would do anything for you, Ruu wanted to tell her. The words tangled up inside him, unable to push their way out. *Please don't ask me to do this.*

"I'll let you know when I'm done," he said instead, scooping up his Nihil gas mask and hooking it onto his belt next to his silver-hilted lightsaber.

He didn't look at her as he left.

Ruu had never told Crash the details of how he and Krix had extracted those access codes from a Nihil prisoner. Now Krix was gone, thank the Force, and Ruu alone carried the secret of that awful interrogation.

Frander's hidden depot was a marvel, if one liked junk and chaos. It was a small space station converted into a shipyard and workshop, filled with old scrap, pieces of vehicles in various stages of being dissected or assembled–Driggit wasn't sure which–and black-market parts. Luckily, she was small, so it was easy for her to slide through gaps in the mechanical tangle and duck under overhangs of dangerously stacked sets of landing gear.

The toe of her boot caught on a loose strut brace, emitting a soft *clang*! Driggit flinched and froze, but when no one came to investigate, she moved on.

A loud argument echoed from the large open hangar door to her right, but Driggit's line of sight was blocked by half of a badly burned starfighter–too damaged to identify the model–and the hangar wasn't her intended destination. Instead, she weaved through the junk until she found what she was looking for: an equally messy desk, several meters long and covered in chalk scribbles. As she drew closer, she recognized the shapes as ship designs in progress. Several were badly smudged, but one looked fresh: it looked like an enormous drill, made to rip through the hulls of other starfighters. The chassis was surrounded by a brace of bulky artillery, patchworked together Nihil-style, which didn't seem to fit with the rest of the design.

Was this the ship the Warden was after?

Driggit turned to the large, bulky computer perched on the desk. It looked as old and weathered as some pieces in the shop–a workhorse of a machine built for durability rather than style. Slicing into Frander's database was easier than she'd expected. Scanning the contents, she found what she was looking for: meticulously detailed schematics.

Dismayed, Driggit realized that the ▸

list of files was nearly endless. "Did this guy keep every draft of every design from the past ten centuries?" she muttered. Luckily, the newer ones were better labeled. And… there! She spotted one marked with "Grend Semant" and a recent date. When she opened it, a nearby holoprojector popped up an image of the artillery-loaded drill ship. *Perfect.*

She fished out the datastick hanging from a cord around her neck. Copying the file would be quick, and then she could get out of here, fast and easy.

The moment the green bar filled up onscreen, indicating the download was complete, Driggit yanked the datastick out of the computer. She was slipping it back over her head when a hand grabbed the back of her scarf, pulling it tightly around her neck. She choked.

"Say, Frander," called the purple-skinned Theelin towering over her. He had several long scars across his face and one tattered ear. He smiled down at her, tightening his grip. "Did you know you have womp rats?"

"Master Conithr? Why do we call lightsabers peacekeeping tools? Aren't they weapons?"

Conithr hummed in response, shifting into the next stance with her green lightsaber held low in front of her. She looked at home in the Corellian temple's training room. Her thick blonde braid swung behind her, reaching almost to her waist. Ruu was amazed that she hadn't accidentally cut it off with a misplaced lightsaber swing. "They are," she replied. "Sometimes we must use weapons to protect those who cannot protect themselves. But they can also be tools. Can you think of any such instance, Padawan Ruu?"

In Eriadu City, Ruu dropped out of the darkness and landed neatly on the balcony of Emple Ortok's apartment. Emple, a tall human man, gaped at him. "Who the hell are you?" the Nihil demanded.

Ruu activated his lightsaber, the glow of its blue blade reflecting off of his own Nihil gas mask. "Tonight, I'm you," he said, and struck.

Ruu had just changed his name a few weeks prior, and hearing his new name–his real name–made him light up inside. When he'd shyly told Conithr, "I'm a boy and my name is Ruu," the Force warmed him like sunshine, matching Conithr's welcoming smile. Now he tried to copy her stance, following along with her movements. His blue lightsaber wavered a bit as he adjusted his footing. "Um, I think… cutting through a door to save someone who's trapped?"

"Very good." She nudged his boot with her own, adjusting his stance even more. "And another?"

Ruu pocketed Emple Ortok's identification card. He left the dead man on the balcony of his untouched apartment and headed west toward a public shipyard. Ortok's identification got him into the man's private vessel, a small, sleek ship built for one. As he took to the sky, the lights of Eriadu City dropped away, and he readied himself for the next step. When a voice over his comms growled something unintelligible over the choppy connection, Ruu entered Krix's access codes. "Requesting permission to cross the Stormwall," he said. It wasn't a good imitation of Ortok's voice, but Ruu passed safely through.

Crash had provided coordinates to Frander's depot, and one hyperspace leap later, the station blinked into view before Ruu. A cluster of other Nihil ships were converging on the location as well. "I've got competition," Ruu murmured. The Force hummed within him, eager. His lightsaber felt like a live wire in its holster. "All right."

"Clearing debris after a disaster? Chopping it into smaller pieces so it can be moved?"

"Also, good. Next stance, Ruu." Conithr stepped forward, bringing her lightsaber up to block an imaginary attack. He mimicked her at half speed, trying to get the movements just right. She winked at him, her sharp red eyeliner flashing in the sun. "That's right. Shift your wrist down a few degrees. One more example, please?"

"Lighting up the dark if we're searching for a missing person?"

"Well done! See? There are many uses for lightsabers. Not just violence."

There were almost twenty Nihil sneaking through the junk maze in

"Who the hell are you?" the Nihil demanded. Ruu activated his lightsaber, the glow of its blue blade reflecting off of his own Nihil gas mask. "Tonight, I'm you," he said, and struck.

Frander's depot, heading toward the hangar. By the time they were halfway there, only fifteen were present. The loud, angry voices echoing through the building masked the sound of Ruu's lightsaber punching through flesh and armor, and he caught each body on the way down to muffle their drop. Fifteen became twelve.

They shouldn't have split up, he thought.

And then, viciously, *They shouldn't have been Nihil.*

Ruu chewed his lip, letting his lightsaber dip. "But what if… what if I have to fight and hurt someone?" he asked softly. "And what if I can't?" He stared at the hilt of his lightsaber in dismay. "Would that make me a bad Jedi?"

Conithr ruffled Ruu's long white hair. "No, Padawan Ruu, that makes you compassionate. Being a Jedi isn't about who can fly a Vector the fastest or fight best with lightsabers. It's about treating people with kindness, because everyone is part of the Force, and the Force is part of everyone."

She parried Ruu's lightsaber suddenly, knocking it out of his hand and into the air. Conithr caught it effortlessly, deactivating hers as well. She sat on the stone floor and patted the spot next to her, inviting him to join her. When he did, she rolled both of their lightsabers across the ground out of reach. "Your lightsaber isn't your greatest tool–your compassion is," she told him. "Never lose that heart, Ruu. That's what will make you a great Jedi."

With each death, Ruu felt the Nihil's lives flicker out in the Force, like pops of static. He thought of the sweet smell of petrichor, and kept moving.

Only eight Nihil reached the hangar entrance, and their shock and fear made it clear that they didn't know what happened to the others. Ruu ducked behind a shelled-out Vector, waiting for his next chance to strike. But then his prey was surrounded, held at blaster-point by another pack of Nihil marauders. Each member of this new group had a slash of purple paint across their scavenged patchwork armor, right below the blue Nihil eye symbol. They moved as a team–or a squad, Ruu realized. Former soldiers turned pirates, perhaps, or a group of mercenaries who'd thrown their lot in with the Nihil.

A huge black ship loomed behind them. Its entire front half was a massive, brutal-looking drill; Ruu caught his breath, recognizing it instantly. A *Spiral*-class Viz-Core Eviscerator, built to shred other ships apart. They'd been banned for more than a century after the Battle of Jedha. But here was one now in the hands of the Nihil, modified with a brace of bulky cannons and a fan of jagged metal spears. It wasn't quite finished yet, but it looked close.

A familiar-looking, green-eyed Lasat stood in front of the ship, arguing with a tall, scarred Theelin. "I'm telling you, Grend," the Lasat snarled, his striped purple fur bristling, "this thing's an abomination. Even if I could build you more, I wouldn't." That must be Frander, the shipbuilder Ruu had come to rescue.

"And I'm telling you that you *will*," drawled the Theelin, thumbing the blaster at his hip. The slashes of paint on his armor matched the scars on his face, and the easy, violent authority in his voice marked him as the mercenaries' leader. "Do it fast, Frander–I've already caught the competition trying to steal your trade secrets."

He shoved a human teenage girl forward. She was small and wiry, with blunt-cut, sandy-blonde hair and the start of a nasty bruise on her cheekbone. Her hands were cuffed in front of her. Ruu thought she was another hostage until he spotted the hook-beaked Nihil mask clipped to her belt.

Grend dipped a finger under the Nihil girl's scarf and drew out a thin leather cord with a datastick attached. With a brisk yank, he snapped the cord from her neck. The girl hissed in pain. "She found the schematic for the new Eviscerator. Unfortunately for her, this datastick isn't going anywhere. Who sent you to steal this from me, little womp rat?"

A huge black ship loomed behind them. Its entire front half was a massive, brutal-looking drill; Ruu caught his breath, recognizing it instantly.

Ruu's gaze darted from the datastick to the Eviscerator, then to Frander. This had become more than a rescue mission. If the Nihil–from any of these warring factions–could manufacture Eviscerators, the consequences would be deadly. He had to destroy the ship. But if the Nihil got away with the schematics or Frander, then they'd be able to recreate them. Which meant that the datastick was a liability…

…And so was Frander.

Light, he didn't know what to do.

The Force roiled within him, urging him to action. Look, it seemed to whisper. Ruu realized that everyone was standing close to the ship: Frander Grend with the datastick, and the other Nihil. If Ruu detonated the ship now, it was unlikely that they would all survive the explosion. An ugly, neat solution to an impossible problem.

Conithr would urge him to choose compassion. But what was more compassionate: saving an innocent life at the cost of thousands of potential casualties? Or sacrificing one to save the many?

Make your choice, demanded the storm.

Ruu did.

He slipped, unnoticed, past the arguing Nihil and into one of the gaps in the Eviscerator's hull. The hyperdrive engine, notoriously fickle and volatile in earlier models, was sealed away behind thick metal paneling, deep in the ship's guts. Ruu drew his lightsaber and activated the blade, piercing through the vehicle's inner wall. "Just like cutting through a door." Conithr was right; sometimes a lightsaber was a weapon, sometimes it was a tool. *Today*, Ruu thought as he lined the hyperdrive with thermal charges, *it was both*.

Ruu slid back out of the ship, disappearing behind the walls of scrap. As soon as he was clear, he wrapped his hand around the detonator in his jacket pocket and pressed the button.

A bright flicker of orange light in her periphery was the only warning Driggit had before the drill ship exploded, but it was enough. She snatched the datastick from Grend Semant and flung herself away from him, rolling behind a heavy, angular slab cut from a shipping freighter. A split second later, the concussive wave of sound and heat rammed into her shelter. She curled into a tight ball around the datastick, desperately praying for survival.

Deadly shrapnel rained down through the workshop, slamming against the shipping freighter. People were screaming. Driggit smelled burning hair.

She hoped it was Grend Semant.

Driggit lay still, playing dead, even after the last bits of metal stopped clattering overhead. She planned to wait until any other survivors left to make her escape, but then she heard an unmistakable sound: the bristling shriek of a lightsaber.

She clambered to her feet, grimacing at all the new cuts and bruises, and ▸

peered around the edge of her shelter. A lean, sharp figure in dark clothes and a Nihil mask lunged through the workshop, a blue lightsaber singing in his hands. He was protecting the Lasat, who was pressed against a far wall. He used a Jedi's weapon, but he didn't fight with the elegant grace of any Jedi Driggit knew from the Valo temple.

He fought like a monster. He tore through the remaining Nihil, hurling himself at them and swinging his lightsaber with the full momentum of his body. The force of his blows left behind deep gashes in the floor. Driggit's eyes widened as he cut down one of Grend's Nihil, slicing a nearby speeder in half in the process.

An arm wrapped around Driggit's neck from behind, cutting off her air. "Gotcha," hissed Grend. He was scorched and bleeding badly, but very much alive. "Give me the datastick–"

Driggit twisted like an eel, thrashing around in his grip until she could sink her teeth deep into his arm. He howled, letting go. She rammed her elbow into his stomach as hard as she could. When he doubled over, she leaped on him from behind and looped the short tether between her cuffs across his throat.

As Grend choked, fingers scrabbling at the tether, Driggit braced her feet on his lower back and pulled with all of her might. "This is for slamming my face into a desk," she snarled. The Theelin's struggles slowed, and he finally went limp. Driggit kept the cord tight against his throat for an extra fifteen seconds, just in case, before letting him slump to the ground.

When she stood up, the Nihil-Jedi was watching her.

"You," he said, his quiet, calm voice distorted eerily through his mask. He sounded like he was in a dream. He cocked his head and moved toward her. His lightsaber burned in the air like a brand. "You're the one who stole the Eviscerator schematics."

Driggit backed up, painfully aware that she was unarmed and her hands were still cuffed. "Yeah? And which Jedi did you kill so you could steal that lightsaber?" she sneered. Void below, it was the same color as Gavi's.

The Nihil-Jedi paused, taken aback. Driggit seized her chance and ran, snatching Grend Semant's blaster from his body as she went. She knew she couldn't outrun the Nihil-Jedi on the ground, but the hangar walls were supported by vertical iron girders. If there was one thing she was certain she could do quickly, it was climb.

Driggit used the loop between her cuffs to haul herself up the girder, finding the tiniest hand- and footholds. She could hear the Nihil-Jedi behind her. But she was faster than him. By the time he made it to the vertical crossbeam near the hangar's soaring roof, Driggit was already on the other side, putting as much distance between them as possible. Except, she realized, there was nowhere else to go.

The Nihil-Jedi paused, taken aback. Driggit seized her chance and ran, snatching Grend Semant's blaster from his body as she went.

"All I want is the datastick," the Nihil-Jedi said. He walked across the beam, perfectly balanced, approaching with his lightsaber drawn.

Driggit clutched the datastick in her left fist. Grend's blaster was in her right. "You don't seem the type to leave behind survivors," she said. When the Nihil-Jedi inclined his head, she glanced down at the Lasat far, far below. "Except for them. You care about this," she lifted the datastick, "and you care about him. So if you could only have one, which would you choose?"

The Nihil-Jedi glanced down sharply, realizing what Driggit already had: that the hangar's east wall wasn't actually a wall at all, but a pair of airlock doors.

"I'd pick now," Driggit said, clinging to the beam with all her might and raising her blaster. She shot the airlock control panel. The doors opened, and the contents of Frander's hidden depot were sucked into space.

Choose.

The schematics were so close. Ruu could reach out and take them if he wanted to, and leave the Nihil girl to her fate. Or he could reach out with the Force and save Frander, who was being dragged rapidly toward the airlock doors. If he did, though, the Nihil girl would escape with the schematics.

"If you could only have one, which would you choose?"

The schematics was the *right* answer. It was the obvious trade-off. And if the only shipbuilder who knew how to recreate them died, then wasn't that the best choice for the galaxy?

But what did *he* want? Who did *he* want to become?

The Force was a storm, and Ruu stood at its eye. For a moment, he and the Force were one, and all he felt was peace.

He chose, and reached out.

Frander froze in midair, only a meter from the open airlock. Ruu held onto him with the Force, fighting the pull of the vacuum. "Can you fix the airlock controls?" he yelled. Frander nodded frantically. Ruu gripped the beam below, struggling to stay balanced as debris rocketed past him. He swung his hand out, maneuvering Frander toward the panel. The Lasat's hands flew over the device, connecting wires and hitting the button on the side of the control panel.

The airlock doors slid closed. Frander collapsed, and Ruu nearly did too. He sagged on the beam, closing his eyes and looking inward.

The Force was no longer a tempest. It had calmed to a strong but gentle breeze, soothing like the smell of wet dirt.

When Ruu opened his eyes, the Nihil girl and her datastick were gone. But looking at Frander, slightly battered but alive, Ruu couldn't make himself regret his decision.

"Let's get you back to Corellia," he said.

That evening in Eriadu City, Driggit waited outside an ornate metal fence, gingerly touching the bruise on her face. It was starting to swell in earnest.

"Kark star, Driggit. What happened to you?" Emelsine Tarkin climbed over the fence surrounding her family's estate, landing on her feet right next to Driggit. She had long, dark hair, sweeping eyelashes, and a constellation of three perfect moles dotting her face. Her sly green eyes usually sparkled with mischief, but now it was just concern.

"Lost a fight against a desk," Driggit said. She batted Emelsine's hand away when the youngest Tarkin daughter–fifteen years old, just like Driggit–reached out to touch her bruise.

"The desk won, clearly," Emelsine said, persisting. Her fingers were cool against Driggit's skin; she tried not to wince and failed.

"Maybe. But I fought a desk and a Nihil-Jedi today–"

"Sorry, a *what*?"

Driggit wasn't sure what he'd been, other than terrifying. He hadn't seemed much older than her, though. It made sense, in an unfortunate way, that there were other kids just as warped by the war as she was. No one was untouched by it. Not even Emelsine, whose family tried to keep her cloistered away from the conflict while they ran Eriadu's political battlefield. All it had done was make Emelsine more determined to help fight back against the Nihil.

Their friendship was unlikely, but mutually beneficial: they met once a week to trade information, with Driggit passing Nihil intel to Emelsine for the Eriaduan resistance. Undermining the Warden by selling out his secrets was rewarding enough; Driggit hadn't wanted anything else. After the first month, though, their meetings had transformed from a business arrangement into something genuine.

"Don't worry about it. Anyway, I got something good." Driggit held out the datastick, pulling it back when Emelsine reached for it. "Which I'll share with you *if* you do me a favor."

Emelsine smirked. Her nose crinkled in a cute and distracting way. "I'm listening."

The Force was a storm, and Ruu stood at its eye. For a moment, he and the Force were one, and all he felt was peace. He chose, and reached out.

"These are schematics for a very dangerous ship. If the Warden gets them, he will build a fleet of them." Driggit dropped the datastick in Emelsine's waiting palm. "I want you to make me a sabotaged copy of the design to deliver to the Warden tonight. He'll have his fleet… with adjustments."

Emelsine winked. "Any requests?"

"I like fireworks," Driggit said idly. She pushed away from the fence as Emelsine began to scale it. "I'll see you later to pick up the new schematics."

By the time the sky darkened completely, Driggit had the datastick back in her pocket. As she left the Tarkin Estate, a cold wind blew down the street, ruffling her scarf. She followed it, letting it guide her through Eriadu City until the breeze died down. She sat on the lip of a nearby stone fountain, wrapping her scarf around her shoulders to ward off the chill. The material was warm and soft, the last piece of Valo–and Gavi–she couldn't bear to part with.

Her face was bruised and her body ached, but for the first time in a long time, she could feel beyond the grief and pain. Something unfamiliar, like hope.

She held the datastick up to the stars and imagined the sky blooming with fire.

"Happy birthday to me," she whispered to herself.

THE END

STAR WARS THE HIGH REPUBLIC

TALES FROM THE OCCLUSION ZONE

"No Big Deal"

By Lydia Kang

Illustration by Jake Lunt Davies

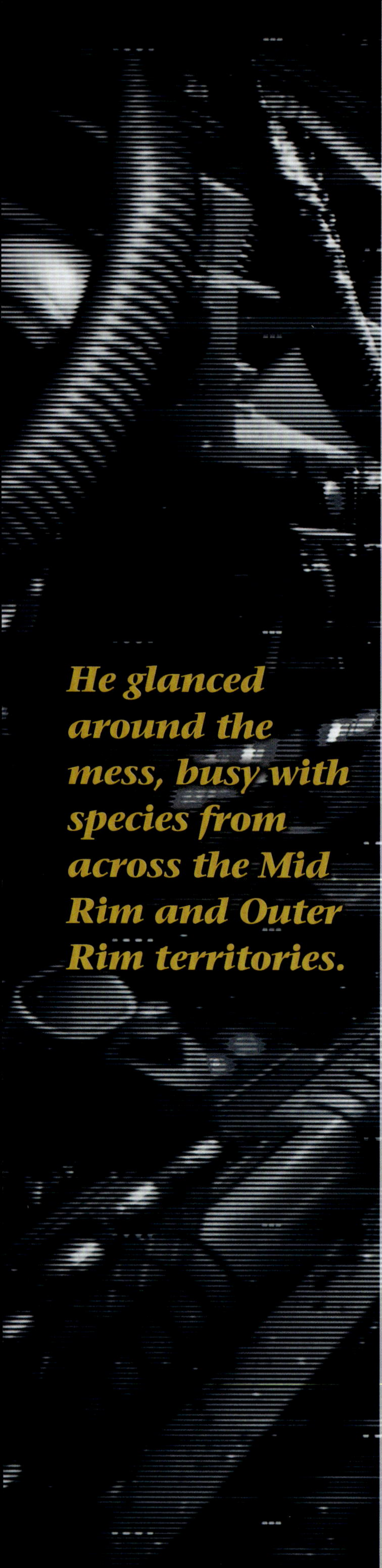

He glanced around the mess, busy with species from across the Mid Rim and Outer Rim territories.

Being on solid ground is supposed to be a comforting thing, especially on a place like Eriadu. Here, everything on the planet was inviting—from the tavern-laden streets of the various cities, to the snow-dusted mountains hiding their inner riches of lommite ore. The place begged you to keep your feet planted and stay.

For Joss Adren, feet solidly on the ground and with a foaming ale before him, he was nonetheless anxious to get back to the *Aurora III*, the Longbeam cruiser he and Pikka piloted for the Republic Defense Corps. Pikka and ship—that was comfort. That was home. She'd always patted the *Aurie*, as they'd nicknamed it, thanking it for saving their lives so many times. Speaking of Pikka, where was she?

He glanced around the commissary, busy with species from across the Mid Rim and Outer Rim territories. Two Ugnaughts, arguing over bowls of stew, another group of RDC officers rubbing their chins and occasionally glancing at Joss. He didn't know them. There were more and more RDC personnel on the planet these days, but they were trying not to stick out too much. Eriadu wasn't a place that enjoyed having a lot of off-world military muscle about. So it was no surprise that heads turned his way when Admiral Kronara and a young ensign at his side parted the crowds by the door and sat before Joss at his tiny table.

Joss was slowly growing accustomed to the rank and file formalities now that he and Pikka had been in the RDC since the fall of Starlight Beacon. But as soon as Joss began to stand, Admiral Kronara barely shook his head. Joss understood. This was not a time to bring attention to themselves.

He only nodded his head, as did the ensign. She looked rather young, her hair tightly wound beneath her RDC cap, lips pressed into a grim line.

"Good to see you again," Kronara said in his gruff voice. "This is Ensign Ebbe Casset. New to the RDC, after working in the Malastare-Sullust Joint Task Force for a few years. Ensign, this is Captain Adren."

"Oh!" Joss tried to rein in his surprise. "Casset...as in..."

"Yes, Hedda Casset was my aunt," she said crisply. Not a sign of sadness on her unlined face. More like resolve. She probably got this response all the time.

"Wow. That must have been...wow," Joss said. The young woman nodded with slight irritation, or perhaps sadness, before the steely resolve returned. Joss turned his head this way and that, looking for Pikka. Where was she? He was not good with being face to face with the discomfort of what had befallen Hedda Casset. If not for her, more would have died during the Great Hyperspace Disaster. She was a true hero. But she was also a reminder of how many lives had been lost in the last two years. Sometimes, Joss shivered at the thought that he and Pikka could have easily been on Starlight Beacon when it was destroyed a little more than a year ago.

"Where is Pikka? The other Captain Adren, that is," Admiral Kronara said. "I believe she was going to be in this meeting?" He waved for a service droid.

Pikka had excused herself to wash up before sitting down, but it had been more than fifteen minutes. What was she doing? Pikka wasn't the type of person to preen before a mirror. More likely, she had found a poorly constructed electrical circuit and was telling someone to get it fixed before they had a wire-fire on their hands.

"Right here."

A slim hand squeezed Joss's shoulder and Pikka Adren slipped into the chair beside him. Joss tried not to beam, as he was wont to do whenever Pikka entered the room. He was terrifically proud of his wife. If it weren't for Pikka, they wouldn't have been able to change the operational code of their Longbeam when fighting the impossibly fast Nihil ships during the Battle of Kur. She pushed her wavy, deep brown hair away from her temples, her blue eyes glancing at Ebbe. Of late, there were dark circles under them. She'd been working too hard, but as always, Pikka never complained. She nodded to the admiral. Of course, she knew to play it casual so as not to bring attention to their group.

Pikka and Ebbe introduced themselves. Pikka's eyebrows went up slightly at hearing Ebbe's surname.

"Thank you for joining the RDC. It means a lot to many people," Pikka said quietly. Unlike Joss, she always knew the right thing to say. Ebbe nodded, her eyes glazing for a moment with moisture. The wait staff droid arrived.

"We're technically on duty, but I wouldn't say no to an ale myself," Admiral Kronara said, running a hand through his silver-streaked hair. "A round for the table?"

"Not during work," Ebbe said, eyeing Admiral Kronara.

"In that case, two jogan juices," Pikka said. She waved at the departing droid. "And some salted wuli nuts! I'm starving. So." She leaned in close. "I take it you're not telling us we have a well-deserved holiday coming. You have a mission to discuss?"

"You do deserve a holiday. As for this mission, it's no big deal," Admiral Kronara said. The ale and jogan juices arrived, and he took a deep pull on his amber drink before speaking quietly. "We've received a distress call from a small ship, close to the Stormwall. We need you to intercept it."

Joss furrowed his brow. The Stormwall. It wasn't that close, but it was too close for Joss's comfort. Lately, they'd been working near Eriadu, running shipments and helping the RDC set up a quiet but active base on the planet. The Nihil had been striking and raiding here and there beyond the Stormwall, but Eriadu was still quite safe. Traders were flourishing here, as were the black markets on the edges of every city and village. There was money to be made in times of conflict. A tale as old as the stars.

"Why us? Any RDC crew could handle a ship in distress in this sector. Surely there's someone closer," Joss said.

Kronara said nothing for a beat too long. And Joss knew, almost the same moment as Pikka did, who pulled her jogan juice closer.

"It's a Nihil ship, isn't it?" she said low.

Admiral Kronara nodded. "Probably a raiding craft that got in trouble."

"No big deal, huh? Who else knows about this?" Joss asked.

"Me, Ebbe, and the technician who picked up the signal and has been ordered to stay silent about the report."

"Why the secrecy?" Pikka said. She leaned in to sip the jogan juice, sniffed it, and then pushed it away in slight disgust. She reached for the nuts instead, tossing a few in her mouth.

Ebbe cautiously tasted her own juice, then eyed Pikka curiously. "There's a chance it may provide the means for us to penetrate the Stormwall and enter the Occlusion Zone. Unless it's a trap, and the Nihil are trying to bait us."

"That sounds more like a job for the Jedi than us," Joss suggested.

"Unfortunately, the Jedi are not at our disposal for this one. We need your answer now," Kronara said. "I can pull rank, but I'd rather you agreed to the mission in this case. I can promise you a long break after this." He hid his face by drinking more ale.

Joss sat back and met Pikka's eyes. Usually they talked things out, but they knew each other so well that sometimes a look sufficed. In this case, he was as hesitant as she appeared to be. Lately, she'd seemed so overworked. Her shoulders drooped from exhaustion. He was hoping for missions closer to the Core Worlds, to do something a bit more stable. The year since Starlight Beacon fell had been so hard on them both. Yes, maybe some time off is what they needed. Vacation first. They needed to be a united front. This was a definite no.

Pikka broke eye contact with Joss, and leaned forward.

"We'll do it," she said firmly.

They had spoken little on their way to the *Aurie*. Joss trusted Pikka, and if she wanted to do this trip, he'd be right at her side. But something was off between them, and he wasn't sure how to broach the subject. So instead, he had put all his energy into prepping for the mission. The Longbeam was still in very good shape, and still one of the fastest ships in the RDC. It was capable of some mind-bendingly abrupt changes in direction for a ship of that size, thanks to Pikka's engineering adjustments.

At the RDC hangar several kilometers outside of town, Joss stood on the boarding ramp of the *Aurie*. He was eyeing a set of crates full of supplies on the ground, while checking their plan on a datapad. He had input the coordinates and they were waiting for a last message from Ebbe before the brief hyperspace trip. Pikka was heading his way, weaving between the jungle of boxes and crates that had turned into a labyrinth of sorts. Joss tried not to laugh.

"Seriously, Joss. You brought enough food for a crew of a hundred! It's just us two."

"You know me. I'm a planner."

She was right, though. There was so much food. Pikka had a tendency to overlook things like this, and Joss sometimes over prepped, just in case. But in his effort to push aside his discomfort about the trip, he'd compensated by ordering too many supplies. There were enough shelf-stable items to last a year. Plus medical supplies. Plus parts for the *Aurie*.

A head popped up from behind a huge box of dehydrated bantha milk powder. Ebbe, still looking as stiff as before, walked purposefully towards them.

"This powder isn't regulation RDC ration," she said stiffly.

"Ebbe!" Joss said, surprised.

"Ensign Casset," Pikka said, giving Joss a soft elbow to the ribs. "Yes, the powder was a particular ask of mine. Did you need to speak to us before the trip?"

"Yes, Captain Adren. And Captain Adren. What's the status of the *Aurora III*?"

"Nearly ready. Engines have been double checked, and Joss had made sure we have enough supplies to feed a whole camp of Wookiees." She tried not to laugh, and then suddenly looked a little green for no reason at all.

"You okay?" Joss whispered.

Pikka waved a hand away. "Fine."

"Sorry about the milk powder," Joss said. "We paid for that ourselves."

"Oh, not a worry. Of course you'd want it. For the nausea. I heard it's particularly soothing to the stomach in your condition." She nodded towards Pikka.

Joss glanced at Pikka. He felt like he'd missed something important. ▶

The Nihil had been striking and raiding here and there beyond the Stormwall, but Eriadu was still quite safe.

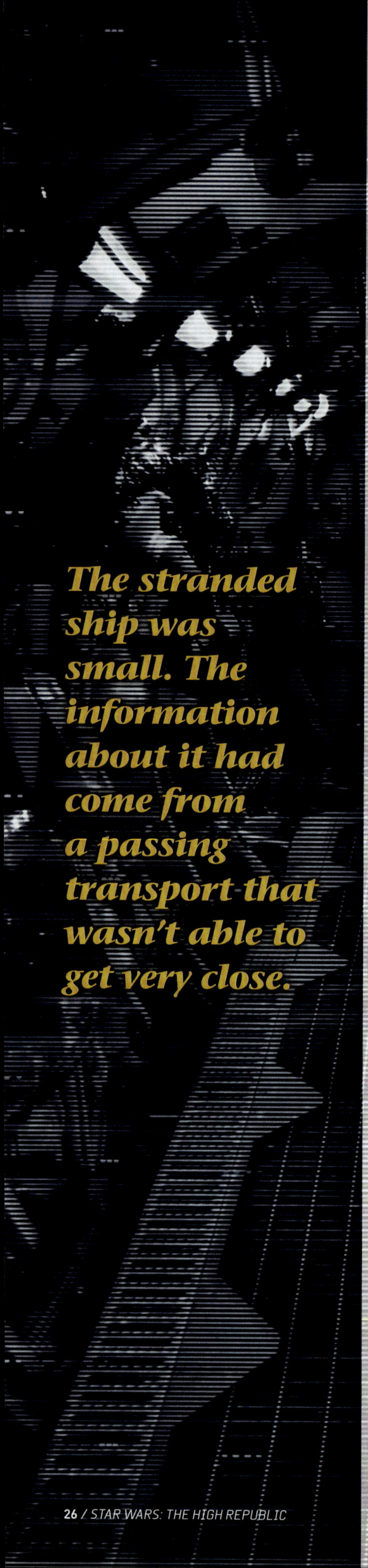

The stranded ship was small. The information about it had come from a passing transport that wasn't able to get very close.

"Don't worry," Ebbe went on quickly. "This will be a brief mission, and I'll ensure that Admiral Kronara will approve a lengthy leave of absence in nine months. Give or take."

For a fleeting moment, Joss wondered why she'd used such an arbitrary figure, and then the credit chip dropped. Nine months. Huh? He spun around and stared at Pikka, his eyes searching.

Pikka went red in the face. "Ebbe..." she said, with a warning in her voice.

Ebbe sounded confused. "For your upcoming family leave. For the baby?"

Joss felt the blood drain out of his cranium. His fingertips tingled, and spots swam in his vision. He was tilting a little, and caught the edge of the *Aurie* so as not to fall off the ramp. Something inside his chest went haywire, bouncing around and trying to burst out of his ribs. Oh. His heart.

"Pikka?" he said, his mouth suddenly dry. He was afraid to speak another word but he had to. "Are you...are we..."

"Yes," Pikka said. Her serious face cracked a smile that was brighter than a double sunrise. She ran up the ramp. "I'm pregnant."

"When were you going to tell me?" Joss said, enveloping her small hands in his. The tangle of four hands trembled.

"When we got going on our trip. I wanted a little privacy and space when I told you. I just found out." She turned her head away from Joss. "Ebbe, how did you know?"

"It was hard not to notice when we spoke earlier," she said. "Signs were all there. I'm sorry for making an assumption out loud. I can organize a mission but I'm, uh, not always good in conversation. But listen. I'll make it up to you. How about I join you? Lift some of the weight there?"

But Joss could barely hear Ebbe. Her words sounded like the distant *wah wah wah* of an insignificant alarm destined to be ignored. Pikka? Pregnant? Several emotions zapped through Joss's body. Joy. Terror. Worry. Terror. Joy. It was a palindrome of happy panic. So this is why Pikka had been looked tired lately. Why she'd spent more time in the lavatory than he did, probably emptying her stomach of jogan juice. It all came together.

Pikka turned back to Joss and raised her eyebrows. "Joss, what do you think?" Pikka said. Joss's mouth opened and closed. No sounds emerged. "Give us a moment, Ebbe?" Pikka gently led Joss to the interior of the *Aurie*. Finally, Joss managed to say something.

"I'm so happy, I don't know what to do with myself. I have a million things going through my head."

"Me too," Pikka said, exhaling a long, held-in breath.

"Are you feeling okay? What can I do?"

"You can help me do this mission, and do it well." She pushed her shoulders back. "I'm all right. Once in a while, I become a regurgitation machine, but other than that?" She patted her lower belly. "I'll be checking in with the *Aurie*'s generic medical screening program. It has an obstetrical application. All is well so far."

"The *Aurie* can't help you give birth, though. We don't have a midwife droid on board."

"Pfft. This is one quick mission, Joss! No big deal. It'll earn us favor with Kronara, who already likes us. We've got many months of work ahead before we take that leave."

"What do you think about having Ebbe with us?"

But Joss had gone back to an internal checklist of prepping for the mission, prepping for *after* the mission, and prepping for the rest of his life that had all suddenly multiplied like a swarm of gizka. Vaguely, he registered that Pikka had descended the ramp to speak to Ebbe. When Pikka returned, she patted Joss on the back.

"I told Ebbe we would do this one on our own. Ready to go?"

Joss nodded. Pikka gently touched his chin, closing his gaping mouth that must have been hanging open for the last several minutes. Joss laughed, and Pikka did too.

"Let's go Captain Adren," she said. "Our mission awaits."

It was time. The supplies were stowed. Pikka had checked the hyperdrive and had run safety diagnostics on the shield generator, while Joss reviewed the information that Admiral Kronara had given him.

The stranded ship was small. The information about it had come from a passing transport that wasn't able to get very close. They had some crude scanning equipment, but there appeared to be no life forms aboard. And it was definitely a Nihil ship. Small sized, but seemingly cobbled together with parts of other ships so it was lopsided and asymmetrical. There was a large cannon burn with damage to the engine on one side. It was far enough away from the Stormwall that Joss felt comfortable not having RDC backup. But it was close enough that it might have drifted out, broken, and the Nihil didn't know or care enough to bring it back in.

He rubbed his chin. Why hadn't the Nihil rescued this themselves? It made him wonder if the vessel was so trashed there was no point, or that the Nihil were either crueler of more disorganized than they let on. If it was the latter, then there was really a chance they could bring in a hyperdrive with the ability to pierce the

Stormwall. Kronara, Chancellor Soh, and the RDC would finally feel like they had a win on their hands.

It could change the entire direction of this war with the Nihil.

It could mean a safer future for Pikka, and Joss, and...another Adren.

"Hey Joss," Pikka said, appearing silently behind him. "We ready?

"Yes. Coordinates are in. I'm ready if you are."

Back in one of the two captain's chairs in the cockpit of the *Aurie*, Joss felt more like himself again. They were ready to go.

Pikka spoke through the comms. "Ebbe, tell Admiral Kronara that we'll send a report as soon as we've made contact with the ship," Pikka added. "Hey...oh never mind." She hesitated, appearing to want to say more. She gave Joss a shake of her head, as if clearing some unimportant thought from her brain. Joss could finish her sentences sometimes, and he could have sworn she was about to say, "If you don't hear back from us..." But no. That was a paranoid thought.

"Very well," Ebbe said. "May the Force be with you."

Ebbe sounded disappointed. Joss could imagine what she was feeling—the desperate need to do something, do anything to fight the Nihil. There were whole planets and systems enveloped by the Nihil in the Occlusion Zone. Who knows how horribly those millions must be suffering. Every night, Joss had nightmares about the Nihil encroaching, closer and closer. But for the first time, he was filled with another level of worry entirely.

They settled into their seats in the cockpit. The *Aurie* soon left the green and brown world behind them, past the several ships coming to and from Eriadu. They soon entered hyperspace with the plasma glow about them. It was a short trip, but Pikka nevertheless dozed off in her pilot's chair for a time. Let her.

A short while later, he announced, "Exiting hyperspace in a minute or two."

Pikka yawned and tossed away the last bits of sleepiness away with a shake of her head. She focused on the bluish-white glow of the hyperlane around them, then the transformation of white streaks as they entered realspace.

"There it is." Joss pointed.

In the distance, there was the small ship, just a speck of gray against the darkness of the galaxy. Pikka looked at the scanners on the *Aurie*'s control board. "Ebbe said that there were no life forms on that ship. She's wrong. There are at least two."

Joss tried not to show his disappointment. This was supposed to be a junk run. Remove some Nihil engine and comm parts and get going. He didn't want a conflict with the actual Nihil. Not now, of all times.

"What about the ship itself?"

"Our sensors say it's cold," Pikka said. "Engine could be broken. Or it could be shut down to appear broken." She looked at Joss, her eyes unsure.

"You can stay on the *Aurie*. I can board and find out what's going on."

"We're both here to do this job, Joss."

Joss shook his head. "The other option is, we can turn around, go back to Eriadu and get reinforcements. Ebbe wanted to come too. I think she knew something was off. I think we should do this with backup."

Pikka frowned. "They wanted this to be done quickly, and quietly."

What if they lost their chance to find out what was on that ship? What if procuring that engine really meant that they could push back against the Nihil, and push back the Stormwall? Joss's decisiveness was softening in the face of the new worry. As much as he wanted to know what was happening on that ship, he also wanted to get Pikka out of here.

"Let's call Ebbe. We ought to be able to communicate from this sector."

They opened up a comms channel. After a few transfers, Ebbe's voice sounded.

"What's going on?"

"The ship has passengers or crew. Alive. At least two," Pikka reported.

"Something feels off," Joss added. "Requesting RDC backup."

"I agree," Ebbe said. "I'll let Admiral Kronara know. He's back on Coruscant. For now, just know that—"

The cockpit filled with the sound of static.

"Ebbe? Are you receiving?" Pikka's voice rose. The static continued.

The control panel of the cockpit suddenly went black, as if they'd lost power. It lit up again and flickered erratically.

"What in the...what's going on? Ebbe, are you there?" Joss tried to run a systems check, but the console didn't respond. He attempted a quick reboot. Again, unresponsive. The electronics continued to act like all the circuits were massively confused. The quiet of the cockpit was still filled with harsh static.

Amidst the flashing chaos, a single red light blinked with certainty. Well, *something* was finally working, but the red light made him feel far worse instead of better. He looked at Pikka, their eyes meeting for one long, panicked moment.

"That abandoned ship isn't alone anymore," Pikka said. "Company's coming."

And then the *Aurie* went dark.

Joss could imagine what she was feeling—the desperate need to do something, do anything to fight the Nihil.

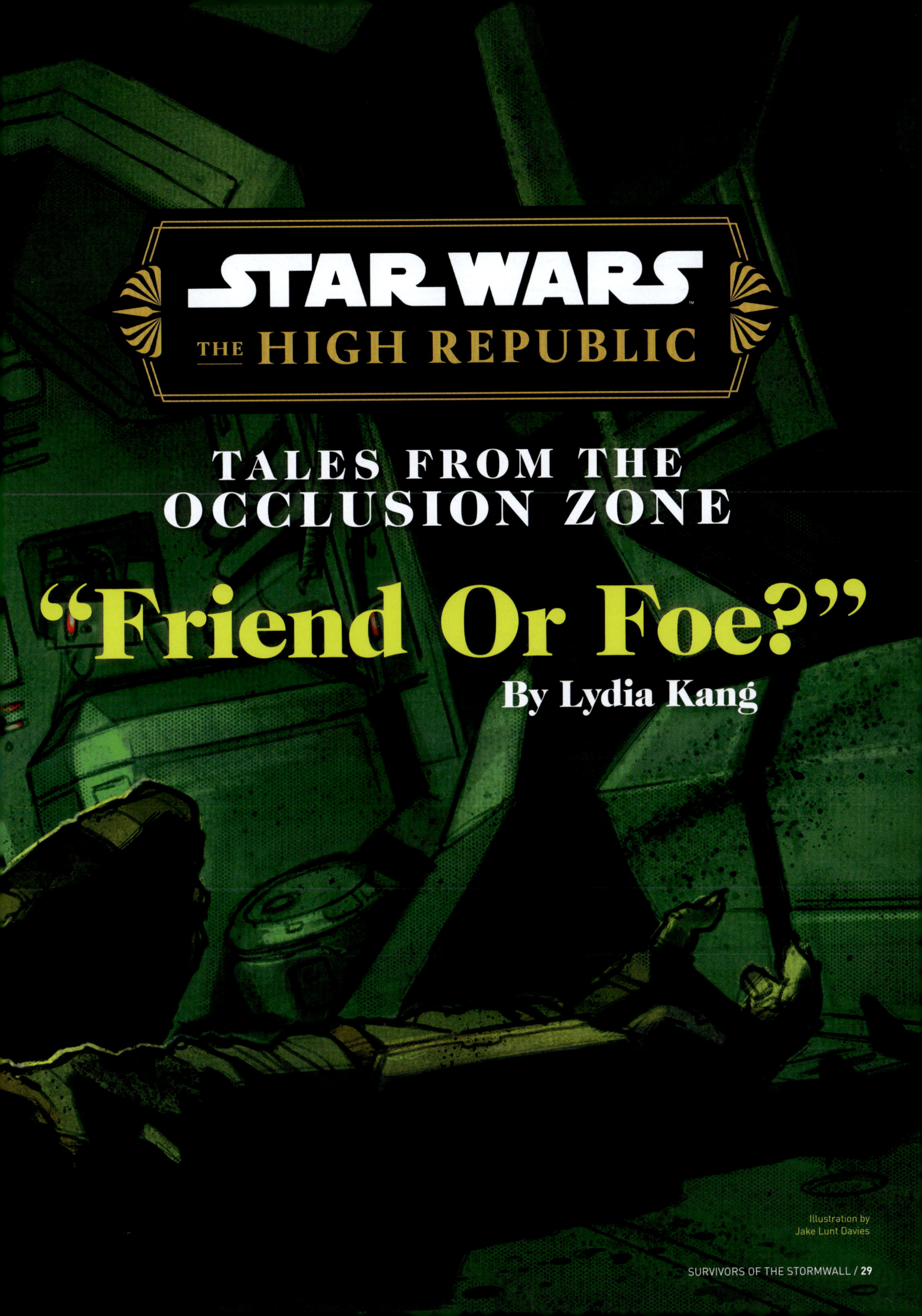

STAR WARS
THE HIGH REPUBLIC

TALES FROM THE OCCLUSION ZONE

"Friend Or Foe?"

By Lydia Kang

Illustration by
Jake Lunt Davies

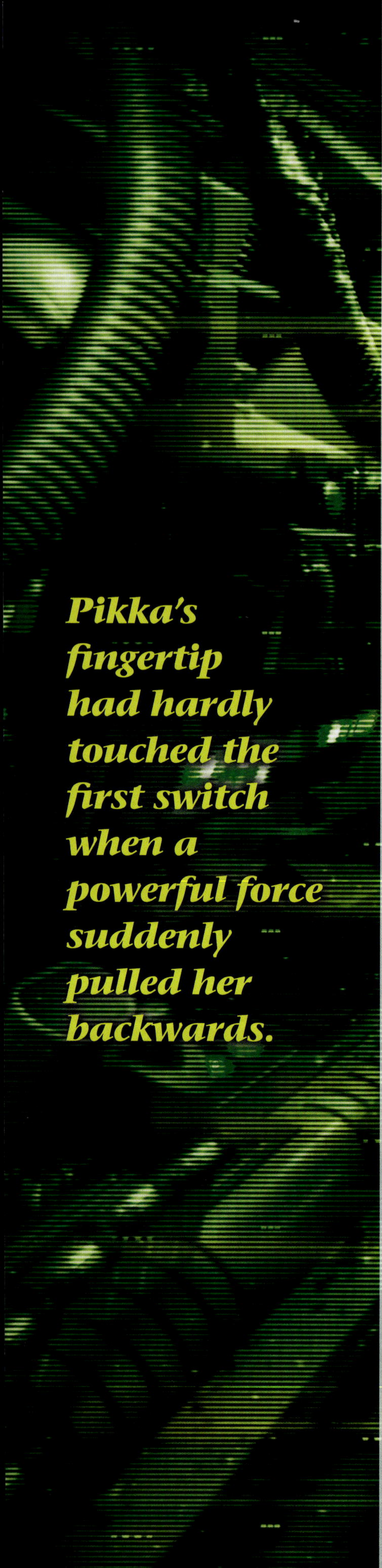

Pikka's fingertip had hardly touched the first switch when a powerful force suddenly pulled her backwards.

Previously, in a galaxy far, far away....

Joss and Pikka Adren are on a salvage mission for the RDC, dispatched to the edge of the Stormwall in their Longbeam, the *Aurie*. But no sooner have they found their target—a stricken Nihil vessel—than a sudden power outage disables their own ship.

Truth be told, Pikka was actually afraid of the dark. All her life, she'd counted on the fact that she could fix things, build things, take them apart. Light was a tool, something she could control to illuminate the unseen. And now she had no control whatsoever. Joss and Pikka Adren were engulfed in darkness.

"The communications are down. The engine is down," Joss said. She could hear him nearby, the frantic tapping of his fingers as he tried to reset the console.

Pikka squinted through the viewport, desperate to get her bearings in the inky blackness. She could just make out the small Nihil ship, drifting nearby. Then she saw something else. A tiny light, far away but getting larger, moving closer, quickly.

"Look," she pointed. "Is that another ship?"

"Yeah… and it's headed this way," agreed Joss. "We should get moving."

"Why hasn't the emergency backup system kicked in?" Pikka wondered aloud.

"Maybe that's fried too," guessed Joss.

"I'm going to the engine room to find out." Pikka blindly felt for the storage locker in the bulkhead and pulled out a glow rod.

"Me too," said Joss. "You can't open those doors without me."

Pikka ran through the ship, Joss's footsteps thundering behind her. He had to manually operate the engine room door, grimacing as he forced it wide. Pikka shimmied inside as Joss propped it open with a hefty power-wrench.

Then something thudded against the hull of the ship. Something small. There was another thud, then another, and the sound of what seemed like little metal feet scurrying across the *Aurie*'s exterior.

"What in the stars is that?" Pikka hissed.

Joss grabbed the glow rod and ran back along the corridor towards one of the ship's gunnery stations, only to return a few moments later. The scurrying noise had turned into buzzing and scraping, getting louder by the second.

"Scav droids," Joss confirmed. "They're swarming all over that stranded Nihil ship. Now they're getting interested in the *Aurie*."

Pikka had heard about scavs but never seen one up close. They were small and incredibly efficient. A dozen of them could skeletonize a small shuttle quickly and cleanly. The *Aurie* was bigger, but it wouldn't take long before the Longbeam suffered a hull breach and the Adrens were dead.

"But those are Nihil tech," said Pikka, her mouth turning dry. "They're only found on the other side of…"

She couldn't say it because it seemed impossible.

"The Stormwall. Somehow, we're on the wrong side of it," Joss exclaimed. He shook his head. "I don't know how, but it must have shifted position while we were on the border."

Pikka's heart had gone cold. "We're *inside* the Occlusion Zone?"

"Never mind that…"

"Never mind?"

"You have to get the ship back up and running," Joss said, quickly. "There might be enough juice in the cannon's emergency backup system for me to blast a few of those scav droids, but I'll need the *Aurie*'s batteries after that."

"On it," nodded Pikka, and she plunged deeper into the engine room as Joss raced to the gunnery station.

"There are only five droids," Joss' voice crackled from the comlink on Pikka's belt, then she heard the boom of their ship's cannon, followed by a high-pitched squeal like a deflating bellows. "Sorry, make that four," her husband added.

For now, she thought.

The scratching was right above her, getting louder. Pikka cast her light beam across the room, searching for the fuel cell manual controls. If she could reset their modulation circuits… The switches had five settings, but if she set them wrong, the capacitors might blow. She heard the *Aurie*'s cannon fire again, but it sounded off.

"Pikka. I have bad news."

"I don't want to know!" she yelled. Gripping the glow rod between her teeth, she reached for the panel. "C'mon, lady. Make me proud and reset like a good

Longbeam," she pleaded.

Pikka's fingertip had hardly touched the first switch when a powerful force suddenly pulled her backwards. She slammed onto the engine room bulkhead, her nails scraping to find a grip as she was dragged across it. With a thump, she landed hard against the propped-open door, and the glow rod was knocked out of her mouth. She made a grab for it, but it slipped through her fingers and was gone, tumbling into the darkness, leaving her alone in the smothering black.

"We have a breach!" Joss's voice yelled from the comlink.

"You think?" Pikka screamed back.

The air roared as it was sucked towards wherever the scav droids had punctured the hull. Pikka could barely breathe, her chest feeling crushed by the rapid decompression. She flinched as tiny bolts and anything else that wasn't secured whipped by, ricocheting off the bulkheads and smacking into her body before flying out through the engine room door. Something sliced her cheekbone—a stray wire, perhaps—on its way out to space.

She could hear the fuel cells shaking in their compartment joists. Soon, they'd break free and fly right towards Pikka, breaking all her bones along with... Her hand moved unconsciously to her stomach, her only thought to protect the new life inside her. Their child.

Then, just when she thought she was done for, the pressure relented. Pikka could stand again. She held her knees, gasping for air.

"How the...?" Pikka began.

"Never mind how. I bought you about one minute. Go!" Joss said, sounding breathless.

Pikka pulled up her sleeves, groped her way through the dark, and reached for the mod circuit switches behind the fuel cells. There were four. They'd have to be reset simultaneously, but she had to do it by feel since she couldn't see a thing.

She pressed them into place and held her breath for a beat, then switched them back on.

Nothing happened.

Pikka closed her eyes. "Joss," she whispered. "I'm sorry, I..."

With a flicker, yellow emergency lights flared into life. The *Aurie* was operational again.

"Yes!" Pikka yelled in triumph. "Joss, get those scav droids off our ship!"

"With pleasure," Joss hollered back, and the sound of blaster fire had never been more reassuring.

With the immediate threat dealt with, they would have time to assess the damage and figure out how to get out of this mess. Occlusion Zone or no, at least for the moment they had a fighting chance to survive.

ONE MONTH LATER

Pikka Adren was in a storage compartment, welding together yet another patch for the hull. The fifth in just the last week. Sweat beaded on her forehead beneath her welding mask. Despite the noise, she was all too aware of the yawning expanse beyond their ship. They were so very alone now, and she had to keep the simmering panic at bay every minute of this new life.

It had been more than thrity rotations since Joss and Pikka had departed on their mission to investigate a stranded Nihil ship on the border of the Occlusion Zone. Admiral Kronara himself wanted discretion, and everyone had hoped there might be some Nihil tech to help the Republic and Jedi finally penetrate the impenetrable barrier of the Stormwall.

Oh, they penetrated it all right. Just not on their terms.

There were no other Republic Defense Coalition ships anywhere nearby. Their hyperspace capability was shot. The one time they'd considered trying to make a jump, they'd discovered the nearest hyperlane coordinates were thick with Nihil ships and scav droids. The *Aurie* could never fight that much firepower and destruction. The nearest planet was years away by travel at sublight speeds, but they weren't going anywhere while they continued to hide from the Nihil.

In effect, they were trapped, along with millions of others whose planets and ships had ended up in the O.Z. the moment the Stormwall showed up.

There had to be another way to escape.

"Hey," Joss shouted from the corridor. He poked his head into the compartment, holding a canister of soup. "You need a break."

Joss fanned the steam her way. Dumplings, with rehydrated greens and lots of spices. It was one of the only foods lately that soothed her stomach. Her pregnancy tended to make her insides feel like they were a herd of fleeing galoomps. Not a great feeling. But not as bad as the idea of giving birth to a baby inside Nihil-

In effect, they were trapped, along with millions of others whose planets and ships had ended up in the O.Z. the moment the Stormwall showed up.

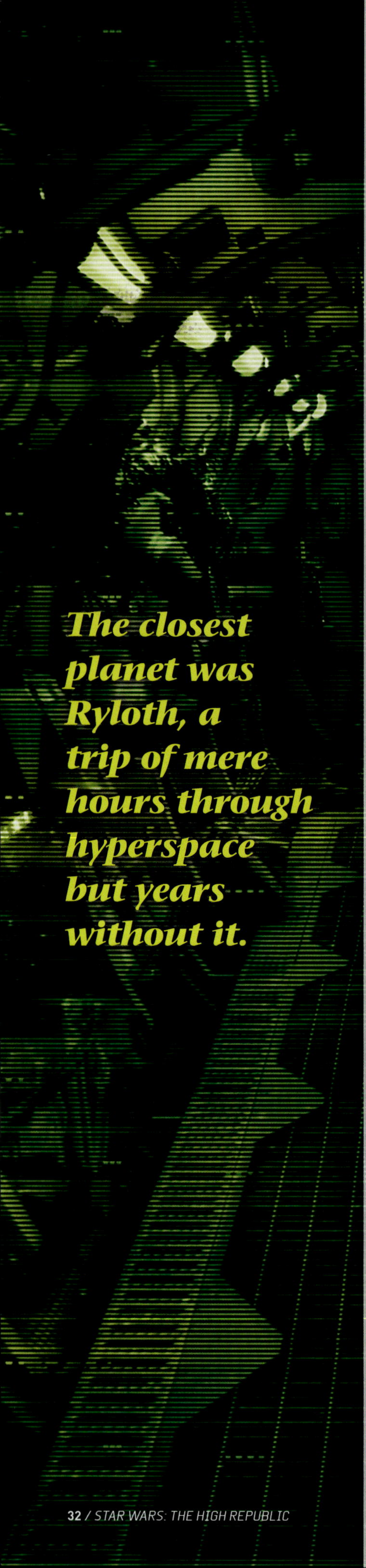

The closest planet was Ryloth, a trip of mere hours through hyperspace but years without it.

controlled space. In only one month, the waistband of her uniform had already been stretched out by several centimeters. There was nothing like a pregnancy to document the passage of time and their growing worries.

"Okay. Just a few more minutes," Pikka said, turning back to the shard of duralloy in her hand.

"I think you need a break, *now*."

Pikka turned to stare at her husband. Standing tall with this hair overgrown in a slightly bushy mass around his head, his wide shoulders touched the sides of the door. His usually serene face looked concerned.

There was more bad news, wasn't there?

She stood up and stretched, accepting the soup, and walked with Joss back to the cockpit. She ate as they went, managing not to slosh it all over her clothes.

"Did you catch something on the scanners?" she asked.

"I did."

"Nihil?"

Joss took a breath. "Yes. A cloud of scav droids coming our way. We need to move."

Within minutes, they had navigated the *Aurie* into the nearby asteroid field. Lately, they'd learned it was helpful to cozy up to anything they could hide behind—uninhabited moons; space debris; gas clouds. As they entered the field, Pikka watched the swarm of scav droids change direction to follow them. The ship swerved its way through the spinning rocks, taking a twisting route to avoid getting pummeled. She was relieved to see that the droids were dropping off in number as the *Aurie* ploughed ever deeper.

"There. That's perfect," Pikka said, pointing out a particularly large asteroid, shaped like a rotten jogan fruit missing one huge bite, most likely thanks to a glancing blow from one of its sister asteroids.

"It's probably not safe long term, but it'll do for now," Joss said.

The *Aurie* swooped around the lip of the crater as Joss maneuvered the Longbeam into a crevasse large enough to protect the ship from debris. There was a slight jolt as the craft nestled into place.

Pikka exhaled. Joss did too. They glanced at each other in relief.

But it was a brief respite.

"Um, Joss!" said Pikka. "Take a look at this!"

Pikka magnified the image on the topography scanner before her. The reading revealed an impossibly regular bump against the battered surface of the asteroid.

"What is that?" Joss asked. "A Nihil ship?"

Pikka pulled a knee up to her chest, thinking. "If it is, there's no reason for it to be hiding, so why isn't it attacking us?"

"It looks damaged. It may be waiting for help?" Joss suggested, nervously. "Just not help from us."

"*Another* incapacitated ship." Pikka sighed. "Look where that got us the last time. There might be something onboard that we could use, though. Nihil codes, maybe even a way to pass through the Stormwall. Which would mean…"

"We could get out of here," said Joss. "But it's just the two of us. If we go aboard, we could be outnumbered and outgunned."

"We only have enough supplies for a few more weeks," Pikka reminded him.

They both knew they could only hide for so long before they starved to death. The closest planet was Ryloth, a trip of mere hours through hyperspace but years without it. They'd barely be able to make it halfway before their fuel and food ran out, or they got picked up and killed by the Nihil.

Joss and Pikka looked at each other. Their hand was being forced. They had no option but to scavenge that ship.

Pikka and Joss had armed themselves with blasters before proceeding cautiously into the belly of the crab-like wreck. The *Aurie*'s life-form scanners had been glitchy ever since they'd wound up in the Occlusion Zone, so they were only too aware that the ship could be crawling with the enemy.

The first thing they noticed was the pervading stench.

"It smells like something died in here. A while ago," said Pikka, trying not to gag.

"Or someone," Joss replied.

Beams of yellow light from the lamps they carried were the only illumination as they entered what looked like a hold, and it was a mess. A platter heaped with rotten food lay in a corner with mold-covered fruit peelings. Another pile of discarded clothing—rich velvets and metal cuffs and jewelry—lay next to several broken blaster rifles. Vases, crystalline orbs, and containers overflowing with trinkets and enameled ornaments were piled in the corners of the room. "That's some trophy," said Pikka. "I wonder if every Nihil ship has a hoard like this?"

Makeshift bunks of torn blankets suggested some very large Nihil had slept there. Everything was covered in dust. Joss poked at a discarded crimson robe, embroidered with frayed golden threads. "Doesn't seem like anyone alive has been here in a while."

"We'll find out soon enough," Pikka remined him. She gripped her blaster and pointed her light towards an open door to the rest of the ship.

Click, click.

A faint sound, quite some distance away, like the reloading of a blaster, or the flick of a switch.

"We are not alone," she whispered.

They stepped through into a long corridor. The stench was only growing stronger. Pikka didn't say aloud what they were both thinking—there had been a massacre here, or worse.

Joss pointed his lamp, illuminating a partially open door just ahead. He nodded at Pikka, and she moved forward, peering inside. Looking pale, after a few moments she holstered her blaster and entered the room.

Two bodies, bloated and quite dead, sprawled on the floor of the compartment, riddled with blaster burns. Both wore helmets, one of which was decorated in the grotesque form of a human skull, with horns that looked as if they belonged to felled staga. Clearly Nihil.

Suddenly, from behind, Pikka felt a heavy, fetid pair of arms make a grab for her shoulders.

"Joss!" she screamed, unable to free herself from the weight of the body pushing her to the floor.

Joss was upon them in a flash, landing punches on the assailant as he fought to pull the attacker away from his wife. But there was no resistance, and the figure fell away like a deadweight.

Pikka's blaster was already pointing at the corpse, despite her hands shaking. In the pale-yellow light of her lamp, the Nihil at their feet took on the aspect of an apparition.

"He's…he's…" Pikka couldn't finish the sentence.

"He's not alive, that's for sure." Joss prodded the Nihil's thickly booted leg with a foot. The body was stiff, rancid smelling, still clad in heavy garments—a fully articulated set of armor that looked ancient, possibly of Rakatan design. This one wasn't wearing a mask, however. It didn't even have a head.

"You okay?" Joss asked.

She nodded nervously, brushing the dust off her. She couldn't wait to get back onto the *Aurie* and wash away the odor of death that clung to her.

Click, click.

There it was again, coming from somewhere further down the corridor.

"What *is* that noise?" Joss said. He looked almost as relieved as Pikka felt.

"Doesn't matter. We've got to keep going," she said.

Maybe that clicking sound was some last-ditch function of the ship. Nothing they needed to worry about, she told herself. But Pikka couldn't shake the bad feeling she'd had since the second they'd stepped on board. "Come on. This place is empty. We need to find out what we can salvage. Let's head to the command deck, see what we find there, then we'll try engineering."

The vessel's bridge was in as much of a mess as the rest of the ship, but at least it was empty. Pikka lowered her blaster while Joss made for the captain's chair and sat down with a grunt. He looked like he'd aged a year. She cast her gaze over the unfamiliar control panels, noticing that the main console looked as if half of it had been reconstructed from spare parts and trash.

"I wonder if I can get these panels working?" she wondered aloud.

"That would be a very bad idea," a voice intoned from the rear of the command deck.

Joss jumped up as Pikka spun around, and both trained their blasters towards the shadows where the voice had come from. Two Nihil emerged from the darkness; their own blasters aimed steadily at the Adrens. Both were tall, and wearing the unmistakable, garish attire and helmets favored by the marauders. Goggles and breathing ports hid their faces like hideous death masks. A dark gray protocol droid lurked behind them, studying the intruders intently.

Click, click.

The noise was coming from something broken inside the droid's chest.

"Drop your weapons," said the first Nihil.

It seemed Joss and Pikka had walked into a trap.

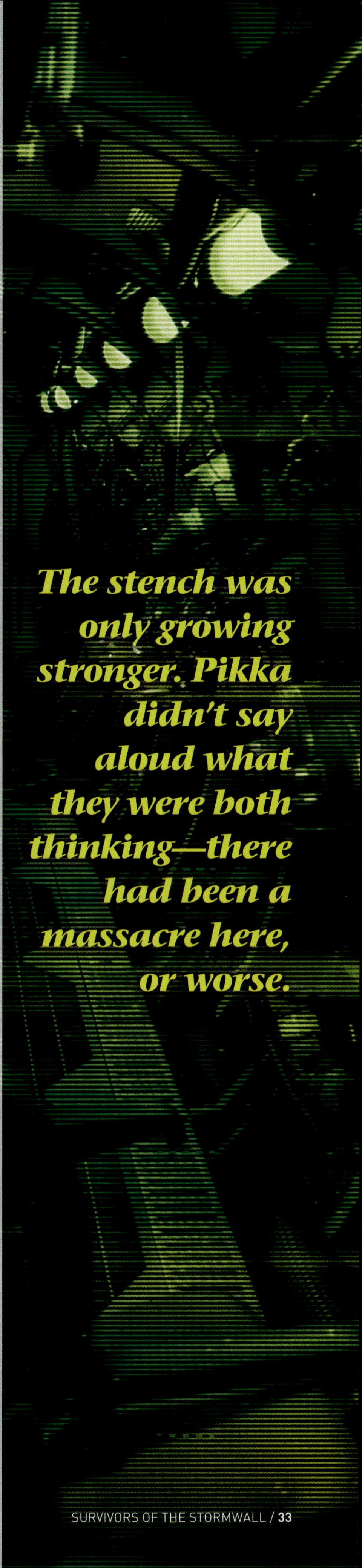

The stench was only growing stronger. Pikka didn't say aloud what they were both thinking—there had been a massacre here, or worse.

STAR WARS
THE HIGH REPUBLIC

TALES FROM THE OCCLUSION ZONE

“Survivors”

By Lydia Kang

Illustration by
Jake Lunt Davies

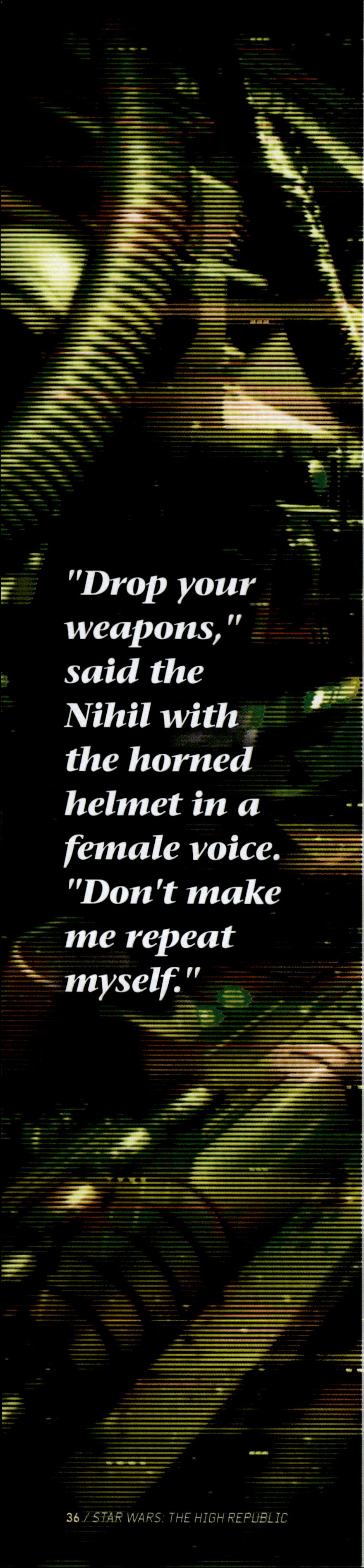

"Drop your weapons," said the Nihil with the horned helmet in a female voice. "Don't make me repeat myself."

Previously, in a galaxy far, far away....

Trapped within the Occlusion Zone, Joss and Pikka Adren have discovered a seemingly abandoned Nihil ship, littered with corpses and the spoils of war. But not all aboard are dead...

***C**lick, click.* **That odd sound continued to echo from the silver protocol droid's chest. Right now, it felt as loud as a gong in the cramped cockpit.**

"Drop your weapons," said the Nihil with the horned helmet in a female voice. Scuffed armor covered her torso, with chain mail protecting her legs. "Don't make me repeat myself."

The other Nihil was taller and slimmer, wearing a helmet with three eye holes and wide ear covers, as if made for a Gran. This one seemed far less confident than the other Nihil, and kept looking towards their companion, as if questioning whether her commands were appropriate.

"I would strongly recommend you follow her orders," the silver protocol droid stated, dryly. *Click, click.* "She hasn't eaten today and she's quite cranky."

"Shut up, Six-En," the female Nihil snapped.

The taller Nihil cocked their head, motioning with their blaster towards a faded area on Pikka's upper arm, right where her Republic Defense Corps patch used to be. She and Joss had removed them weeks ago, as a precautionary measure in case they were ever captured. RDC prisoners would be valuable to the Nihil, in the worst possible way.

"What's that?" asked the tall one. They had a soft-spoken male voice that lacked the hard edge of their companion.

"Aren't you a little young for a Nihil?" Pikka said, raising an eyebrow.

"Enough. Identify yourself," the female interrupted, her blaster still aimed at Joss.

The Adrens said nothing.

"Very well. If you won't do as you're told..." She turned her blaster towards Pikka.

Joss's heart raced, but Pikka raised a single finger, a sign to Joss that things were about to go sideways—on her terms.

"Drop your..."

Pikka dropped to one knee, firing her blaster simultaneously. The bolt struck the female Nihil's weapon, sending it spinning out of her hand, and she staggered backwards into the cockpit wall. The taller Nihil seemed confused, and Joss stepped forward, striking the marauder's blaster hand to one side and punching him hard in the faceplate. The Nihil fell to the ground, moaning and clutching at his Gran-like helmet. Joss kicked his blaster safely into the shadows.

"Awww, flark! That really hurt!" he whined. "What's the point of a helmet if it doesn't protect you?"

"Who are you?" The female asked, nursing her stinging hand.

"We'll be asking the questions now," Joss said as he yanked the taller Nihil to his feet. In doing so, a piece of flimsy armor pulled away from the man's shoulder. The pauldron clattered to the floor. On the gray fabric of his upper arm were loose threads in a familiar rectangular pattern, just like the emblem they had carefully removed from their own uniforms.

"You're RDC?" Pikka asked.

The tall Nihil shrugged and pulled off their helmet, revealing the face of a human male, so young that he appeared to be barely out of his teenage years. "We are," he said.

"Elping!" The female Nihil snapped in frustration at her companion.

"What?" The young man protested. "They're the ones holding the blasters now! And, *you* just told them my name," he added. "Plus, I think they're RDC, too."

Pikka glanced at Joss, who tipped his head. Might as well show their hand now. And like the kid said, they had the blasters.

"Yeah. We're RDC," Joss admitted. "Captain Joss Adren."

"I'm Captain Pikka Adren," Pikka said. She relaxed her stance a little, but only a little. "Want to tell us who you are, and how you got here?"

The female Nihil pulled off her helmet, revealing a grim-faced Arkanian woman. She possessed the telltale white eyes of her species, and her snowy hair hung in waves around her neck, contrasting against amber skin. She tucked the Nihil helmet under an arm and stood to attention.

"Lieutenant Visma Tarko," she said, tilting her chin up. She was proud of her name, though it meant nothing to Joss. "This is Corporal Elping Tsoo."

The young man raised a hand, almost sheepishly. "Hi. Sorry about that blaster business." He slouched a bit, as if to make himself smaller next to his senior-ranking colleague. She glared at him, and he immediately straightened up and pulled his shoulders back.

Joss finally let his blaster fall to his side—but he didn't trust them, not by a long shot.

Trust had to be earned, even if they were fighting on the same side. "So. How did you find yourselves in the O.Z.? Are there more of you?"

Elping shook his head. "Just us. And Six-En," he said, gesturing to their protocol droid.

"See-Zerosixen. Protocol droid for the Tarkos family. I am temporarily at your service." Six-En tipped his head forward. "For as long as we are stuck in this death trap situation together."

Visma rolled her eyes, and Elping cringed.

"That's temporarily generous of you, Six-En," Pikka said dryly.

"You're quite welcome. Though I must mention I am far more likely to survive however long we spend together, being altogether far more useful to both sides of the conflict."

"Thank you, Six-En. That's quite enough," Visma snapped. The droid bowed graciously.

"He's why we're stuck here," Elping said. "Visma and..."

Visma cleared her throat, and Elping corrected himself. "I mean, Lieutenant Tarko and I had been assigned to a station near Yerbana. We were on a transport with Six-En when our shuttle was attacked by Nihil. We got out in an escape pod."

"We've been running ever since," Visma said. "Hiding out on one of Yerbana's moons. We stowed away on a ship that got recaptured, escaped again, hid again. We managed to steal a shuttle but were attacked and taken aboard this Nihil ship."

Pikka swiveled her head. The cockpit had the body of a fallen Nihil in the corner. It looked like the man died of a blaster shot to the gut.

"So, you've been in the O.Z. for how long?"

"Months," Elping said.

Joss noted that he had hollows under his eyes, and his Nihil disguise hung loosely on his thin frame.

"Sounds like you've had a hard time of it," Pikka said. Her eyes were sympathetic. Elping was just a kid yesterday, it seems. But Visma shrugged it off.

"Every Nihil we came across on this ship is dead. What happened?" Joss asked.

Visma crossed her arms in defiance. Elping rubbed his chin thoughtfully, his eyes looking elsewhere while nonchalantly pointing with his finger at Visma.

Pikka and Joss exchanged a quick glance. They were both very glad they weren't Nihil.

Whether they liked it or not, they were now a party of four. Five, if you included Six-En. Joss and Pikka's first priority was to find out more about this broken Nihil ship.

"How functional is the engine?" Pikka asked, as Visma casually stepped over a dead Nihil. She pulled off a metal panel to reveal a tangled jumble of wires.

"Barely," Visma said. "It works, but the Path drive is broken. We can't use any of the hyperlanes here."

Pikka's face, which held a hesitant optimism, drained of color. "You mean to say, we can't get past the Stormwall in this ship."

Elping nodded. "Whatever advantage we gained capturing this ship doesn't add up to much. But we do have this." He led them to a room off the cockpit that was lined with metal boxes fitted with wires, pointing to one that was oddly shaped. "This thing sends out some kinda signal that protects the ship against scav droid scanners. We're not sure how it works, but we've not had trouble from those mechanical rats since we got stuck here."

"Anything else?"

"Lots of war spoils, if you're into that sort of thing," Visma said. "The next step is going to be ditching these corpses and loading your supplies on here as soon as we can, so..."

"Whoa," Joss said, holding up his hands. "Who said we're moving off the *Aurie*?"

Visma threw him a look, and not a very nice one.

"That is Lieutenant Tarko's way of saying that your circuits must be malfunctioning if you disagree with her," the droid explained. Click, click.

"I figured that, thanks Six-En," Pikka said.

Visma took a step forward. "Isn't it obvious that we have a far better chance of survival on this ship, hiding from the Nihil in one of their own, rather than on your Longbeam?"

"The *Aurie* has survived this far pretty well," Joss said. "It can outmaneuver any ships they have by a mile. And Corporal Tsoo says this ship doesn't offer us any advantages."

"I've been out here longer than you have," Visma said, bristling.

"We," Elping said quietly.

"What?" Visma retorted.

Elping seemed to regret his small vocal rebellion but repeated himself anyway. "I said, 'We.' We've been out here this long."

Visma rolled her eyes.

"Let's take an inventory," Pikka said. "See if there is any real worth in keeping it.

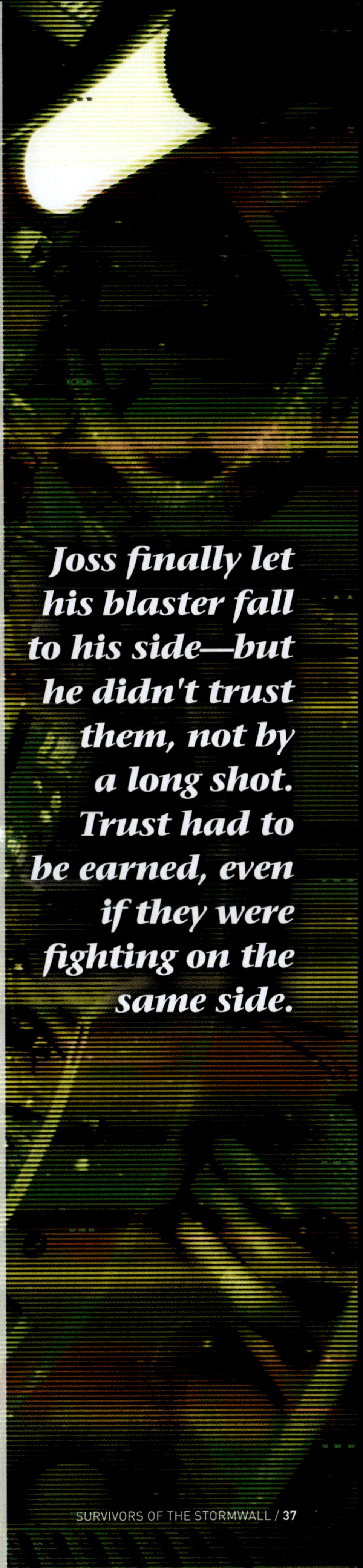

Joss finally let his blaster fall to his side—but he didn't trust them, not by a long shot. Trust had to be earned, even if they were fighting on the same side.

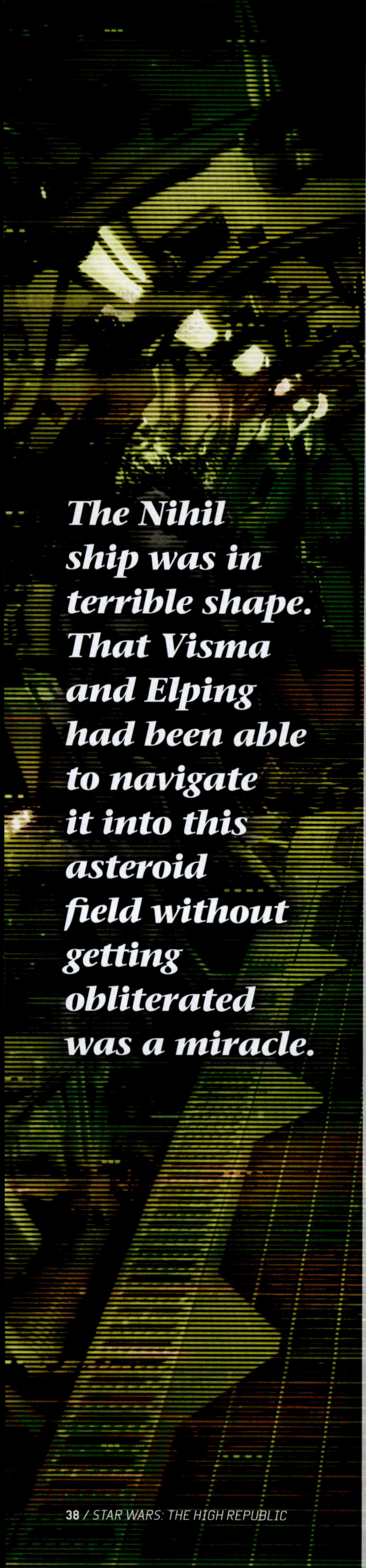
The Nihil ship was in terrible shape. That Visma and Elping had been able to navigate it into this asteroid field without getting obliterated was a miracle.

And then Captain Adren and I will make the decision." Visma opened her mouth to argue, but Pikka firmly stared her down. "As higher-ranking officers, what we say, goes. Got that, Lieutenant Tarko?"

"Yes Captain," Visma conceded, though Joss was pretty sure her teeth were clenched as she spoke.

"Lieutenant Tarko outwardly agrees but internally thinks you are filled with..."

"Interpret this, Six-En. I'm shutting you down for a while." Visma reached out and deactivated the protocol droid. "Just be glad I don't yank out all your core circuits permanently while you're napping."

The Nihil ship was in terrible shape. That Visma and Elping had been able to navigate it into this asteroid field without getting obliterated was a miracle. The engine was cobbled together with slickplast and hope.

"At least this Nihil communications decryptor should come in handy," Pikka said, detaching the device from a cockpit control panel.

"We should gather up what loot we can," Visma suggested, holding a box that was spilling over with sparkling Naboo jewelry and statuettes carved from purple stones. "Since credits are useless over here, we can trade them for goods."

"We should really return them to where they were stolen from," Pikka said. "We can trade work, instead."

Visma said nothing to this.

Joss and Elping lifted a crate at both ends, loaded with potentially useful items, and started to make their way back to the *Aurie*. Joss noticed the young man wincing.

"This too heavy for you?" Joss asked.

"It's not the weight," Elping answered as they maneuvered their way past yet another inert body, a Nihil corpse lying face down in a pool of dried blood.

Joss instantly understood. "War is a terrible thing," he said.

"When I signed up for the RDC, I thought I could help," said Elping. "I didn't expect... this!" he admitted.

"What's your background?"

"I'm an... I was an ecologist," Elping said regretfully. "I was cataloging native species and researching interplanetary evolution in the Outer Rim. Like when a scrap rat stows away on a ship and ends up living on Mandalore. I guess I'm more interested in that sort of thing than killing anybody."

Joss laughed. "I'm sure your expertise will come in handy. In any case, we have to focus on the goal right in front of us."

"Winning the war against the Nihil?" Elping asked as they set down the crate in the *Aurie*'s main hold.

"Survive living in the Occlusion Zone, one day at a time," said Joss, grimly. "Help people when we can. And, eventually, get out of here."

Elping nodded. He seemed relieved to be on the *Aurie*, Joss thought. Who wouldn't be, after spending months surrounded by the corpses of the enemy on a disabled ship. Six-En didn't seem like particularly agreeable company, and Visma wasn't the kind of person who could provide solace under life-threatening circumstances. It was clear from the state of the Nihil crew that she was a formidable individual.

After several days of pulling what they needed from the Nihil ship, they finally left the asteroid and put the field of tumbling rocks behind them. Pikka had wired the scav droid-evading tech into the *Aurie*'s systems, the hope being that it would keep them safe from any roving droids that might be flying out ahead of any Nihil ships in the region. But with two new RDC members on board, they'd soon be out of rations if they didn't find more supplies in the next few weeks. Ryloth was probably a month away if they flew straight there and didn't get into trouble. A big *if*.

With the *Aurie* on autopilot, the new companions finally sat down for their first collective meal together. Rehydrated tubers and a pormork stew, with a side of wuli nuts for Pikka. Joss wondered if their future child would be part wuli nut when it finally made its entrance into the galaxy, in just a few short months. But he didn't like to think on it too much. The fact that they were here, and not in safe space, worried him to no end so he simply did what he'd told Elping to do. Think survival first. One day at a time.

Visma sat ramrod straight in her chair and ate her meal like it was a mission. Quickly, efficiently, and without any apparent enjoyment. Elping ate voraciously, as if he'd only eaten scraps for months on end. He'd also brought the Nihil comms decryptor to dinner and was adjusting the dials between bites.

"Mmf," he mumbled. "This is so good, even if it's all Republic rations. Thank you." He looked at Visma, encouraging her to say something.

Visma rolled her eyes and sighed. "This meal has the appropriate ratio of protein to carbohydrates, fats, and nutrients."

This time Elping rolled his eyes. "She means, 'Thank you.'"

"I guess it's been pretty slim pickings, food-wise," Pikka said.

"It was..." Elping started to speak, but Visma shot him a warning glance. "It was fine."

"We have performed as per our RDC guidelines given our arduous circumstances," Visma said.

Joss leaned closer to the Elping, who continued to tinker with the decryptor. "You don't have to work during the meal, you know."

"In circumstances like this, time can't be wasted," Visma stated, flatly. She pushed away her empty plate and stood. "I should be double-checking the inventory."

"Why don't you sit for a while longer," Joss said. "Tell us about yourself."

"There's not much to tell," Visma said formally, as if interviewing for a new position. She sat down stiffly. "I've risen through the ranks of the RDC faster than any other Lieutenant. If not for being behind the Stormwall, I'd be a Captain commanding my own ship by now."

"I see," Pikka said. "That is admirable. And what about your family?"

"The Tarkos have been one of the most illustrious families on Arkania, for centuries. There have been Generals, Governors, and top scientists in our family. Even Jedi."

Joss nodded appreciatively, keen to put her at her ease. "What do you miss most about Arkania? I've never been," he asked.

Visma's expression changed, a subtle transformation. For a moment, Joss saw a young girl before him, not the severe lieutenant.

"I don't understand the question," Visma replied, confused.

"Hey," Elping suddenly interjected excitedly, as an even tone replaced static on the decryptor. "It's picking up a transmission."

Visma seemed relieved to not have to answer Joss. They all leaned in to hear the garbled voice coming through the speakers.

"This is Prison Transport 7X-533. Are you receiving?" crackled a worried voice. "Causalities are growing. We have only a skeleton crew left and more are succumbing. Please respond."

Joss and Pikka looked at each other. Elping adjusted some dials above the small display.

"It's local. Very close. But the signal is weak and on an old wavelength, which is probably why it's not reaching other Nihil right now," Elpin said.

More static, then "...only one prisoner left alive...Republic...Starlight..."

"Did he just say something about the Starlight Beacon, or am I imagining things?" Joss said. "What in the stars is going on in that ship?"

"They are in great distress," Six-En said.

"That's obvious, and it sounds like we should steer clear of whatever trouble they're in," Visma insisted. "It could take us down too."

"But there's a prisoner on board," Pikka said. "Probably one of us. They said 'Republic.'"

"One?" Visma said, nearly laughing. "Versus risking the lives of the four of us? Plus, we've got barely enough rations to get us to civilization as it is. We can't risk a side mission. Tactically it would be wiser to ignore the transmission and continue to Ryloth. Get supplies, weather the storm, and make it out of here alive."

"We're that prisoner's only hope. We have some basic protective wear and respirators," Joss offered, but his suggestion masked thoughts that were a mess of largely negative outcomes. What about Pikka? What if whatever was taking down the Nihil, went for her? Or him? Was it worth the risk?

"Boarding a functional Nihil ship would give us access to a Path engine. We could leave the O.Z.," suggested Elping

Everyone went quiet.

"It's a risk, but that ship is in trouble, and we have a good chance of overtaking it," Pikka said. "A Path engine could change everything."

"Lot of good that did us when we tried the same tactic," Visma said. "The engine on that Nihil wreck was barely functional and its hyperdrive was toast."

"Not all Nihil ships are going to be in the same state," Pikka said. "Plus, this one's a prison transport. It's likely to be in much better shape." She paused. "I think we should vote on this one."

Six-En waved a hand. "The frown on Lieutenant Tarko's face suggests she would rather dive head-first into a sarlacc pit than go after that prisoner."

"Thanks, Six-En," Joss said, shaking his head. "But we need a real vote, not your interpretations right now. All in favor for intercepting that ship and saving the prisoner, raise your hand."

Pikka did so. Elping followed her lead and, surprisingly, Visma raised her hand too.

But Joss did not.

"I'm sorry Pikka... I just can't."

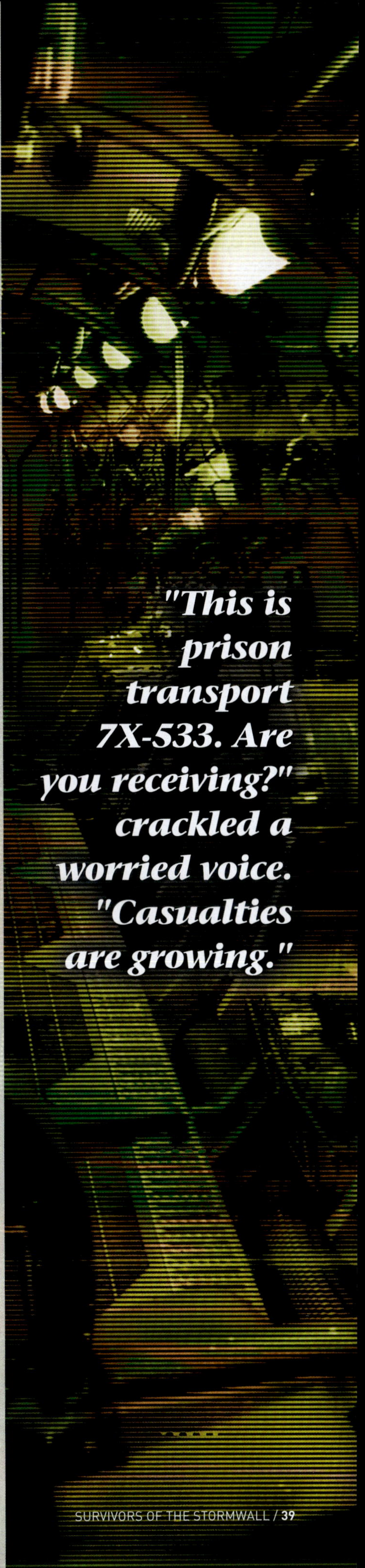

STAR WARS
THE HIGH REPUBLIC

TALES FROM THE OCCLUSION ZONE

"Pathogen"

By Lydia Kang

Illustration by Jake Lunt Davies

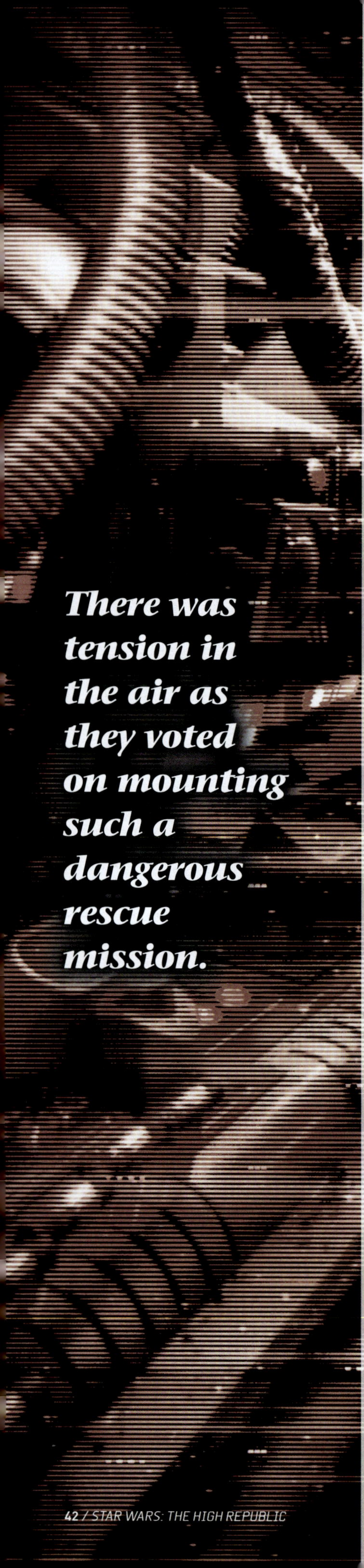

Previously, in a galaxy far, far away....

After rescuing a cell of RDC operatives stranded on an asteroid, the *Aurie* has detected a Nihil prison ship, stricken by a scourge that has decimated its crew. But there is one sole survivor—a prisoner who could unlock the secrets to escaping the Occlusion Zone...

"All in favor for intercepting that ship and saving the prisoner, raise your hand," Joss said, his face grim.

Corporal Elping Tsoo looked at the others uneasily—Visma Tarko, his frosty RDC superior of the past few months; the protocol droid C-06N; and their recent saviors Captains Pikka Adren and Joss Adren. He'd been relieved to meet the couple after spending so long in Visma's cool company as they hid in the wreckage of another Nihil ship, but now there was tension in the air as they voted on mounting such a dangerous rescue mission. Visma and Pikka had already argued over the potential benefits of boarding the ship when Elping had suggested it might have a functional Path drive that would take them out of the O.Z. But the fact was that *something* was taking out the crew and its cargo of prisoners, and they had no idea what that was. The transmission begging for help had mentioned the crew *succumbing* to something. The description had leapt out at Elping, suggesting it was more insidious than an attack. An unknown pathogen perhaps? It was an idea the scientist found unexpectedly exciting.

There was tension in the air as they voted on mounting such a dangerous rescue mission.

Pikka raised her hand, and Elping immediately followed suit. To his surprise, Visma raised her hand too. Only Joss did not. The room fell silent.

"Joss?" Pikka said, looking at him quizzically. "Why?"

"I'm sorry, Pikka... I just can't. It's too much of a risk. Who knows what's on that ship. I have a feeling that by the time we get there, that prisoner will be dead. We have a responsibility, beyond just you and me." He gave Pikka a look that Elping didn't understand.

Did he mean me and Visma? Or someone else?

"Well, then we can scavenge the ship, like we did the last one," Pikka suggested. "There will be food, resources..."

"You really want to eat something from a Nihil galley?" Joss interrupted, incredulous.

Visma put her hands on her hips. "If we don't make it to another planet by the end of the month, we are going to starve."

"It doesn't feel right. I don't think it's a good idea."

"*Feel* right? We need to make an objective decision," Pikka told her husband.

"We already did. You were just outvoted, Captain," Visma reminded him. Elping recognized the flick of her hair she made when she'd won an argument. There had been a lot of hair flicking when they were stuck on that asteroid together.

"Whatever is on that ship might kill us," Joss said.

"Or save us," Pikka countered.

The couple stared down each other, their faces drawn with frustration. Just when it seemed he might explode, Joss turned on his heel and left in the direction of the *Aurie*'s cockpit.

"Is he okay?" Elping tentatively asked Pikka.

"Don't worry. I'll deal with Joss. You keep listening to that transmitter. Gather whatever info you can find about that ship," Pikka ordered before turning to Visma. "Prepare for boarding."

Visma crossed her arms once Pikka had departed. "I'm worried this won't go well if they can't agree on anything. It was easier when it was just the two of us," she said.

"You mean when you were the only officer and could boss me around?" Elping raised his eyebrows.

"I did what I did for our survival. There's no room for disagreements in hostile territory."

"I get the feeling they'll sort it

out," Elping said. "They seem like they care about each other. A lot."

"There's no room for that either," Visma said dismissively as she skimmed through the *Aurie*'s inventory of supplies.

Elping's mouth dropped. "You don't really mean that."

"Caring gets in the way. We do what's best for our RDC team. Period. Feeling and fluff make for messy soldiering."

Ah, Elping realized. That would explain why Visma had never asked him a thing about his life in all those months they'd spent together. She didn't care that he'd chosen to leave his ecological work to help the RDC because it was the right thing to do after the fall of Starlight Beacon, abandoning his frail, elderly parents on Coruscant. Or that he absolutely hated it every time he had to pick up a weapon, and how he was sometimes so homesick, the ache seemed like a gaping, burning hole in his chest.

Elping knew he wasn't much of an RDC crewmember—naive and probably a liability. If it hadn't been for his corporal stripes, she probably just saw him as being "in the way."

"You'd better get to work then," he told her, pointing a petulant thumb at his own chest. "This 'mess' has some prep work to do, too."

He ignored the tall Arkanian's sharp glare as he left.

It took as long to prepare for the coming mission as it did to intercept the ship. Joss and Pikka had been locked up in the cockpit the whole time, talking, while Visma had concentrated on how many weapons she could reasonably carry while boarding. As for Elping, he had retreated to one of the spare cabins to plan ahead, happy to be alone. He enjoyed the silence. It helped him think.

He glanced out of the cabin viewport and spotted the prison transport looming nearby. It was a featureless, oblong box of a ship, its hull a mosaic of mismatched metal plates with no viewports save for a cockpit at the front. It clearly wasn't built for speed or maneuverability, but to carry as many prisoners as possible, probably not comfortably. And it appeared to be drifting aimlessly.

He turned back to the Nihil decryptor beside him, teasing the dials in one last search for a communications signal coming from the ship. The original channel had been silent for more than an hour now. Probably not a good sign.

"It's time," Pikka's voice echoed over the comms.

Elping felt the *Aurie* lurch as it locked onto the Nihil vessel. They were ready to board. He glanced about the cabin—a simple room with its lone bed and wash station. It would do. He made some final adjustments on the control panel just outside the door and headed to the supply room.

The four of them gathered at the airlock. Joss looked miserable, Pikka defiant at his side. Visma, grim-faced and tense as a coiled spring, appeared ready for battle, armed with no less than five blasters and a long knife sheathed to her thigh.

C-06N fussed nearby, looking like he'd given himself a polish for the occasion.

"You are all very stressed," the droid advised them. "Objectively, you look terrible."

Joss tilted his head. "Does he need to be here?"

"We'll need Sixen if we meet anyone who doesn't speak Basic," Pikka said. "That is, if anyone is still alive in there."

"Oh. That reminds me," said Elping, presenting an armful of white fabric evac suits and respirators to the group. He was already wearing one. "We don't know how hazardous the atmosphere might be."

"This is overkill," Visma said. "The Nihil probably just mutinied and killed each other."

"It doesn't matter," Elping said. "It's basic protocol. You have to put it on."

"Says who, Corporal?" Visma said through clenched teeth.

"Says *me*," Elping replied

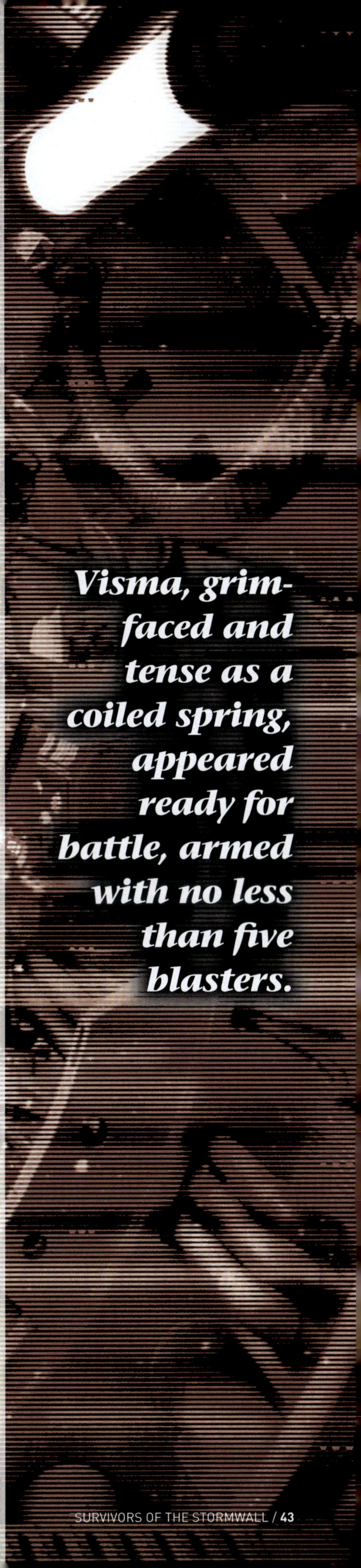

Visma, grim-faced and tense as a coiled spring, appeared ready for battle, armed with no less than five blasters.

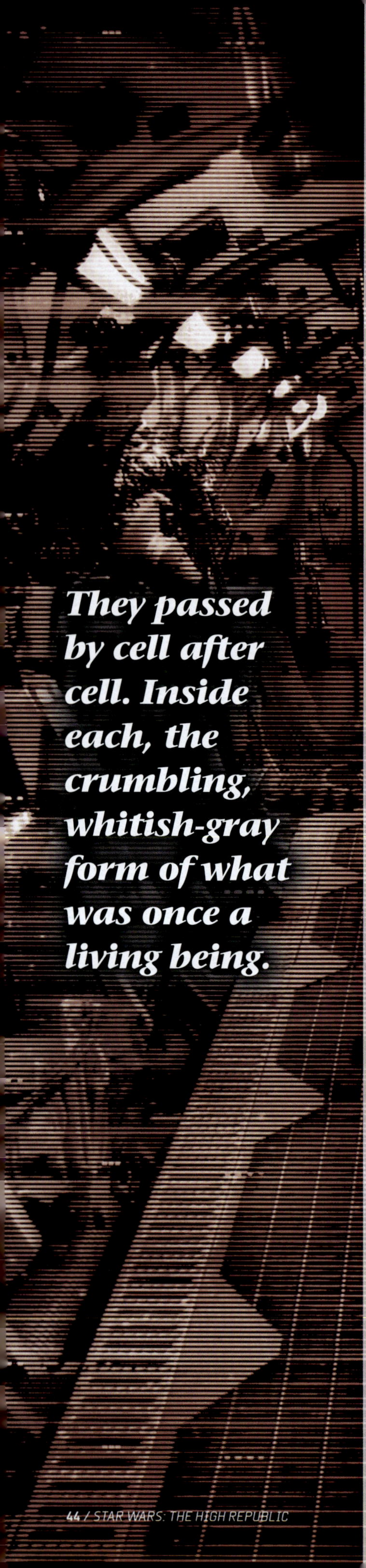

They passed by cell after cell. Inside each, the crumbling, whitish-gray form of what was once a living being.

pointedly. "I'm the highest-ranking scientific officer on this ship." He shrugged his shoulders. "I'm sorry, Captains. That goes for you too."

Pikka crossed her arms. "Very well. What is the protocol?"

"Protective equipment, including respirators, for all the those who board. I will collect samples, if at all possible, but only if it's safe to do so," Elping said, showing them a medkit hanging from his belt. "I've got a double-layered containment bag with a ventilator for the prisoner, if they made it, in my backpack. I've also outfitted one of the cabins near this loading area as an isolation ward, with negative pressure venting into space." Elping handed a single protective jumpsuit and respirator to Visma, then to C-06N.

"I am a protocol droid! I do not wear garments!" C-06N cried out in dismay when Elping attempted to hand the droid a protective suit.

"Non-organic material might be affected too. Wear it, Sixen," Elping insisted.

"I applaud your authoritarian tone of voice, but I must protest—"

"Wear it, or we'll remove your legs and carry you in a backpack," Elping replied, firmly.

"And on it goes!" the droid said, wrangling the jumpsuit over its silver body, far quicker than Elping ever expected.

With just one set of gear left, Elping turned to Joss and Pikka. "One of you must stay on the ship. Protocol, again. And I would suggest, although it's up to you, that it's Pikka who stays behind, due to…" Elping cleared his throat. "You know."

Pikka gave him a quizzical glance. "How did you know?"

"Know what?" Visma said.

Pikka looked at Visma, and her hand moved protectively to her lower abdomen. "I'm pregnant."

"*In the O.Z.?*" Visma exclaimed. "This zone isn't exactly child friendly!"

"We didn't *exactly* plan to be here," admitted Joss, with a sigh.

"I'm sorry, Captain Adren," Elping said to Pikka. "I was reviewing the medical protocols to prepare for the prisoner, in case they're sick. And your prenatal-screening update was visible when I turned on the monitor. I was going to tell you that you need to turn off the program for privacy's sake, but things got busy."

"If you think I should stay back, I will," Pikka reluctantly agreed.

"It would be the safest decision," Elping nodded. "Your immune system isn't as strong as ours. It's a fact. Someone must stay back, in any case."

"Okay, I said I'll stay" Pikka replied, glancing at Joss, who was clearly relieved. "I'll be ready to detach the *Aurie* as soon as you give the order."

Joss looked at Elping gratefully, then grabbed his gear. "Let's get on with this," he said, suiting up.

The first thing Elping noticed was the absence of sound. He imagined a prison should be filled with noises. Inmates complaining, if they hadn't been subdued into silence. The thump of boots from guards. Doors shutting or closing. Beeps and alarms. But it was quiet as death.

The second thing Elping noticed was the *substance*.

He wasn't sure what else to call it. They entered an airlock, and then a corridor that led to metal ladders going up, left, and walkways with barred prison cells. But the strange substance was everywhere. An off-white, crumbly residue that Elping first saw on the door of one of the cells. Then he saw a body inside it, covered in the stuff. There was a console that was once manned by a guard, now with speckles of the thing all over it. The individual, or what used to be him, lay prone on the floor.

Visma, uncharacteristically, held back and stood behind Elping, as did Joss.

"What is it?" Joss asked.

"I don't know. I've never seen anything like it. It doesn't look quite like a fungus, or an ameboid parasite. Maybe a sprayed weapon of some sort? I just don't know."

Visma was staring at a wire that hung from the ceiling, curving down. The substance was clinging to part of it, like a clump of fluffy sand nearly ready to fall off. She extended a hand,

and Elping immediately shot out an arm, holding her back.

"Don't touch it, Visma. Nobody touch any of it."

His arm continued to hold her back, and she clutched at his wrist. Not in anger, but in fear. How odd, Elping thought. All their months together, Elping and Visma had always kept their distance. No friendly pats on the back, hugs of affection, or angry cuffs. It was unusual for her to show anything aside from steely determination. Whatever this substance was, she couldn't outsmart it. She couldn't tackle it, stun it, kill it. Visma's eyes widened with apprehension. She shrank into a smaller space.

"Stay behind me. Only step where I step," Elping instructed her. Visma gave him a grateful look, and a surprised one. As if she expected him to take this opportunity to get rid of her, or weaken her. Is this what went through her mind, to be on defense all the time? It sounded exhausting. And utterly lonely.

"How silent of you, Lieutenant Tarko!" C-06N said.

"Speaking of silent, shut it, Sixen," Elping said. "The sensor said there was one life-form on this ship. It's on the far side of this hold."

Joss took out his blaster. "Let's go."

They passed by cell after cell. Inside each, the crumbling, whitish-gray form of what was once a living being: a human, a Trandoshan, a Chagrian. All dead. All covered with the thing. Or consumed by it, or transformed into it, it wasn't clear. What worried Elping was that while it appeared to only affect biological organisms, it had spread onto the ship's surfaces too, across the cell walls, the ceiling, and the wiring. Perhaps it was devouring micro bacteria on those surfaces in order to spread?

"I don't like this one bit," C-06N said. "Not one bit."

"I agree with you," Joss murmured.

"Thank the stars we have these respirators on. Watch where you step, too," Elping said.

They made their way around the rectangular scaffolding. Each and every cell contained calcified remains. All dead, their faces and bodies now a dull grayish-white, like volcanic ash or stone.

"The sooner we leave, the better," Joss murmured. He placed his hand against one of the few cell doors that was devoid of the strange substance. It moved. "The cells are open. I wonder if there was a last-ditch effort to let the prisoners free?"

"Doubtful," Visma said. "More likely a glitch that happened when that Nihil guard died."

A strange, wheezing sound emanated from a cell further down the hallway.

"What's that?" Joss asked.

It was followed by a groan. Visma and Joss readied their blasters as the group walked forward. Joss peered inside the cell, his blaster before him.

"We found 'em. The survivor. I don't think we're going to need these," he said, lowering his blaster.

Elping moved forward for a look. Inside the cell was a person, but Elping had difficulty even comprehending what species they were. The body was curled up like an unhatched tadpole. A very dry, desiccated tadpole. The arms and hands were immobile, frozen in place by dried skin that had thickened, peeling in places, almost like an ill-fitting shell. The creature was wheezing, their breath limited by shrunken, hardened skin—as if wearing armor that was far too small for its torso. There was a large, faintly bluish head with bulging, cloudy eyes. They could not see. It looked like the off-white substance had been slowly making its way onto their body, but only affecting the tips of the feet and hands.

Elping cocked his head. He saw barbels hanging off its face. "I think... that might be...a Mon Calamari. A really sick Mon Calamari."

Joss stood by the door, staring. His face behind his respirator slowly changed from confusion to utter shock.

"Captain Adren?" Elping said, thoroughly worried by his reaction.

"Ghal?" Joss whispered, placing his hands on the bars of the cell door. *"Ghal Tarpfen?"*

Elping moved forward for a look. Inside the cell was a person, but Elping had difficulty even comprehending what species they were.

STAR WARS THE HIGH REPUBLIC

TALES FROM THE OCCLUSION ZONE
"Family Ties"

By Lydia Kang

Illustration by Jake Lunt Davies

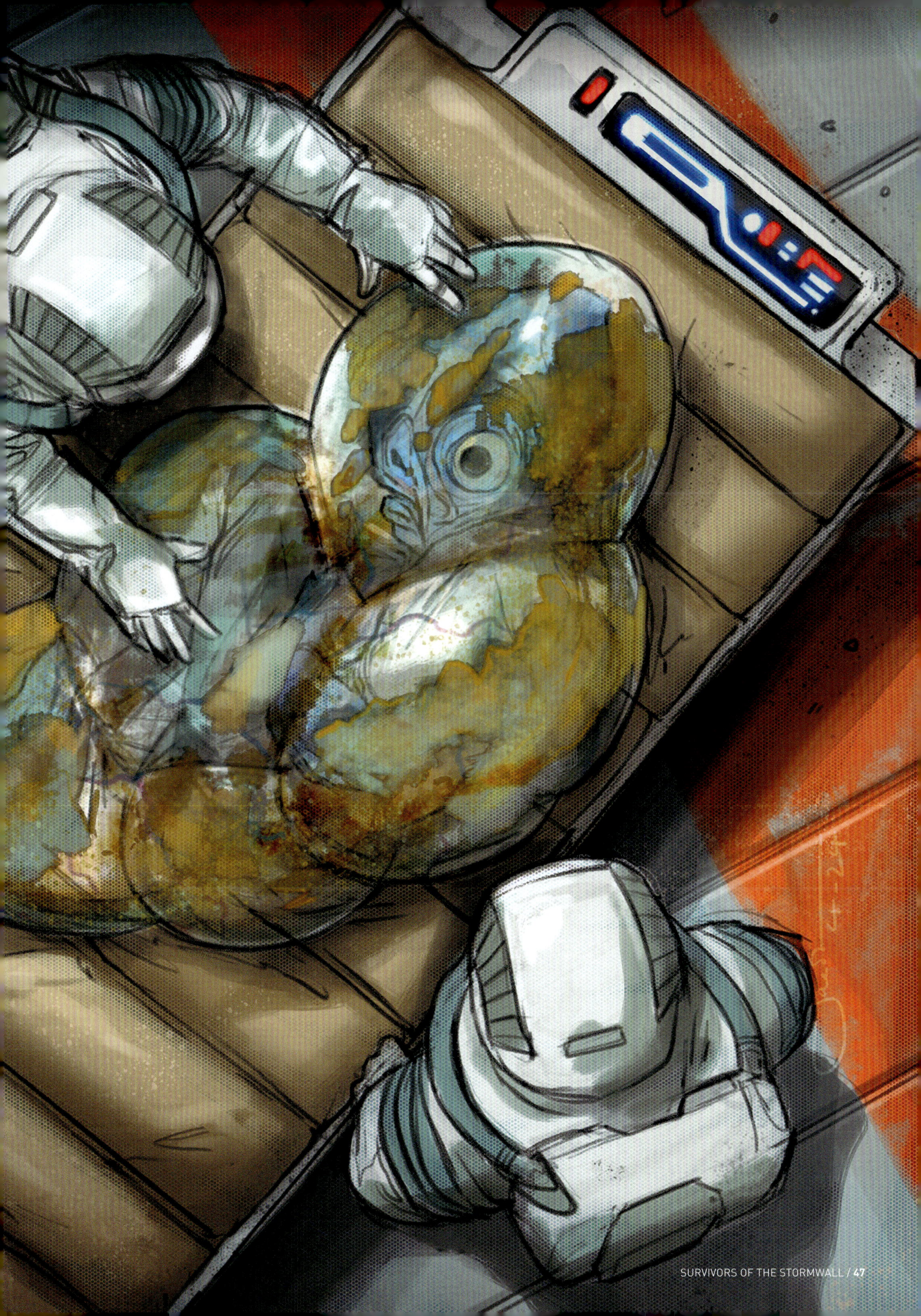

Previously, in a galaxy far, far away....

Missing and presumed dead, Chief Ghal Tarpfen is alive but critically ill. Rescued by the RDC crew aboard the *Aurie* in Nihil space, they race to save her despite being confounded by her mysterious affliction. Will they be able to find out what happened to Ghal—and a way out of the Occlusion Zone—before they all succumb to the mysterious blight?

"I don't like this. I don't like this at all."

Visma had lost track of whether she was muttering out loud or screaming inside her head. She stood on the Nihil prison transport ship as Corporal Elping Tsoo and Captain Joss Adren accompanied the desiccated but living body of Ghal Tarpfen onto the *Aurie*. The small portable hover gurney held the Mon Calamari, who lay in a state of biostasis within a hibernation shell that her body had extruded. In the airlock, Joss spoke aloud, his voice muffled by his protective respirator.

"Pikka. We're in. Close the airlock, and stay where you are. There was definitely some sort of pathogen or bioweapon on that ship that caused the death of the crew."

Pikka's voice sounded guarded over the comms. "Is it truly Ghal Tarpfen? I thought she was dead!"

"I have a gut feeling it's her. I just hope we can save her."

And for what? Visma thought bitterly. They had located the prison ship's Path drive, but it was speckled with the grayish stuff that had infected nearly every area of the ship. They couldn't bring it back and take the chance that it would cause the *Aurie* and its passengers to succumb.

"Pikka, stay right where you are," Elping said. "We'll take the patient to the isolation room."

Visma peered through one of the less-opaque areas of the bulbous shell that was wrapped around Ghal. A low moan could be heard, followed by garbled, muffled words. Visma concentrated, trying to make sense of what she was trying to say.

"It's coming...someone has to tell them...get away...the Stormwall..."

Elping's biosensor beeped a warning. "Vital signs are getting weaker. We have to work quickly."

Pikka had set up a protected corridor from the airlock to the makeshift medical cabin. The door behind them slid closed securely. Visma could feel the pressure in her ears pop a little. She noted an air current in the room, a sign that the ventilation was being directed out of the room and out of the *Aurie*. The Mon Calamari had stopped moaning and murmuring. Elping locked the hover gurney in place.

"She's quiet now. Maybe that's good?" Joss said.

"Maybe that's bad," Elping said grimly.

"The...substance. It's not all over her, but it's definitely on her. Look at her hands. Her feet," Visma said.

Ghal was still in the same position she'd been in when they found her in her prison cell—like a tadpole that had dried out in a tight curl beneath layers of peeling, hardened skin. Specks of the grayish matter that had infected the prison ship clung to the tips of her webbed feet and hands. She wore no boots, and scraps of clothing clung to her body as if painted on. Her yellow eyes were unblinking beneath a dried shell of tissue surrounding her head.

"Why does she look like this? Did the Nihil do this to her?" Joss asked.

"I don't think so," Elping said, studying the translucent shell-like covering encasing Ghal. "The Mon Calamari are an amphibious species, and sometimes amphibians can undergo a sort of state of hibernation or stasis in times of severe drought. In this case, perhaps stress or illness."

His biosensor began beeping an even louder warning. His eyes widened, and he stared at Ghal through the protective layer cocooned around her.

"She's stopped breathing!" Joss said.

"We don't have a medical droid!" Visma said. "What are we supposed to do?"

"Sixen," Joss hollered. "Don't you know any… medical speak? Can't you help?"

"I am quite helpful!" C-06N replied cheerfully, still wearing his protective garb over his silvery body. "I am capable of conversing with other programs, but I was specifically designed by my maker to help the Tarkin family with interspecies communication, regarding the particular cultural nuances and linguistic dynamics--"

"Sixen!" Elping cut off the droid. "Go plug yourself into the wall, cross reference the medical program on the *Aurie* and tell us anything actually helpful!"

C-06N tossed his head indignantly and shuffled over to the side of the small room. Soon, he was plugged into a port. "Oh! Well, look at this. An interspecies algorithm for medical emergencies. Splendid! Step one. Is the patient breathing if gaseous respiration is possible?"

Visma spun around to stare at Ghal. Inside the hardened exterior, the Mon Calamari's chest was no longer moving.

"She's not breathing!" Visma said. Her own heart began to race. Visma could shoot down an enemy combatant at eight hundred meters in the dark. But what was happening to Ghal was beyond anything she could fight or outsmart. She was so out of her league, and the helplessness made her want to scream. She'd felt that helplessness before. When she was a child, when her family was taken from her. When her whole life changed. No one had done anything to help her. The sensation was so familiar right now she could hardly think straight.

"But if she's in stasis—maybe she doesn't need to breathe?" Joss said.

"Step two," C-06N announced. "Does the patient have a pulse, if a liquid pulsatile vascular system exists?"

Elping searched the scanner in his hand. He touched a few buttons, and it began blaring.

"No pulse. Even if she was in stasis, she would still have a faint

"Visma could shoot down an enemy combatant at eight hundred meters in the dark. But what was happening to Ghal was beyond anything she could fight or outsmart."

one. She's dying," he whispered. "We have to do something."

Joss and Elping exchanged ideas back and forth, talking so fast, it was a cyclone of words and questions. They were holding back, afraid to touch Ghal for fear the substance might affect them too. But then, what was the point of bringing her on the *Aurie* if they were just going to stand there and do nothing?

"Breaking the shell? I don't have the data for that, Captain Adren," Elping was saying about something. "What if that kills her?"

"You have a better idea?" He pointed at the curled, lifeless form of the Mon Calamari woman. Just looking at her, Visma felt a tightness in her chest, as if some mighty unseen being were squeezing her. She took a breath of air, but the respirator felt too confining. She had to force herself not to yank it off. But she couldn't breathe, watching Ghal dying before her.

"Mon Calamari, on rare occasions in times of historic drought, prior to the development of modern environmental controls, have gone into suspended animation in the mud of exposed seabeds," C-06N said.

"It's too confining. This isn't some drought on Mon Cala and she isn't a cocoon of wet mud. The air here is dry as dust," Joss argued.

Visma could barely hear any words. Blood rushed to her ears,

pounding so loudly it was a rhythmic churning that drowned out the argument between Elping and Joss. Unblinking, she stared at the Mon Calamari woman dying before her. Perhaps already dead.

There was a lip of thickened, dried shell over Ghal's torso. The dangerous grayish pathogen clung to the tips of her hands and feet, but were absent from the rest of her body. Beneath the translucent tissue, Ghal's chest had indeed stopped expanding and shrinking. The yellow eyes had started to dilate. If they did nothing, Ghal would die. She was being abandoned right before her eyes. Before she could think, Visma shot out a hand and grabbed the lip of dried skin. She began pulling with all her might.

"Visma! What are you doing?" Elping reached out to stop her. But Visma was stronger than Elping and held him off. She pried open the thick shellac of skin and a cracking noise sounded. Joss didn't hesitate. He, too, began to pull at a section of the hardened shell, and the crack extended around Ghal's chest and up across her face. A gluey, clear substance oozed from the crack, and soon they had a huge section free around her mouth.

Ghal's lips opened, and she gasped for air. Under the shell still enclosing her face, the yellow eyes blinked once.

"Help her!" Visma yelled.

Elping grabbed an insulated containment bag. "Put the pieces in here! Don't touch that gray stuff, whatever it is."

"Ghal turned to see a monitor on the wall. On the other side, a stern-faced Arkanian woman in RDC gear stared back at her with arms crossed."

Together, Elping, Joss, and Visma freed Ghal from her shell. Elping rinsed fluids over her as they continued to remove pieces, the liquid being collected in another containment bag. The gray material clung to the tips of her left fingers and left toes.

"We have to remove that. She might die," Elping said.

"Or infect the rest of us," Visma said.

They all nodded, grimly. Quickly, after administering a nerve block to her arm, Elping used an instrument that simultaneously amputated and cauterized several fingers. They repeated the process on two left toes. She would still be able to walk, eventually. The removed digits were dropped into the containment bag. With Elping's guidance and the readouts from the *Aurie*'s medical program, Ghal's hand and foot were bandaged carefully.

"Heart rate is back to a normal range. Respirations stabilizing," Elping said. He closed his eyes for a moment, and Visma knew exactly how relieved he was. She felt it too.

Ghal went from being a curled up tadpole shape to an exhausted, panting Mon Calamari on the gurney, utterly spent.

"Thank you," the Mon Calamari wheezed, "for saving my life. And now…" She took several more gasps, before finding the energy to speak more, "It's my turn to save yours."

Ghal could not speak another word, losing consciousness a moment later.

She did not know if she awoke after a few hours, or days. Her body felt tender and sore. Pain blossomed from the tips of her webbed appendages. Her left hand and foot were bandaged, and she peeked beneath them to see that she was now missing the tips of several fingers and two toes. Those were the areas where the blight had touched her, but it was gone now. She tried to move, and found that she could. Her chest was wondrously free of the confining shell of her hibernation layer. She took a deep breath and it was marvelous.

She opened her eyes and found she was no longer in the small medical room. She was now situated in… an escape pod? Ah, it made sense. Not that she thought her rescuers planned on jettisoning her out into space, but rather, they considered this a makeshift quarantine. A hydration mister had been set up instead of an IV line. She was comfortably clothed in RDC garments. Her insides no longer felt like syrup, and her skin was growing more elastic and hydrated by the minute.

"You're awake."

Ghal turned to see a monitor on the wall. On the other side, a stern-faced Arkanian woman in RDC gear stared back at her with arms crossed.

"I am, thank you. Where am I?"

The Arkanian's eyes narrowed. "Please state your name and rank."

Ghal blinked. Her eyes felt sandy, her vision slightly blurry. "You already know my name, Lieutenant Tarko. Ask me a more useful question."

The hard look on Visma Tarko's face was replaced with surprise. "How did you…"

"I am Ghal Tarpfen. I was Chief and Head of Security on Starlight Beacon before it fell, and a ranking member of the Republic Defense Coalition. I was on the committee that cleared your promotion to Lieutenant. One of the youngest promotions in the Coalition, as I recall."

Visma opened her mouth, but had nothing to say.

"You don't remember me, do you?" Ghal chuckled.

The young Arkanian woman was visibly uncomfortable. "I…am Visma Tarko, you're right. You are now on board the *Aurie*. We are in the Occlusion Zone, about 300 parsecs away from Valo."

Ghal used to do the same thing. When anything was uncomfortable, just lean into protocol. Protocols and rules gave her backbone when sometimes she might not have the strength to stand on her own. She recognized fear when she saw it. This Arkanian wasn't simply afraid of Ghal, or the blight that had attacked her. She guessed that Visma lived in a constant state of fear, hidden by a sheen of formality and coldness. For Ghal, it had been a constant state of heartache that had the same effect.

She reached for a canister of hydration fluids and drank deeply, her eyes closed. It was infused with dried kelp. After draining it, she sighed. "By the depths, that was so delicious." Ghal turned back towards the monitor. "How long have you been in the O.Z.?"

"Several months. The Captains Adren, for less so." Visma leaned in. "What were you doing on that prison transport ship? How did you survive? What do you know about—"

"The second RDC lesson of interrogation, Lieutenant, is to ask one question at a time," Ghal said, her expression hardening. "The first lesson is to get to know your subject. You know nothing about me, do you?"

Visma stiffened. Ghal raised her injured hand. "I'm sorry. I'm not trying to be difficult, but clearly I am. Some habits are hard to shed. I'll answer all your questions. In the meantime, I'd like to thank you for saving my life."

"Well, it wasn't just me. It was Corporal Tsoo, really, who—"

"You don't need to parse the details. You saved my life. I was aware enough to know that much. I am grateful, Visma."

The lieutenant seemed a little taken aback at being addressed so informally. She even smiled a little.

"You're welcome?" the Arkanian answered uneasily.

Behind her, two human RDC captains and a younger corporal entered. Ghal remembered the captains well. She smiled when the entered, and the smile was warmly returned.

"Captain Pikka Adren, and Captain Joss Adren. I can't tell you how glad I am to see you, under the circumstances," Ghal said.

"It seems like a miracle that you're here. We were all distraught when we thought you'd died," Pikka said through the monitor. "When Velko Jahen received your message—"

"She did? It went through?" Ghal said, her hands shaking.

"Not all of it. It was filled with static, but enough of your message ▸

came through for us to know that you were kidnapped. That the Senate was compromised."

"Ghirra Starros, Jeni Wataro. And more," Ghal said quickly.

"We know that now. But we also thought—we'd lost you," Joss said.

"I thought my end was coming, too," Ghal said. "You changed that."

"Your vital signs are stabilizing," the younger RDC man said, smiling. "I'm Corporal Elping Tsoo. Your body's defense in creating that protective hibernation shell probably saved your life."

"It almost ended my life, too," Ghal added.

"Nevertheless, there are no other survivors on that Nihil prison ship. How are you feeling, Chief Tarpfen?" Elping asked.

Ghal touched the newly blunted ends of her barbels with bandaged fingertips, but she was thinking of Shenrick, the King of Mon Cala, and their ill-fated time together. She thought of Velko, and all the things she wished she had said back on Starlight Beacon. She still might never see her friend and colleague again. She thought of all the Nihil and their prisoners on the ship, their cold, lifeless bodies now adrift in the O.Z. "I've lost some things, but not as much as others have. I'm all right."

"Can we ask what happened on that ship?" Pikka inquired, arms crossed.

"I don't know when the sickness began. It was insidious. No one knew where it came from—if we were seeded with it, or we were...infected with it somehow. Other prisoners succumbing, turning almost to dust. I saw it starting to affect the wiring, and there were spots on the walls of the ship. The commanders asked for help, and were ignored by the other Nihil. We were all left adrift to die."

"You don't know what it is?"

"No. None of us did. It was definitely spreading, but it seems you need to touch it to be affected. Honestly, I'm not completely sure. The second it began to affect my hand and foot, my body shut down. That's how you found me, I guess."

Everyone looked slightly relieved. Perhaps Ghal really had left the blight behind her, and the Nihil. But it didn't mean there weren't more bad times ahead. On the monitor, she saw Joss bring a seat over to Pikka, who sat down on it, looking slightly tired and slightly more round-faced than before. Pikka leaned into the monitor to speak.

"We've put a lot of distance between us and that Nihil ship. If you have the strength, tell us what happened to you."

Ghal took another drink of her kelp infusion. "They had kidnapped me from Starlight Beacon. I was on a Nihil ship. Even though I'd freed myself, I ended up facing three vessels ready to fire on me. And they did, but I managed to get in an escape pod. In the aftermath of the wreckage, it drifted in space for days. I was picked up by another Nihil ship and imprisoned on a transport. They tried to get more information from me about the RDC, and the Jedi." She lifted her chin. "I wasn't cooperative."

Ghal didn't say what methods they had used to force her to speak. They'd withheld water until her skin peeled and bled painfully. Used injections to try to get her to reveal RDC secrets. Made up stories about finding Velko, finding Ghal's family members, and threatening to murder them using every horrific detail they could imagine.

In the silence, Joss looked sorrowful. He seemed to guess what she wasn't saying. "I'm so sorry, Ghal. As long as you're with us, you're safe."

"Don't be so sure of that," Ghal said. "The entire O.Z. is unsafe, but some areas are worse than others. You mentioned our coordinates. We're close to the Stormwall."

"Yes. Heading to Valo, for more supplies," Elping said.

"No. You have to turn around. Immediately. I thought you were headed in the opposite direction." She held her head, which began to spin. Maybe she had dreamed of telling them about the danger? About staying away from the Stormwall? By the depths, perhaps she had only told them in a fever dream.

"Ghal. What are you talking about?" Pikka said, her face blanching with concern.

"I heard things on the Nihil ship. Whispers of a plan that had something to do with the Stormwall. We have to get as far away as possible. Please. Everything you fought to save..." She swallowed, her throat feeling like a desert now. "We'll lose everything if we don't turn around."

Joss and Pikka glanced at each other, and now Joss went pale. Visma barked, "The decryptor. We haven't been checking it for the last few hours!"

"Ghal touched the newly blunted ends of her barbels with bandaged fingertips, but she was thinking of Shenrick, the King of Mon Cala."

Pikka, Joss, Elping, and Visma left Ghal in the emergency exit bay, running as fast as they could to the cockpit where the decryptor had been synced up with the ship's central computer. Elping began adjusting the knobs, trying to find a frequency with Nihil transmissions. It was nothing but silence and static. He checked the past feed, but nothing had come up. A fragment of optimism filled his face.

"Maybe we're okay?" he said, hopefully.

Joss and Pikka looked more worried than ever. "That doesn't mean anything."

"Who knows what Ghal could have heard? She was so sick for so long. She could have imagined it," Visma offered.

"Ghal wouldn't have said it if she didn't think it was a legitimate concern," Joss said.

"Which is what worries me, too," Pikka said.

Suddenly, a channel of static was replaced by the sound of yells and screams. At first, it sounded like a recording of a massacre.

"What is that?" Pikka said, covering her mouth. "Who are they killing?"

Visma reached out her arm, as if to hold back an unseen foe. "No. Listen." She paused, ear cocked to the vocalizations. Screams, yes, but also—whoops. Hollers.

Laughter.

"They're celebrating," Visma said. Confusion filled her. She turned to face Elping. "Why are they celebrating?"

Alarms began to blare from the console, and Visma felt her body react, an immediate reflex. She would have grabbed her blasters if she was armed. "What's going on?"

Joss's hand flew over the console, his eyes searching. Blips on the scanner began to appear. Visma knew exactly what they were even before Joss spoke.

"A Nihil ship just appeared in our area. No, two."

"No, *three*," Pikka said, her voice grave. She turned to everyone. "Elping, amp up our scav signal to protect us better."

"*Protect us?* We're a Republic Longbeam! We can't hide!" Elping said, hands up in helplessness.

"Blast, there are more ships appearing!" Joss said, his voice rising.

"They've come to find us. To destroy us," Visma said, grimly. "They must have known we rescued Ghal. She's a prize for them." Just when Visma and Elping had found some safety. Just when Ghal did, too. She noticed Pikka's hand unconsciously go to her belly, as it tended to do more and more often.

"I...don't think so," Pikka said, looking over the glowing blips on the screen. She pointed. "It's too much firepower to chase after only one ship. They're not here to surround us. Look at the formation. They've come here for something else." She looked Visma, Elping, and Joss and her face went ashen. "They've come for something bigger. Much bigger. And we're caught in the middle of it."

STAR WARS THE HIGH REPUBLIC

TALES FROM THE OCCLUSION ZONE

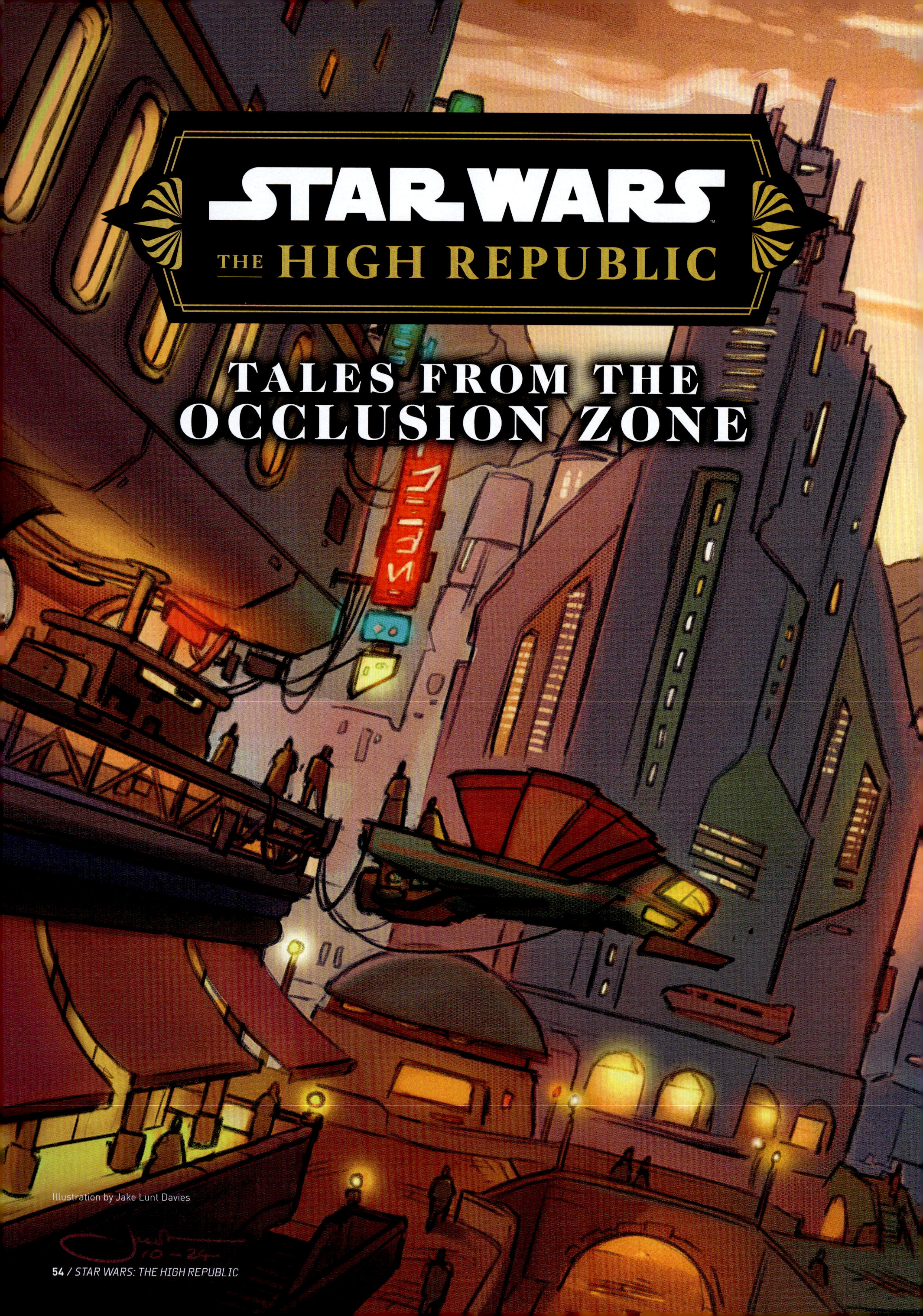

Illustration by Jake Lunt Davies

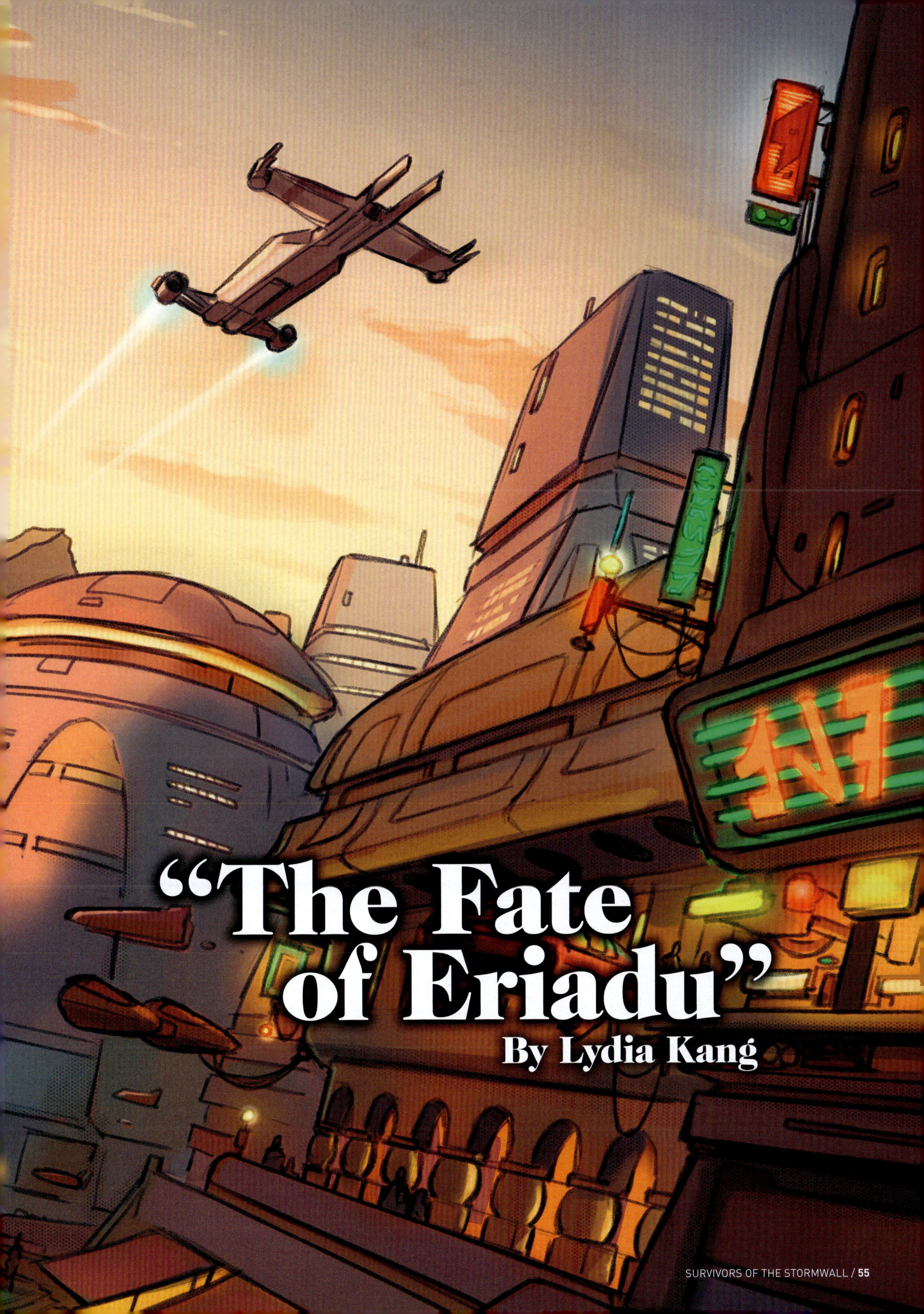

"The Fate of Eriadu"

By Lydia Kang

The tall Weequay grimaced, which was her version of smiling. "Got a new ship coming in. Republic Longbeam. It's covered in scav-droid scars."

Previously, in a galaxy far, far away....

The Republic Defense Coalition crew trapped inside the Occlusion Zone has traveled far to find a safe haven as supplies run dangerously low. With Pikka closing in on her due date and the survivors on the *Aurie* in ragged shape, they've finally made it. But Eriadu may not be the sanctuary they were hoping for...

Skrood licked the meat juices off his fingers as he rested his metal-clad boots on the control panel of the *Sickle*. He chose not to eat with the rest of his Nihil crew, as he was a suspicious commander. He might be poisoned, or worse, his food might be swiped when he wasn't looking. Skrood was smallest of his crew, which was common enough when you were a Lannik, but he'd sliced and hacked off enough fingers, noses, and appendages to fight for his rank. Diminutive or not, he was a vicious, dirty fighter. He gnawed off the last bits of flesh from the roast foot of the siler—some striped beast from Eriadu that the Nihil culled by the dozens to feed themselves—and followed with a sonorous, wet burp.

As if she'd been signaled with the gastric vocalization, one of his Nihil underlings appeared. The tall Weequay grimaced, which was her version of smiling.

"Got a new ship coming in. Republic Longbeam. It's covered in scav-droid scars."

"Excellent. I'm boarding this one. Last time you killed too many and we lost bargaining chips."

The Weequay grunted at the criticism, then punched at the communications controls of the *Sickle*. The Longbeam responded immediately by opening its comms channel.

Skrood smiled internally. *So pathetically eager to give up, these Republic vermin.*

"You are an unidentified vessel in Nihil space," Skrood said. "Surrender and prepare to be boarded, by order of Marchion Ro, the Eye of the Nihil. Your crew and your ship will hereafter belong to the Nihil. If we allow you to live, you will be confined to the planet of Eriadu until further notice." Skrood knew his voice was harsh and triumphant. Steady. The voice of someone who was winning a war.

As the *Sickle* and fifteen other Nihil ships orbited the brown and blue planet of Eriadu, now comfortably within the Occlusion Zone, this ship's passengers had little choice. The Nihil were well-fed, well-equipped, and always prepared for a fight.

There was a long pause. What was there to think of? Die, or be subjugated.

A woman's voice spoke from the Longbeam.

"This is the Republic Defense Coalition Longbeam designation *Aurora III*. We accept the terms of surrender."

She sounded exhausted and defeated. *How very excellent*, he thought.

A ragtag group including Skrood and ten Nihil—all wearing battle-scarred, mismatched armor and masks, with a single, unifying blue, spiral, angry eye—boarded the Longbeam. Despite having done this multiple times before, they weren't quite sure what to expect. Some ships they'd captured had dozens of crewmembers who fought back; others had only corpses of inhabitants who had starved to death or died of battle injuries.

The crew of the Longbeam were something in between.

There were only five, plus a shiny silver protocol droid. One was a human female with curled brown hair and heavily gravid, and the only one who appeared healthy. Two human males, both with starved looks in their eyes: one tall and broad-shouldered, and one much younger with black hair. An Arkanian woman with a fierce expression stared with her white eyes at the Nihil as if their very existence was an insult to *all* Arkanians. And finally, lying on a hover gurney, a sickly-looking Mon Calamari female wheezed with every painful breath. Her normally yellow eyes had paled to a color akin to watery mucus. The Nihil wouldn't have been surprised if she died right there in front of them.

The droid stepped forward. "I am See-Ohsixen, specially programmed for high-level communications, servicing the Tarkin family. I am delighted to be home, I might add, and—"

"His programming is irreversibly malfunctioning," Joss warned. "But you're welcome to have him."

"*Malfunctioning?* I would very much like to rebut that statement! I am in *magnificent* condition! The caliber of my circuits is pristine and beyond dispute! I am categorically perfect in every way and I..."

"You can have him if you want," the human woman said, rather dryly.

Skrood looked at the droid and waved his hand, like C-06N was damaged goods. "State your name and rank," Skrood barked at the rest of them.

"We have...no rank," the woman said. "I am Pikka Adren. This is Joss Adren, Elping Tsoo, Visma Tarko, and Ghal Tarpfen."

"You really expect us to believe those are your real names? And that you're not RDC? In this ship?" Skrood asked, scrutinizing them. They certainly weren't wearing uniforms. They all looked like service crew. Still, they could have torn off their insignias.

"We were only delivering this Longbeam to Eriadu, when we were overtaken by the expansion. We've been stranded ever since," the taller male said.

"Search the vessel," Skrood said. "Take everything."

The Nihil scattered, ransacking all the compartments, finding a single serviceable blaster, a few nearly empty bags of protein powder, dried fruit, and vitamin packets. One well-worn game of Shah-tezh. Even the medical fluid supplies of intravenous dextrose had been drunk. The crew looked like they were ready to eat the walls of the ship. Skrood studied them. The others had starved so the gravid one could have more to eat. Ah, they were tender hearted. What a horrific sentiment. Now, they looked like they could barely stand. He laughed at them, and the sound of his mirth made them wince.

"Skrood," said one of his soldiers. "We have a record of one of these names in our system. Ghal Tarpfen. She was our prisoner who was on that transport that went adrift some months ago and...succumbed."

"She's as good as dead," the Weequay Nihil said, sneering. "Eriadu is a prison anyway. *Our* prison. Enjoy your slow death."

Pikka took control of the *Aurie* as soon as the Nihil were gone. They left a rancid smell in the air that made her feel queasy. Thank the stars they weren't feeling bloodthirsty. None of them were in shape for combat right now.

"I can't believe they let us through," Pikka said.

"Sometimes the truth is the best plan of action," Joss said. "Saved them the energy of an argument."

"And a bloody mess. They are so drunk on power, I think that murder has gotten boring," Pikka said. She thrust her chin forward. "Hey. There it is. Eriadu."

Over her shoulder, Joss leaned on her pilot's chair and stared at the enlarging green and brown marble of a planet before a spray of stars. Pikka put a hand on her belly and looked at her husband. Her beautiful Joss, usually strong as a lifter droid, thinning from starvation. His hands had balled into fists, ready to fight. Always ready to defend. But this time, they had to land on Eriadu no matter the cost. The Nihil ships were now far behind them. Visma and Elping appeared in the doorway of the cockpit.

"You don't sound relieved, Pikka," Visma said. They'd stopped using their RDC ranks for weeks now. The tightness of their quarters made honorifics and such seem ridiculous ▸

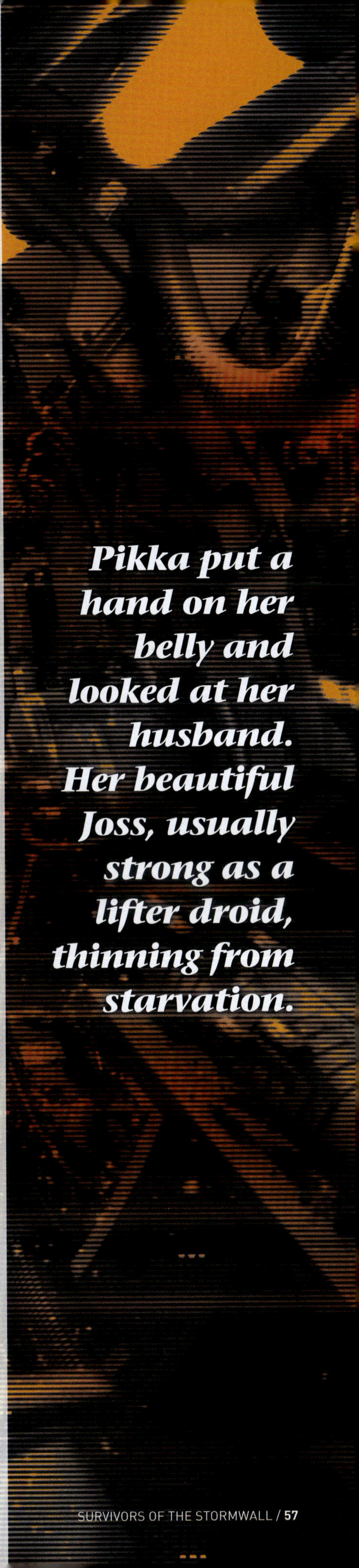

Pikka put a hand on her belly and looked at her husband. Her beautiful Joss, usually strong as a lifter droid, thinning from starvation.

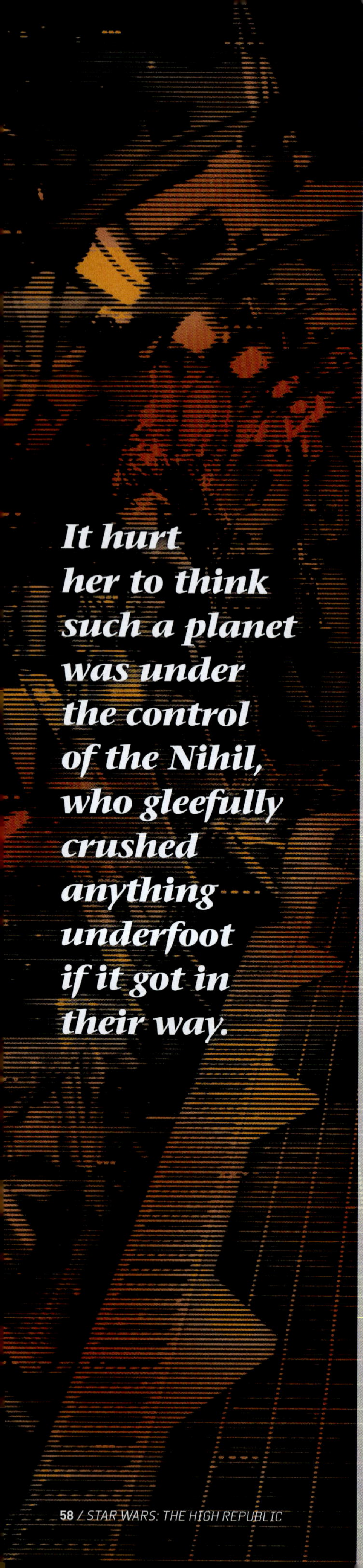

It hurt her to think such a planet was under the control of the Nihil, who gleefully crushed anything underfoot if it got in their way.

after a while. The Arkanian's cheekbones were sharp, and her once close-cropped hair now touched her shoulders as she crossed her arms.

Elping shrugged. The young RDC corporal had aged years in a few months and had lost the bright curiosity in his eyes. "Eriadu isn't the Eriadu from a few months ago."

As they descended towards the planet surface, Visma and Elping stared out the viewport. Pikka had noticed in the last few months the two younger RDC crewers in a detente of sorts. They fought less and often checked in on one another in silence, as if to make sure that they were, indeed, still alive. Still surviving.

Eriadu was a beautiful planet from above—mountainous areas, vast seas, and greenery that made Pikka feel almost hungry after so much time in space. The last time they'd been there, they were free. Now it hurt her to think such a planet was under the control of the Nihil, who gleefully crushed anything underfoot if it got in their way.

At first glance, Eriadu City and the neighboring Bri-Phrang seemed relatively unchanged, sprouting its metropolis around the inlet of the Orrineswa River and threading its borders into the wilder edges several kilometers out. But on closer view, there were scattered buildings that had crumbled into rubble, and fires smoldered here and there in what used to be homes. Ships flew low and cautiously over buildings of varying height and shapes, creating an irregular skyline. Pikka landed the *Aurie* at an airfield north of the city, crowded with vessels. Some ships appeared to have been pilfered by the Nihil for parts.

"We have to hide the *Aurie* as soon as we can," Joss said, and Pikka nodded in agreement. An Eriaduan man met them when they disembarked. Elping and Visma pushed the hover gurney with the weakened Ghal between them.

"We just got your clearance to land," the Eriaduan man said. "This is the *Aurora III*?" Joss nodded. "There's plenty of space here for you to keep your ship, though it can be confiscated by the Nihil at any time. Or worse—" he motioned to the ships that seemed to be missing entire engines, ion cannons, sections of fuselage, and hyperdrives.

"We need urgent medical assistance," Elping interrupted, "for this Mon Calamari. We think she's suffering from some profound vitamin deficiencies due to eating only human food for months."

He gave an appraising glance to their group and raised his eyebrows. "Looks like you *all* need medical help. How long were you in the O.Z.?"

"Too long," Visma said.

A woman in the distance shouted. A flaxen ponytail flew out behind her as she ran to the group. She wore baggy work pants and an oversized smock. She looked familiar, but Pikka couldn't place her.

"Joss! Pikka!" The woman embraced both of them and they awkwardly accepted the hug with arms stiff at their sides. After she'd released Joss, he squinted his eyes at her as if seeing through a haze of time and distance.

"Ensign Casset? Is that you?" he asked.

"Shh," she said. "No ranks. Not while we're being occupied. Just call me Ebbe."

She seemed older by years since they'd last said goodbye to her right here on Eriadu, before that fateful day when they'd left to investigate a Nihil ship, only to get swept into the Occlusion Zone. Her clothes made her look like an ordinary citizen on Eriadu, but her upright posture told them she was still RDC to the core.

"I thought you were all dead," she said. Her eyes were glassy. "I thought I'd sent you both—and your little one—to a death sentence."

"It wasn't your order. It was Kronara's. And our decision," Pikka said. "No one could have predicted the Occlusion Zone was going to expand like that."

"But it was my idea," she admitted.

"It doesn't matter," Joss said. "Right now, we have other things to worry about. Like Ghal."

The Eriaduan in charge of their processing looked at his datapad, running the list with their IDs. His face went pale, and his eyes widened.

"Ghal...Ghal Tarpfen? The Head of Security from the Starlight Beacon?" His mouth dropped open. "I thought—I thought—"

"I am not dead, but I will be if you keep gawking," Ghal rasped, her pale eyes reddened at the edges.

Ebbe yelled sharply to a group of medics nearby, who came running. They whispered to each other as they approached her.

"Is it true? This is Ghal Tarpfen? She's actually alive?" said the taller one.

The other replied, "She was a hero when she was dead. She's a beacon of hope if she's alive."

Elping and Visma stayed at Ghal's side.

"We're not leaving her," Elping said.

"We're going to make sure she's okay, then find you later," Visma said. She lowered her voice. "We'll find out what the RDC is doing here. I think there are probably more hiding on Eriadu than we realize."

Ebbe spoke quietly too, glancing around with a paranoia that they all seemed to carry with them. "There are. And plenty of places for us to hide." She glanced behind her, but nobody was there there—only an Eriaduan mountain range beyond the city's borders. "We have to stay quiet for now." She looked at Elping and Visma. "We'll get you debriefed after you get some rest. I'll find you later."

Visma and Elping followed the medics to a shelter nearby.

Pikka frowned. "I hope they remember to get a square meal and take a shower. They stink."

"We're not smelling that much better," Joss said. The sound of clanging came from inside the *Aurie*, and C-06N emerged, arms up and making a direct line to Ebbe.

"Finally! I shall be reunited with the Tarkin family! It has been a trial, these last months."

"Really? You weren't semi-starving, Sixen," Joss said.

"Worse, I have been cohabitating with people who have no respect for my translational skills."

"We saved you from being Nihil scrap metal." Pikka rolled her eyes. "Take him. Please."

Ebbe waved the droid forward.

"We'll return you back to one of the Tarkin households," she said. "Head to that hangar over there for eval and processing." C-06N walked away so fast he was a blur of metal legs and waving arms. "Come on. I'm walking you to the infirmary to get checked out. And then..."

"And then, we lay low," Pikka said. Though they were no longer on the run, she felt anything but safe. "Find a place to live. Hide the *Aurie*. And figure out our next steps."

Three weeks had passed.

Joss had woken up inside their tiny quarters on the outskirts of Eriadu City. It wasn't much, but it did the job. A small bedroom, a space with a kitchen, place to eat, and a long workbench that spanned an entire wall, where they continued to make a vast number of repairs that the *Aurie* needed. After so many scav-droid attacks, there was plenty to do. Joss and Pikka had found a small space nearby that served as a hangar for the Longbeam.

Joss made himself a large caf and breakfast for Pikka, whose belly was seemingly enlarging every day. She sat down at the tiny table and sighed, her curly dark hair rumpled and gorgeous. Another day alive. Joss chose to lean against the wall and stare out a long, narrow window barely wide enough to stick his hand out of. He liked to look at the mountains and get a glimpse of green when he could.

"You know, we haven't had a chance to talk to Ebbe in a few days."

"She's busy." Pikka gave her husband a meaningful look.

Ever since Ebbe had quietly mentioned it, Joss and Pikka had carefully asked around. It was Elping and Visma who ended up telling them the truth—that the RDC had stashed several ships and hidden RDC personnel inside the abandoned lommite mines and hidden mountainous passageways. Those mountains *looked* uninhabited. No buildings, no houses. Just scars from the lommite mines, but beneath

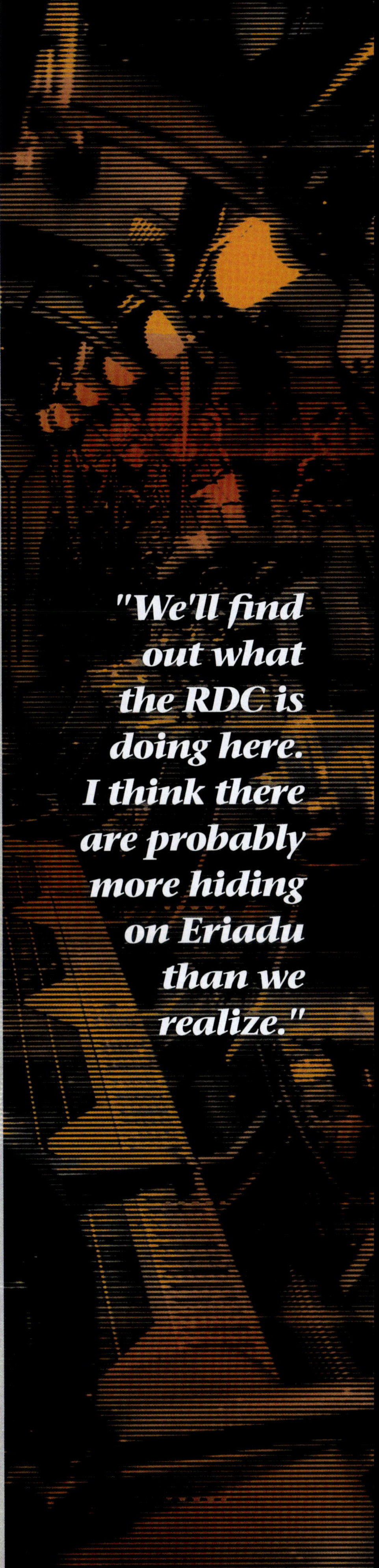
"We'll find out what the RDC is doing here. I think there are probably more hiding on Eriadu than we realize."

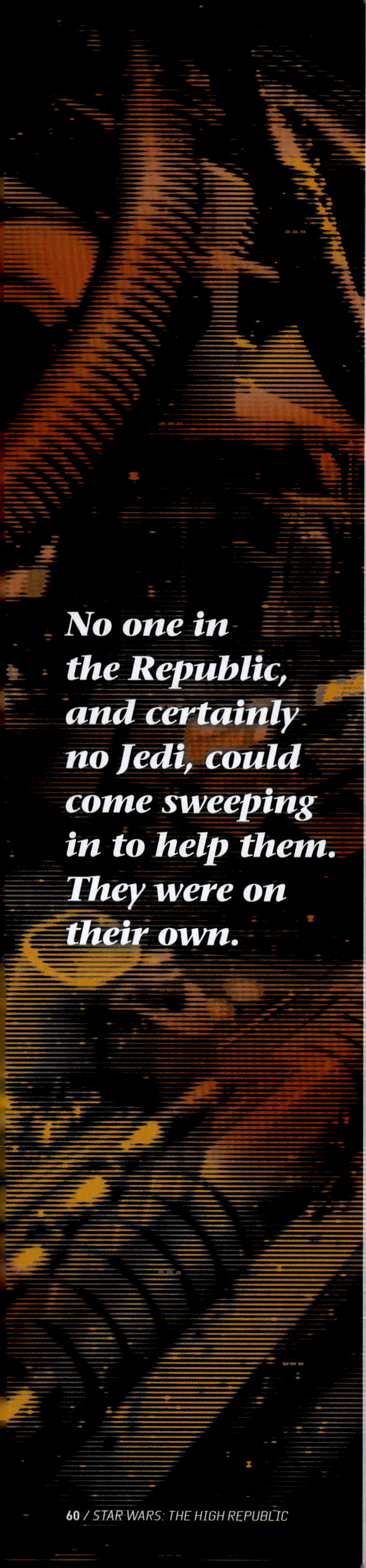

No one in the Republic, and certainly no Jedi, could come sweeping in to help them. They were on their own.

them was an arsenal. Waiting... for something.

Just then, there was a knock at the door.

Pikka and Joss froze, his mug stopping halfway to his mouth.

They had been careful to live quietly in Eriadu City, where the Nihil might sweep in at any moment to take all your things or throw you into confinement. Mostly, the Nihil seemed to leave the Eriaduans alone, but Joss and Pikka had already been subject to one raid and had gotten away unscathed. But now they had other reasons to worry.

Knowing there were more RDC than the Nihil knew existed felt like a shout on the tip of Joss's tongue, and yet he had to keep his mouth shut. Even Ebbe Casset couldn't tell them what the plan was. Plus, they didn't know if they had enough support from Eriaduans to overthrow the Nihil. And even if they did, Eriadu was still in the Occlusion Zone. No one in the Republic, and certainly no Jedi, could come sweeping in to help them. They were on their own, and currently, an uprising might be tantamount to suicide. But they were ready for the call, and that made their existence all the more precarious. They *knew* things now.

Someone knocked again on the door.

Joss stood up, quietly took his blaster where it was stowed beneath their bed. He'd carefully hidden his WESTAR under a bolted section of the *Aurie* so the Nihil wouldn't discover it, and now he hid it in a holster against his left ribs. He touched a screen by the door where Pikka had rigged a camera showing them a view of the hallway outside their quarters, as well as the alley behind the building. Just in case.

It was Visma and Elping. Elping was holding a basket.

"We come bearing gifts!" Visma said.

Joss opened the door and they entered, handing over their gift of hard-to-get fruit and a small jug of jogan juice, Pikka's favorite.

"Good to see you!" Pikka said, waving them in. Just as the door closed, a silver droid arm prevented it from closing, and C-06N barged in.

"Sixen! What are you doing here?" Pikka said, so surprised she nearly dropped the juice. She looked at Visma and Elping. "Is this what you meant by 'gifts'?"

Visma frowned. The Arkanian woman had shorn her hair short again and appeared so much stronger than when they'd landed. Good. She wore an old RDC uniform with the insignia ripped off.

"I have been to several Tarkin abodes—so beautifully designed—nothing like the squalor I have lived in these past weeks and months—"

Here, Joss was very tempted to reach over and shut off the droid for insulting the *Aurie*. Pikka gave him a warning look and he backed down.

"—and the Tarkins have decided that my services are no longer of use, and I may be deployed to other acquaintances." The droid looked at Joss and Pikka. "The Adrens."

"Oh, no." Pikka waved her hands around. "There's hardly room here. Why don't you stay with Elping? Or Visma?"

"He has," Elping said. He closed his eyes for a full few seconds, and Joss knew he was *this far* away from tossing the droid in a dustbin. "For two weeks now. Fourteen days. Twenty thousand, one-hundred and sixty minutes after he was fired."

"I was not *fired*," the droid said irritably. "The Tarkins are so well-versed in social and political communication that I was simply superfluous to their excellent discourse. Though I tried at every instance to intersperse my nuanced understanding of tactical wordplay and subtle repartee—"

"Ywareah," Visma said, rolling her eyes. "He was fired."

"And now you're trying to bribe us with jogan juice to keep him?" Joss said, arms crossed.

"Please?" Visma said, wringing her hands. Her white irises darted between Joss and Pikka. "We have a lot of work to do." She lowered her voice. "And we need to keep things quiet. The last thing that Sixen is good at."

Pikka gave Joss a look that said, *I will murder that droid if he stays here.*

Joss cleared his throat. "Tell you what. We might need more help after the baby comes. How about in one month?" He leaned to Pikka and whispered, "Maybe we figure out how to alter his programming by then."

"One month," Pikka said, decisively. "In the meantime, perhaps you could shut him down for a bit to preserve his, ah, circuits? I hear Eriadu can get very dusty in certain areas and cause a rapid decay of certain processing units."

It was decided then, though Elping and Visma both looked so disappointed. They found out that Ghal was feeling much better after reverting to a Mon Calamari diet of Eriaduan crustacean soup and proper vitamin supplements. Joss longed to go with them and find out more about what the RDC was able to do while hiding on Eriadu, but Pikka was already looking like she was getting a stellar headache. And he had some work to do on the *Aurie*.

He watched Elping and Visma leave and couldn't help but think they seemed more like siblings now. When they'd first met the two young RDC officers, Visma was constantly berating the younger Elping, who didn't at all seem like he ever belonged in the RDC. But Visma had mellowed by the harsh months in the O.Z., and Elping had matured. He had a terrible, foreboding feeling as he watched them walk away, as if he might not see them again.

Joss shook his head. *Don't start with catastrophic imaginings. Get some work done. Take care of Pikka and the baby. Figure out what our next move is.*

Which was either as a parent to a newborn child or as a participant in a war. Or, more likely, both.

A few hours later, Pikka could tell Joss felt antsy. He didn't say it out loud, but she knew he felt what she felt. That he wanted desperately to do something except hide and stay low in this dingy dwelling, in this city that didn't belong to its people. But right now, she desperately needed rest. What she wanted to do and what this baby wanted to do were often entirely different things. Usually, the baby won.

When Joss was making way too much noise trying to fix a navigational circuit, or getting a snack, or heck—just *existing*—she called out to him.

"Joss, I think you need to take a walk. Get some air. I gotta get some rest for an hour or two."

He nodded and kissed her gently. As he left the bedroom, she watched him leave. Joss with those huge shoulders, that height, those feet that made *so much noise*. For a fleeting second, she had a premonition.

What if I don't see him again? What if the Nihil get him? What if—

But then she remembered.

Don't start with catastrophic imaginings. Get some work done. Take care of Joss and this baby. Figure out our next move.

And right now, the next move was a nap. In her dreams, she was holding her breath as the Nihil gathered around the *Aurie*, feeling certain that they were truly going to die. But the Nihil ships had not come to destroy the vessel, which had hidden for months inside the Occlusion Zone. They had gathered at the Stormwall and rushed forward when it had suddenly expanded. In the chaos of the expansion, the crew of the *Aurie* had reversed course and turned off their engines to hide quickly and quietly—and it had saved them. This time.

She stirred, realizing this was a memory, not a dream, and the child within her stretched and sprang back into a curled position. Pikka fell back asleep.

This time as she dreamed, she saw Eriadu on fire, the *Aurie* flying like the beautiful machine that she was, and she heard an explosion.

She heard another one.

And then she realized, perhaps she was not actually dreaming anymore. Her eyes flew open, heart pounding. Without thinking, Pikka threw open the door to their tiny living space to see very real smoke and fire rising in the heart of Eriadu City.

The war had begun.

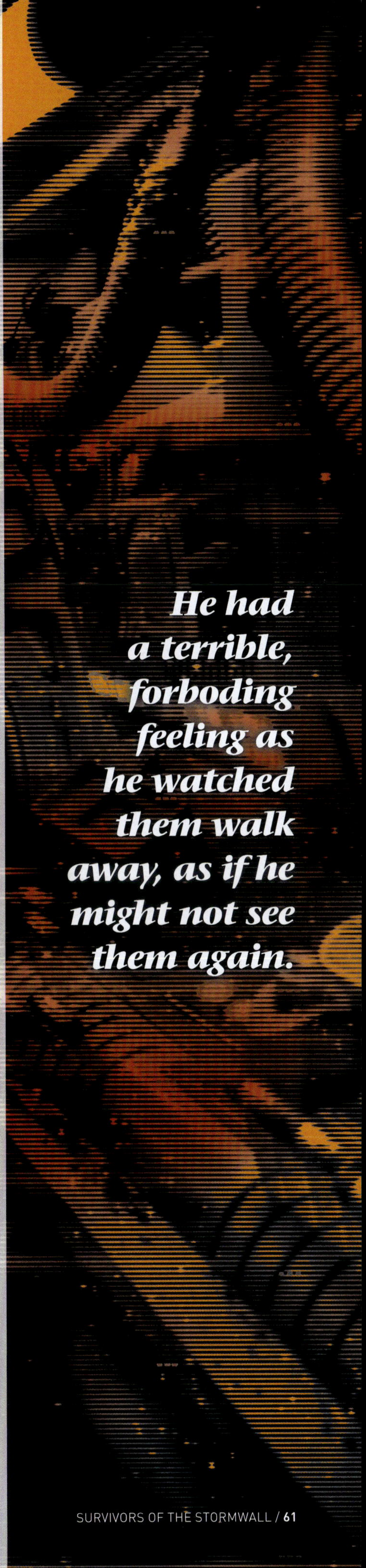

He had a terrible, forboding feeling as he watched them walk away, as if he might not see them again.

STAR WARS
THE HIGH REPUBLIC

TALES FROM THE OCCLUSION ZONE

"Sparks Fly"

By Lydia Kang

Illustration by Jake Lunt Davies

Previously, in a galaxy far, far away….

The Battle of Eriadu has begun. With Joss unreachable, Pikka now faces a choice: join the hidden RDC to fight, hide in order to protect their unborn child, or try to find Joss. But before she can decide, Eriadu has become incendiary, with trouble—and the war—already heading her way.

Pikka stood in the doorway of their small Eriadu home, staring at the smoke. It was coming from the direction of the cantina that Joss frequented these last weeks. She knew he'd be there. Recently, when Pikka needed a moment of peace, Joss had found respite at the comforting establishment. Now, there were distant shouts, followed by blaster fire. But no screams or petulant cries for help followed. The Eriaduans would never wait for aid to arrive; they had always been a coiled spring ready to unfurl. Violently so.

Her eyes darted from tendrils of smoke to a burning rooftop to an explosion several streets over. The fight was coming her way, and fast.

Pikka spoke into her wrist comm. "Joss? Joss, where are you?"

Silence. Either he was not answering or…

She shut that thought down immediately and swiftly scanned their quarters—their rumpled bed, and the long worktable where she and Joss worked on upgrading and fixing circuits from the *Aurie*, their scav-droid-scarred Longbeam hidden in a bunker nearby. She had to get to the ship, but first she had to get out of here. This building was one of the tallest in this district. Housing RDC and Eriaduans, it would be a target.

Pikka ran (as fast as her eight-month-pregnant belly would allow) to a panel on the main wall. She pulled an alarm—one meant to signal there was a dangerous electrical fault somewhere in the building. The Adrens had spoken with everyone in their tower at some point, and each one of them had known it would only been a matter of time until a battle engulfed the city. They'd agreed on a particular alarm that no one would mistake for an oil fryer fire, so she knew that anyone left in the building would recognize the electronic screech for what it was—a call to evacuate and prepare for a battle.

The blaring noise ricocheted throughout the hallways and stairwells. Pikka could already hear boots thumping down the steps and corridors. Good.

She grabbed two blasters, then scanned her workstation and picked up two small objects.

They resembled mechanical versions of the bird she and Joss had seen at the inlet of the Orrineswa river. The Eriaduans called them dagger birds, due to their propensity to dive into the water and spear aquatic creatures for food. But Pikka thought them lovely, with their pointed, blue-black wings and elegant maneuvering. As a pilot and engineer, she thought they were magnificent examples of natural engineering. Joss had added an ability enabling the tiny models to fly. She put her hand on her belly, hoping someday this little one would appreciate such gifts.

Pikka hit a small button, causing the birds to fold into egg-shapes, and pocketed them. She grabbed a go-bag from under their bed already stuffed with clothes, a handful of tools, food

Her eyes darted from the tendrils of smoke to a burning rooftop to an explosion several streets over. The fight was coming her way, and fast.

Pikka dropped to her knee. The Nihil stood there, arms outstretched and ready to fire. She heard the sound of her blaster in her ear, three electrified notes, all the same pitch, a staccato of energy.

and water, then slung it behind her shoulders and ran out the door.

"Ebbe! It's Pikka. What's going on?" She spoke into her wrist comm as she descended, or rather tottered, down the stairs, one hand holding her belly. She wouldn't be able to run in her state, which meant hiding was her best option. The shouts from the center of Eriadu City were growing closer. "Ebbe! Can you hear me?"

Ebbe's voice came after a crackle of static, and what sounded like a blaster shot. "I'm coming your way. Check the alternate channels—check—."

The comm channel went dead.

"Check what?" Pikka said, gasping as she skipped the last step and hit the ground waddling. The blaster fire was getting closer. She ducked behind the stairs, watching as a group of Eriaduans hollered and ran down the street.

"Joss? Joss!" Pikka spoke into her comm. Still nothing.

A blaster bolt whizzed by her head. She ducked, pulling out her own weapon. The shot came from the street. She peeked out from behind the stairwell to see two Nihil on a speeder, shooting Eriaduans as they zoomed by. They were randomly firing up at buildings across the street where a store's tables of fruit and vegetables had tipped over, spilling in a rainbow of color, their juices staining the ground. The storekeeper was shouting, cursing at them, not even ducking when a pyramid of glass bottles exploded in suds and liquor. He was retreating into the depths of the storefront for safety when a small child bolted forward. She held a toy slingshot, and began firing pebble after pebble at the three Nihil. One of the stones clanked against the helmet of the tallest one.

He stopped shooting and slowly turned his head towards to the liquor store. As did his two companions.

Suddenly, the chaotic shooting changed from chaos to focus. The three Nihil aimed at the child. Her father dashed forward, hand stretch out to protect her.

Everything happened at once. Pikka dropped to her knee. The Nihil stood there, arms outstretched and ready to fire. She heard the sound of her blaster in her ear, three electrified notes, all the same pitch, a staccato of energy. And then their three torsos jerked, as if puppet strings yanked them askew. Before blood could darken their clothing, they fell to their knees, then landed face down in the street.

Pikka lowered her blaster.

The Nihil were dead, and the store owner crouched with his arms around his daughter.

"Run!" Pikka shouted. "Get down—"

Something burst right above her head, and rubble rained down upon her. The acoustic shock made her ears feel stuffed and soundless for seconds. A chunk of masonry hit her forearm, knocking the blaster from her hand. The weapon was quickly buried by more falling debris, and when she pulled free the power pack was smashed. She staggered back, shielding her head from more rubble, reaching for her second weapon.

Another Nihil at the cross street near the store was aiming directly at her. He fired again, and Pikka dropped to her knees, the blaster bolt striking the wall right where her heart had been just a second before. The Nihil looked down the barrel of his weapon. He wouldn't miss again. ▸

But one second turned into two, and then three. Pikka squinted in his direction and saw his weapon had jammed—it was a model that possessed more flash than reliability. Too finicky for the Adrens.

She didn't give him a second chance. Pikka pushed herself to her feet and began to run, with the Nihil in pursuit. He would pummel her into the ground if he could. She saw the intense rage etched on his face—a look echoed on countless other Nihil she'd seen in the last few months. And now it was worse, because their coveted possession, Eriadu, was no longer under their control. The Nihil's prisoners were fighting back, and it infuriated them.

Pikka knew she could never be able to outrun him, so she had to outsmart him. She *had* to. The Nihil was gaining on her as she scurried through the alleyway beside their building. He was broad shouldered, with spikes on his gauntlets. Even with a quick glance back, Pikka could see they were stained with the blood of others. The sound of his harsh breathing was closing in, spittle escaping his mouth.

An engine roared close by.

Pikka spun on her foot, falling to a knee. The last thing she saw before dust clouded her vision was a speeder smashing straight into the Nihil, launching him into the air. His body hit the alley wall with a sickening thud before falling to the ground. The vehicle slowed and twirled, turning back towards Pikka, its engines revving.

"Get on," the rider said, removing their helmet.

It was Ebbe Casset.

"What are you doing here?" Pikka said, hurrying quickly towards her the best she could. It was an RDC speeder bike, but painted the color of lommite ore. Likely it had been hidden in the mines for months.

"I told you I was coming your way!" Ebbe said, handing Pikka a helmet. She put it on and straddled the vehicle, but her round belly prevented her from grasping Ebbe's waist. Pikka felt the baby inside her flip flop in protest.

"Nope. Not going to work." She got off and made motion with her thumb. "I'm driving."

"But—"

"Ebbe," she said, her voice low and calm. "I'm driving. And that's that."

The Nihil was gaining on her as she scurried through the alleyway beside their building. He was broad shouldered, with spikes on his gauntlets. Even with a quick glance back, Pikka could see they were stained with the blood of others.

Ebbe pushed her dark hair back where it had fallen out of her ponytail, then put her helmet back on.

"Yes, Captain." She slid onto the seat behind Pikka, grabbing her waist firmly above her pregnant belly. "You know, I came here to rescue *you*."

"Nobody's keeping a tally," Pikka said. It had been years since she'd driven a speeder, but it came back to her quickly. She pressed her boots down onto the accelerators, and quickly exited the alleyway in a smooth arc. "Where to?"

"I wanted to get you and Joss back to the mines," Ebbe said, her voice raised above the drone of the engines. "It's safest there. Even a direct hit from above won't cause a collapse. We've been reinforcing the tunnels."

"Don't you think we would be better off helping, instead of

hiding?" Pikka shouted.

"Well. We could use the help of your Longbeam."

"Oh, is *that* why you came?" She chuckled. "We can get to the *Aurie*. It's nearby." She revved the engines and the speeder flew down another alleyway. They could see red sparks and flares every time they passed a cross street. "I'm far safer in the *Aurie* than twiddling my thumbs under a bunker."

"Let's do it," Ebbe agreed.

They started down a street, swerving to avoid a group of citizens bunkered behind a downed vehicle, aided by a well-armed RDC woman she recognized from their landing a few weeks ago.

"Have they been dispatched? All the RDC?"

"I'm not sure. It's all happening so fast."

Someone spoke urgently through Ebbe's wrist comm. "Lieutenant Casset! This is West Command. We are in need of backup at our bunker by Port Sawwer. Five of our people are down. Another officer is surrounded. There are Eriaduans in the vicinity, but not enough to repel the Nihil."

Pikka tilted her head towards Ebbe, waiting to do what they both knew they needed to do.

Ebbe shook her head. "We can't. Captain Adren is with me. I need to get her to shelter—"

"We're on our way. Send your coordinates," Pikka shouted over Ebbe.

"Pikka!" the latter yelled.

"Hey. I'm driving, aren't I?" she said, shouting into Ebbe's wrist comm. "Send those coordinates!"

Eriaduans were angry. It felt like a swarm had arisen from the quiet streets and they could no longer be tamped down.

"Thank you, Lieutenant Casset. I'll let them know you're on your way."

"Lieutenant?" Pikka asked.

"Promoted," Ebbe said, rolling her eyes. "Who cares. Let's go!"

Pikka leaned forward, her toes tipping the accelerator pedals downward. They quickly traversed the city, with Ebbe providing cover with her blaster as they zigzagged past the skirmishes that were breaking out on nearly every corner. Eriaduans were angry. It felt like a swarm had arisen from the quiet streets and they could no longer be tamped down.

Pikka, with her newly sensitive nose, could smell the Orrineswa river before she saw it, reeking of old wood and algae, moisture and metal. The Nihil had destroyed barges and sunk boats that river folk had been using for decades, for no better reason than to ruin everything good. The hulls of the vessels had broken the surface in the shallows, covered in muck and rust.

Nearby, the bodies of three people lay slain on the shore. Two Nihil were shooting at a cluster of Eriaduans who had taken shelter behind a stone wall that led to a pier. Two other Nihil were grappling with a Mon Calamari wearing an RDC uniform. They had abandoned their weapons for some reason, and one had the Mon Calamari in a headlock while the other pulled out a long, sharp, dagger-length pike, panting heavily.

"You ought to have died on that prison ship," the Klatooinian Nihil muttered. His helmet was on the ground in two clean pieces, and his cheek had a deep gash that was dripping blood. "The great Ghal Tarpfen, failed Security Chief of Starlight Beacon. You like what we did with your beautiful Beacon? Littering the galaxy with its corpses? You'll be one soon enough."

It *was* Ghal. Pikka hadn't seen her in weeks, not since she'd been rushed away by the medics after they'd landed in Eriadu City. She'd had been near death, having become so severely malnourished during their time in the Occlusion Zone. Evidently she was now clearly well enough to fight, and to incite ▸

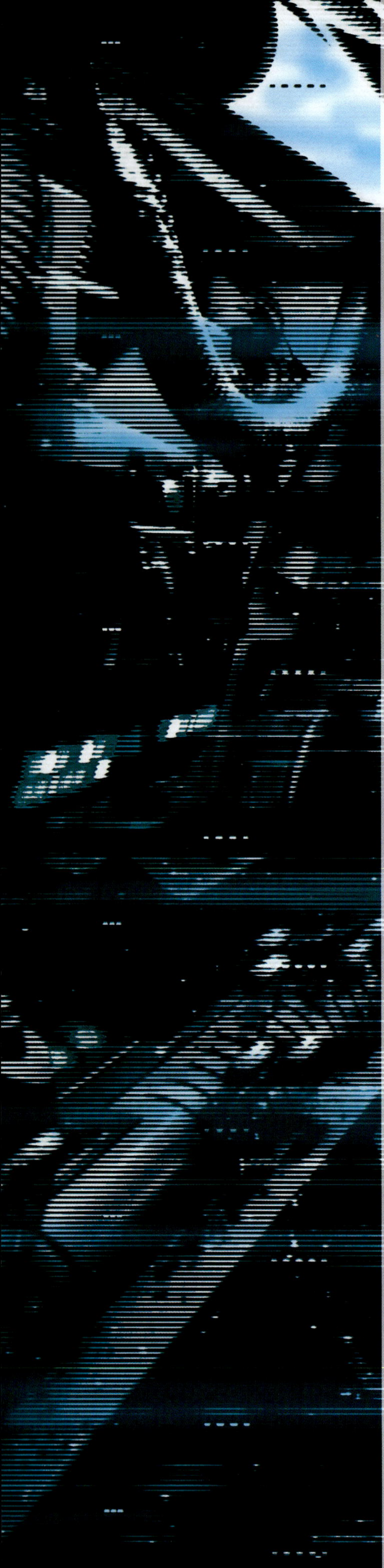

sentiments of vengeance on the part of the Nihil.

Ghal's yellow eyes were bright again, and flashed with anger. One of her hands was missing several fingers, a result of being struck by the blight. She looked thinner than the Ghal Pikka had known on Starlight Beacon, but she had some fight back in her. The Mon Calamari had survived so many things, she wouldn't die here. Pikka would make sure of that.

"Ebbe. You take the group at the wall. I'll take care of Ghal."

Ebbe said nothing, a silent acquiescence. Pikka accelerated, drifting into the air as far as the speeder would allow, surprising the Nihil fighting at the stone wall. Ebbe popped a booted foot onto the speeder seat, then jumped down to the ground, blasters firing from both fists in a spray of bolts.

Shocked out of their stance, the Nihil ducked for shelter. It was enough of a distraction that the other Eriaduans could finally lean into their offense. The Nihil were defeated in less than ten seconds, but Pikka could already see there were more coming in the distance. Ebbe would have her hands full while she directed her attention to helping Ghal.

Pikka accelerated, drifting into the air as far as the speeder would allow, surprising the Nihil.

Pikka turned around, heading back towards the water's edge. The Nihil grappling with Ghal shouted a warning, pivoting and raising his blaster; she couldn't respond in time. Pikka quickly pulled the speeder's nose up, braked hard, and then dived onto the ground. The vehicle exploded in a shower of sparks and fire.

"Ugh!" Pikka gasped, reflexively cradling her belly. The crushing weight of the speeder had rolled in the opposite direction. Stars, that was a close call. She reached for her blaster.

Ghal had seen her. She yanked at the assailant's arm choking her and rasped two words. *"Behind you..."*

Without turning around, Pikka snapped and fired. She heard a shriek and a thud, and risked looking back. A Nihil that was nearly upon her fell to his knees, toppling face first. A blaster bolt whizzed by her head, felling the marauder who had shot her speeder. That was thanks to Ebbe, who came running to her side.

"Are you okay?" she asked, her eyes wide.

"I'm fine. But Ghal—"

They turned to see her slowly wrestling the Nihil she was fighting, both moving closer and closer to the water. Ghal dug her booted heels into the soil, kicking and pushing. The river soon lapped at their shoulders, then drenched their torsos. Ebbe made to run forward, her blaster poised to take out the Nihil, but Ghal shot the lieutenant a cautioning glare with her deep, yellow eyes, and shook her head slightly.

And then she smiled.

Ghal's body spasmed and she kicked hard below her. She flipped the Nihil over her head and splashed into the shallows of the river. As he flailed about, trying to find secure footing in the water, Ghal disappeared beneath the surface. The Nihil found his balance, searching left and right, trying to locate his opponent.

A fraction of a second later, his body was abruptly jerked beneath the water's surface, as if he had been swallowed whole.

"Never fight a Mon Calamari in her element," Pikka murmured, grimly. She looked over to Ebbe. "Tell the others—anyone who can hear—to drive the Nihil into the river. Even ankle deep. Let's go!"

"They're scattered! How are we going—"

"They're not scattered," Pikka said. "There are two main groups. I'll bring them closer. Get everyone to drive them into the water."

Pikka took out her two toy eggs.

She tossed them both into the air where they hovered for a second before cracking open. The two mech-Dagger birds took flight, Pikka guiding them with a remote on her wristband. The birds zipped quickly toward the far side of two groups of Nihil, and a couple of them stared quizzically at the toy birds, not sure how to react. Pikka touched the controls.

The birds exploded with a bright light, as glittering filaments shot outward, blinding anyone who was standing too close.

"Now!" Pikka yelled.

The Nihil were off-kilter and disoriented. Ebbe and the other Eriaduans began to fire their weapons as the Nihil fell back towards the river. Once the group was knee deep, some began to swim to escape, hoping to brave the current and make it to safety on the other side.

They didn't reach it.

One by one, they fell beneath the surface, never to reappear. A dozen Nihil became ten, then five. Then none.

The second group began to realize the trap, desperately fighting to exit the water, but they too succumbed, screaming and clawing at the surface. The thrashing quieted. Their last exhalations, contained in bubbles spreading along the rushing river's surface, were all that were left after several minutes.

Finally, there was a relative silence. The fighting and explosions could still be heard in the city beyond them. Ghal Tarpfen slowly emerged from the river. Her eyes were glassy with vibrancy, but there was no triumph in them.

"Pikka," she said simply when faced with her friend. They embraced quickly, then let go. Ebbe approached them, tired but ready for another battle.

"Those were some impressive... uh, toys, you had there," Ebbe said.

"Toys, yes. Not for cuddling. For education," Pikka said, feeling a little defensive. Should she have been sewing together soft blankets these last weeks? She had made what came naturally to her when she thought of her child. The intricate, the beautiful. Engineering craftsmanship.

Joss's voice suddenly came through. "Get out of the way!" he yelled. She heard the telltale blasts of his WESTAR-28 firing.

Sure, they were weapons, but even sticks and stones—the playthings of children across the galaxy—could be weapons too. Perhaps the next time she built them, she would make them not so explosive.

"Pikka, you shouldn't be out here fighting," Ghal said. "Not in your condition."

"You're right," she replied. Pikka looked up at the sky, and listened to the sounds of chaos emanating from the city center. "I need to be fighting in the *Aurie*."

Ebbe nodded, and soon a sturdy, scarred landspeeder was brought their way. She and Pikka climbed in.

"Let's get you there," said Ebbe.

Pikka nodded, lifting her wrist and speaking into her comm. "Joss? Are you there? I'm headed to the *Aurie*." *Please be alive,* she thought.

It was silent and the light on the comm was red. The signal was either being jammed, or something else. *Please don't be something else.*

"Joss," she said, trying again. The red light suddenly winked out, and a crackle of static came through. The static was soon replaced with the sound of laser fire. Of screaming. Of chaos and pain.

Joss's voice suddenly came through. "Get out of the way!" he yelled. She heard the telltale blasts of his WESTAR-28 firing.

Pikka sucked in a breath, on the cusp of speaking, when Joss's voice came through the static one last time. *"No!"*

STAR WARS
THE HIGH REPUBLIC

TALES FROM THE OCCLUSION ZONE

"Out With A Bang"

By Lydia Kang

Illustration by Jake Lunt Davies

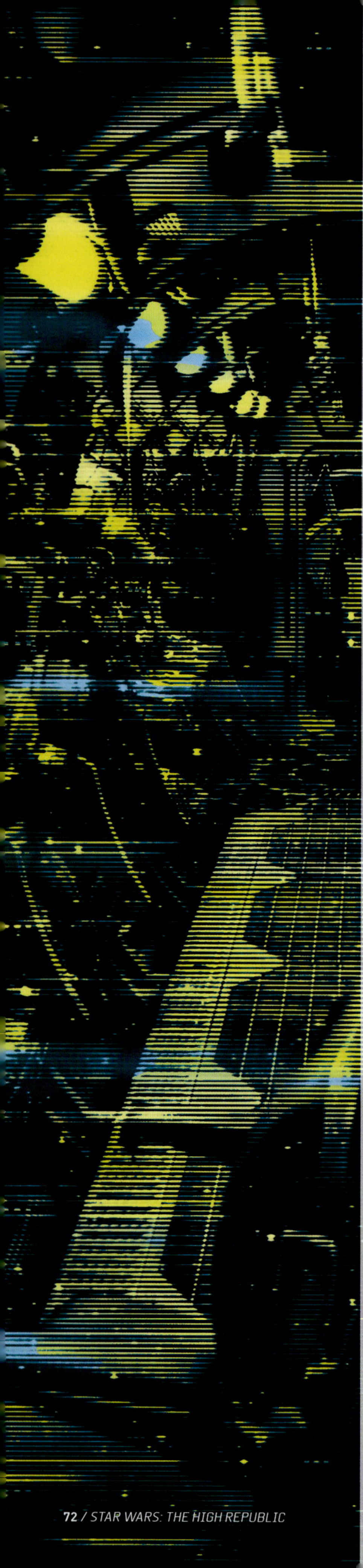

Previously, in a galaxy far, far away....

The battle on Eriadu has spread. Pikka Adren is fighting back aboard the *Aurie*, while desperately searching for her husband, Joss. Meanwhile, on the ground, Lieutenant Ebbe Casset and the RDC have taken advantage of the sudden uprising of the Eriaduans in an attempt to overwhelm the Nihil, but the tide of the conflict is taking a turn for the worse...

"Incoming!" Corporal Elping Tsoo's yell sounded like a roar above the din of battle. To Visma Tarko, it was almost more shocking than the bombs pummeling the airfield from Nihil starships. The countless attack runs were pulverizing the few functioning ships the RDC had on the ground. Back when they'd been hiding out on an abandoned Nihil vessel in the Occlusion Zone, Visma had found her meek, science-minded colleague to be almost intolerable. Now, he was barking orders to medical personnel and pulling together fighters to cover them, dropping to his knee to blast a Nihil sniper on a building roof twenty meters away.

"You good?" Elping asked.

"I would prefer to be inside, where it's safe," C-06N replied indignantly. The droid was hiding behind a large boulder that was once the corner of a utility building, curled up like a silver ball.

"I wasn't asking you, Sixen. Get back to the caves!"

"But I am here to be of service!" he cried between explosions. "I have, of late, been adding programs to my databanks..." *Boom!* "...so that I may be of more service than a standard protocol droid..." *Crash! Bang!* "...now that the Tarkins have no use for me."

"New programming? Can you fight?" Visma asked, returning fire at a group of Nihil taking cover behind a downed RDC ship.

"Goodness gracious, no," C-06N protested in shock.

"Then can you fix this?" Elping threw a broken blaster at the feet of the dusty droid.

"No, indeed."

Elping shook his head in frustration. "Anyway, Visma. You good?"

She rolled her white eyes. "Well, at least I'm not bored."

Elping's eyes twinkled for a fraction of a second before he turned back to the fight. Visma remembered those long, dull months on the abandoned Nihil ship. She'd used to say that boredom was going to be the death of them both. Give a Tarko a task, however—a reason to succeed, a hill to climb—and she was good. Given the Nihil's repeated aerial salvos, and the ground forces they couldn't seem to hold back, it didn't look like she was going to be bored for a *long* time.

To make things even worse, the Nihil's line had been bolstered by strange and dangerous machines. It took Visma a few shoot-outs to finally work out what they were—recommissioned scav droids.

The hope had been that the RDC would regain control of the native defense grid from the Nihil and send these invaders back into the skies. But they hadn't been able to wrest it back. What's more, the ground assault had to pause whenever Nihil bombs were being dropped, so any traction made was lost when carnage intermittently rained down from the sky.

To make things even worse, the Nihil's line had been bolstered by strange and dangerous machines. It took Visma a few shoot-outs to finally work out what they were—recommissioned scav droids, the kind that used to attack non-Nihil ships in the Occlusion Zone, scurrying over unfortunate vessels like lava ants on a carcass and decimating them, one square meter at a time. Only these had been modified into something far more monstrous, and programmed to take apart people. Lethal blades and cutting equipment sprouted from additional limbs. Some packed a single blaster; others had four. And some of the larger, more lethal scavs were fitted with defense shields as well. Visma even spotted a few with short, pliable electrowhips and pikes for close combat when their blasters no longer functioned. Just like Nihil armor, the machines looked like they'd been cobbled together—a mash-up of metal plating, with legs of varying lengths. Some scurried silently, striking in stealth; others attacked in every direction at once. Each one so different that whatever tactics a half dozen RDC and Eriaduans used to take one down, they couldn't defeat the next one the same way.

The comms crackled to life.

"Ebbe Cassett here. Report."

"They've deployed ground scavs to attack us. We're being inundated!" Visma replied as a blaster bolt whizzed by her head. She jerked back, her white hair momentarily swept before her eyes. "Where are they coming from?"

Elping appeared at her side, crouching down. "That hair of yours. It's like a beacon, Visma. Cover it up," he said, handing her an RDC helmet, painted in the green and brown colors of a Eriaduan mountainside. Visma dropped it.

"I hate helmets. I can't think when I'm wearing one."

Elping glared at her. He was right. Lately, he was right a lot. She sighed and jammed it on, clicking shut the chin clasp.

"So, the ground scavs. I've been tracking them," Elping said. "They're all over the place."

"Send me the coordinates of the ones you've encountered," Ebbe ordered. "Something Admiral Kronara has told us from day one, 'Even in the chaos, there is order.' There's got to be a pattern to their movements. We've got to find it."

"Ebbe, we're seeing more scavs here than in the southern part of the city," Visma said grimly. "Does that count?"

"*Look out!*" Elping shouted.

An explosion sounded all around them, directionless, as if they were at its epicenter. Close by, two RDC soldiers lay dying, ten meters away from a scav that was steadily creeping towards them like a lumbering, rusty metal spider. Visma looked over to where Elping was laying on the ground, and he wasn't moving. Breathlessly, she crawled to his side.

"Elping!" Visma gasped, trying to rouse him. Her friend was dazed and unfocused, but alive, albeit with a darkening patch of red spreading across his uniform. He was bleeding profusely.

"Ah! Now I can help!" C-06N declared. "I believe Corporal Tsoo is losing blood at approximately twenty milliliters per minute, which means he will be unconscious within thirty minutes. Perhaps sooner."

"Come here" Visma growled. She dragged the droid forward, pushing its dusty, metal hands onto Elping's bleeding shoulder. "Put pressure here, you bag of bolts." ►

Close by, two RDC soldiers lay dying, ten meters away from a scav that was steadily creeping towards them like a lumbering, rusty metal spider.

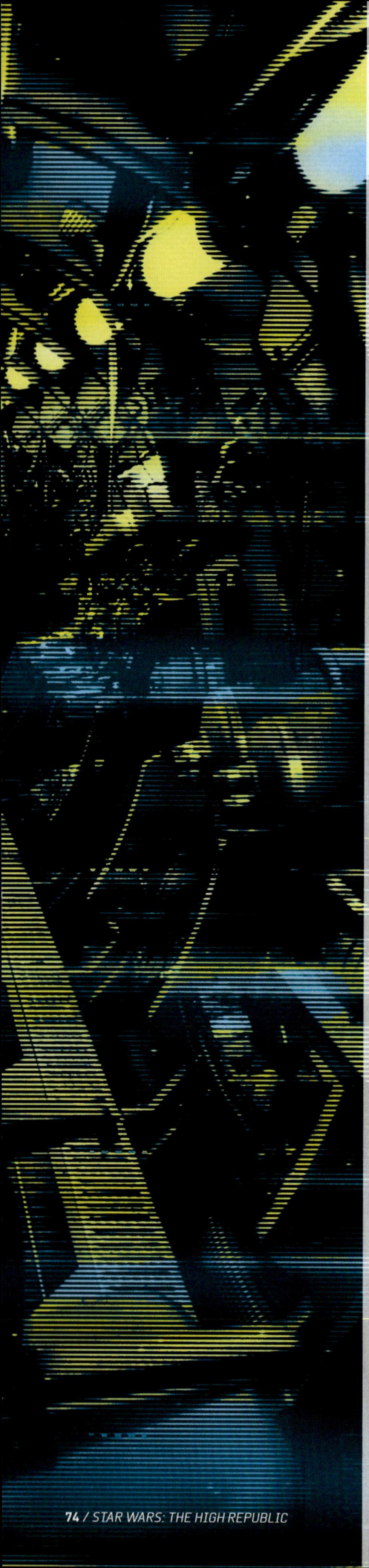

"Wait!" Elping said, cringing in pain. He raised his good arm, reached over, and touched the datapad on his injured arm. "Ebbe. Coordinates sent."

"I'm on it," came her response on the comms. "Sixen, I'm going to need you. Get the fastest transport and meet me at the coordinates I'll be sending you shortly."

Visma yanked off her helmet and stood, grabbing Elping's blaster and striding toward the ground scav with a weapon in each hand.

Visma met Elping's eyes. "Don't you dare die, Corporal."

"Never without your permission, Lieutenant." He winced, as a medic came to his side and shooed C-06N away. "Get that ground scav for me, will you?"

"My pleasure."

Visma yanked off her helmet and stood, grabbing Elping's blaster and striding toward the ground scav with a weapon in each hand. She wanted that damned droid to see her, to be the last thing its photoreceptors registered before she turned it into a ball of molten metal. One by one, she blasted at its appendages, exploding one leg, taking out another.

A Nihil shot from across the battlefield whizzed too close, but her Arkanian eyes quickly pinpointed the heat of the shooter's body, and she blasted him from a distance that no human could. Visma pivoted back toward the ground scav, now dragging itself forward on only four legs. It brandished and swung its electrowhip right at her before she could dodge the flailing weapon. Her hair sizzled, near her ear—too close a strike. Suddenly furious, she sprang lithely onto the droid's back, balancing her booted feet on its shield-like body. The droid tried to spin her off, left, then right, then it made a grab for Visma's ankles. It jerked its electrowhip again, trying to lash upwards, but she leapt into the air and pointed her weapon straight down at the center of its carapace, firing repeatedly.

The ground scav convulsed, crumpling in a shower of sparks.

Feeling satisfied, Visma shook her head and looked up, only to see three more ground scavs pointing their blasters straight at her head.

Smoke rose in coils from every direction in Ebbe Cassett's view. Wounded Eriaduans and RDC were being shuttled into the deeper tunnels for safety. The last that Ebbe had seen of the very pregnant Captain Pikka Adren she'd taken off in her Republic Longbeam, the *Aurie*, which had been hidden in a secret hangar near her home. Or what had once been Pikka's home. The building was now in cinders, a thick column of smoke marked its previous footprint, like many other Eriadu City buildings laid waste in the sudden conflict. If they were lucky, perhaps Pikka would swing back to give them air cover soon. They needed all the help they could get.

Ebbe looked at the information Elping transmitted to her.

Even in the chaos, there is order.

"But where?" she thought to herself. Ebbe examined the dots marking where the droids had been fighting. It looked like an aimless sprinkling over a quarter of the city, yet they hadn't been dropped by Nihil ships. She held the datapad upside down, then turned it yet again. There was something vaguely familiar. She squinted and blurred her eyes. It reminded her of an intricate fan she once saw being used by a dancer at the Republic Fair on Valo, before the event dissolved into utter destruction.

A fan. And every fan has a center

point, a hub. "They're originating from a single area," Ebbe murmured, and quickly double-checked the Eriadu City map against the battlefield data. The incendiaries from the Nihil ships had been raining down in waves all over the city, but little bombardment had occurred anywhere near the lommite processing plants. "That's it!" she whispered.

Ebbe leaped onto her heavy speeder and gunned the engine, and before long was heading towards a northern enclave of the city where there was nothing but lommite plants. If that was where the ground scavs were dispersing from, and she could stem the flow, it might turn things around.

Ghal Tarpfen's voice sounded from her comm. "We've secured the river's edge. Anything we can do for you?"

"Roger that," Ebbe said. "Follow my beacon."

"I'm headed your way," confirmed the Mon Calamari.

She accelerated through a maze of buildings, some of which were nothing but rubble. With the fighting now concentrated in the heart of the Eriadu City, its northern tip was eerily quiet. Hiding her speeder against a pile of refuse, Ebbe continued on foot, blaster in hand. The ground was covered in lommite dust, which sparkled like snow. In the distance, she saw the entrance to one of the large processing plants. Its door was askew, and several giant containers that normally held raw lommite were tipped on their side, contents strewn across the ground as if a giant had kicked them over. Boulders of lommite lay near the door, gray chunks suffused with clear crystals, destined to become transparisteel if Eriadu City was ever peaceful and productive again.

At the sound of Ebbe's approach, the scav spun its body around and took out its weapon. Before it could fire, she unleashed three blasts in rapid succession.

A scuffling echoed from inside the plant, like metal on metal, then a voice cried out.

"Not my eyes, you unintelligent ball of wire!"

Ebbe knew that voice. "Sixen!" She pushed between the heavy doors to see a scraggly ground scav viciously attacking the silver droid. It was picking apart the wires connecting C-06N's head and torso. One of the protocol droid's eyes was detached, lying a few steps away where it had been flung. At the sound of Ebbe's approach, the scav spun its body around and took out its weapon. Before it could fire, she unleashed three blasts in rapid succession, sending it spinning away from C-06N's body. The droid landed on its back, one of its limbs shattered. The light in its center eye went dark as its legs curled inward, black smoke leaking from its insides.

"Bless my circuits!" whimpered the protocol droid.

"You alright?" Ebbe said, hurrying to C-06N's side. She reached for his disembodied eye, but its connectors were hopelessly frayed.

"I do believe that beast was going to turn me into scrap metal!" C-06N complained. "No respect whatsoever!"

"Anything damaged in there?" Ebbe asked, touching a gouge in Sixen's chest. A hole pierced through the droid's upper-left torso, right where a human heart would have been.

"I have no vital systems there," C-06N huffed. He stood up, trying to brush the sparkling lommite dust off his scuffed limbs.

"No, don't do that," Ebbe said. "I need you looking as scruffy as possible."

"But that's goes entirely against my programming!"

"Trust me. I have an idea," she assured the droid.

They crept deeper into the plant, passing by smelters and giant metal ▸

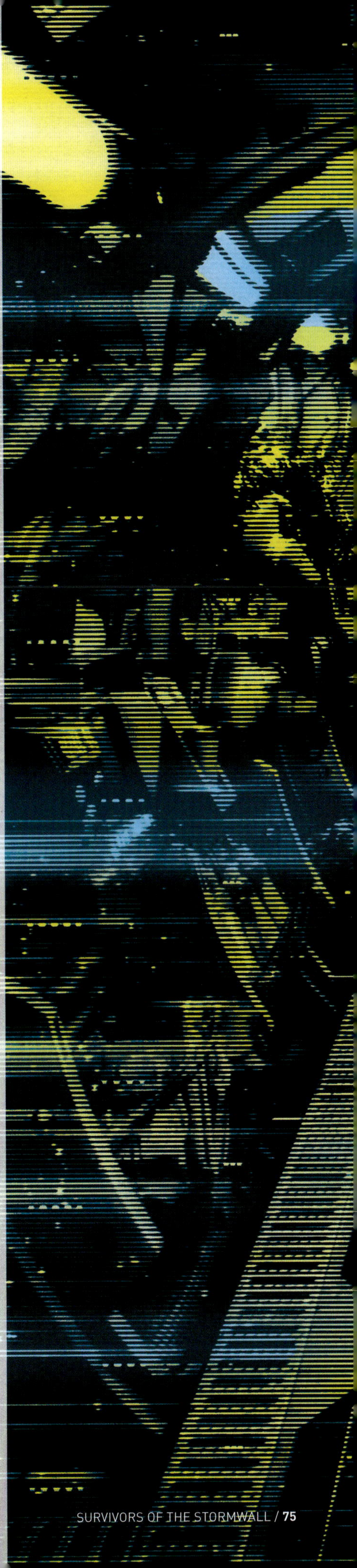

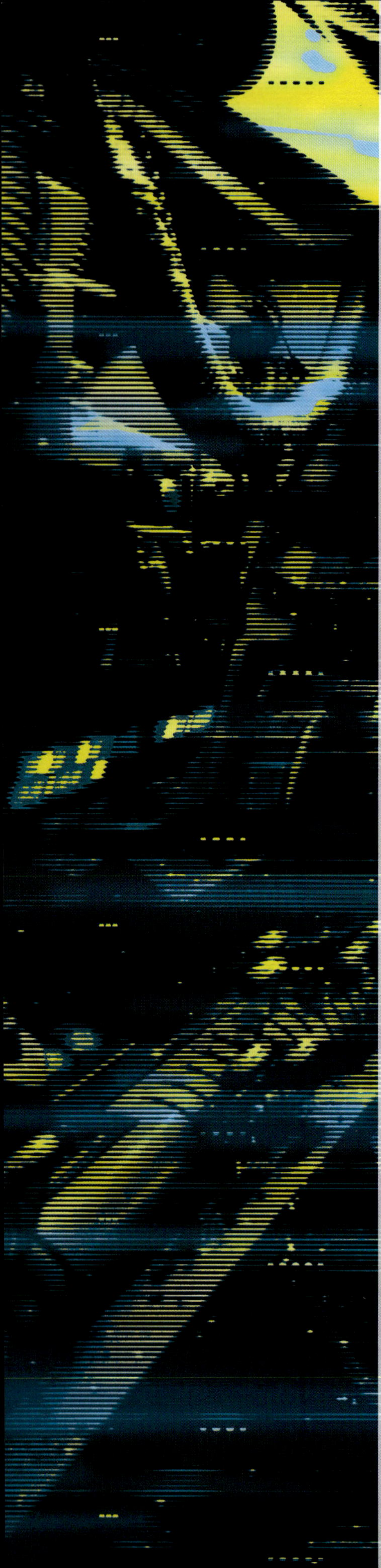

processing machines that looked like teeth, which were used for grinding the lommite into dust. But the factory was quiescent, its workers battling for the life of the city elsewhere. Tube-like corridors with conveyer belts connected this part of the facility with another manufacturing building, and as they moved along one of them, Ebbe could hear coarse talking, and the sound of machinery clanking. Ducking behind the cover of a pile of rough, unrefined transparisteel sheets, she spotted two Nihil guards standing guard outside a door into the building. The clanking was coming from whatever was happening on the other side.

They crept deeper into the plant, passing by smelters and giant metal processing machines that looked like teeth.

"Go tell him you're here for spare parts," Ebbe whispered to Sixen. "Get him to open the door."

"I'll do no such thing. I'm too useful to be spare parts! I have new programming!"

Ebbe rolled her eyes. "We need them to unlock the door."

"I shall not be used as bait!" the droid protested.

"You want your eye back?" Ebbe tossed the loose droid eye in her palm, then pocketed it. "Then go. Or you *will* be nothing but spare parts."

The droid shook his shoulders, irritated. "This is so beneath me," he muttered, and stepped out from behind their hiding place.

The Nihil noticed C-06N and raised their blasters.

"Halt there. What do you want?" the larger one asked. He was tall and broad shouldered, face covered in a helmet with the Eye insignia roughly painted across the side. "Walking junk?"

"Yes. I am... damaged. I was told I would be of use here."

"Who told you?"

C-06N hesitated, and Ebbe held her breath. What if he only told the truth?

"Speak up or we'll use you for target practice," said the shorter Nihil, sneering through his face guard.

"Like we did with those RDC yesterday," said the larger one. He snickered. "And like the seven I killed this morning. Would have preferred it had been seventy."

Ebbe squeezed her fists, wishing they were around the Nihil's neck.

C-06N looked from one Nihil to the other. "One of General Veiss's satellite ships landed and ordered me here. She is greatly disappointed, stating the ground forces will suffer dire consequences if your special droids fail. She mentioned a rather primitive means of execution. You are a Weequay, are you not?"

The large Nihil guard shifted uncomfortably. His scaly, thick skin showed between the plates of his armor. "Yeah."

C-06N straightened up. "I do believe slime midges were mentioned."

The other Nihil looked at his companion curiously. "Whassat?"

"Oh!" C-06N nodded vigorously. "They're tiny parasites that infect the Weequay by burrowing between the folds of their skin, biting and chewing and defecating their way straight through to their—"

"Fine, you can pass," the Weequay Nihil said, so quickly that Ebbe blinked in disbelief. His companion took a step back, as if the Weequay was already infected.

As they opened the door, Ebbe stepped out of her hiding place.

"What...?" Both Nihil blinked in confusion at the unexpected intruder, but before they could turn their weapons on Ebbe, she dispatched them with two rapid-fire shots.

"That was probably less painful than death by slime midges," Ebbe observed. She looked behind at C-06N. "You did a good job there."

"The Tarkins had me programmed

to allow for a modicum of falsehoods, so long as it serves the greater good."

"You could be a politician, Sixen. How in the stars did you know about slime midges?"

"Another upgrade!"

Ebbe shook her head. Why that was necessary to know, she couldn't imagine, but strangely enough it had helped. They crept into the large warehouse. There were several rooms full of spare droid parts, but no more Nihil. They passed half a dozen rooms full of junked material before the corridor opened into a large warehouse. Ebbe inhaled sharply.

Inside were dozens of ground scavs in various stages of repair and refurbishing. Some barely as high as Ebbe's waist, and others far larger and much taller than she was. All with several spindly arms retrofitted with weapons. A single clank echoed from the other end of the warehouse. A trilling sound came after.

"I told you, I'm not to be disturbed if you want these droids ready in the next six hours—"

Inside were dozens of ground scavs in various stages of repair and refurbishing. Some barely as high as Ebbe's waist, and others far larger, much taller than she was.

A Cosian in dusty work clothes ambled out from a line of droids, waving a wrench when he froze at the sight of Ebbe and C-06N. His eyes blinked upwards in surprise.

"RDC?" he asked, trilling afterwards, likely a cuss in his language. Or an exclamation of relief, perhaps. He dropped the wrench with a clang, as if eager to surrender. Ebbe preferred this. Less bloodshed.

"Yes. We are seizing these droids. Our forces will be here in minutes." This was a slight fib; she had no idea how long it would take for Ghal and others to get here. But perhaps she'd already accomplished what needed to be done.

Still, this was typical Nihil, cocky as all hell, the way things were set up in this place. Only two guards, only one droid patrolling, and only one mechanic at work who gave up as soon as you looked at him sternly. Poor thing was probably being worked to the bone.

Behind him, the factory doors were ajar. The light of the Eriaduan sky shone through, and for a moment, Ebbe saw the *Aurie* flying across the clear sky. Pikka! Hopefully with Joss. They were still okay! They were fighting. But then she frowned at the sight of three Nihil ships chasing the *Aurie* at close quarters—Pikka couldn't seem to shake them. The marauders were closing in, with the Longbeam performing a corkscrew maneuver straight upwards in a last-ditch, desperate effort to escape its pursuers. The dogfight swept out of view and a cloud darkened in Ebbe's heart, suddenly afraid that the Adrens weren't going to make it.

A voice echoed from the other end of the room. "Ah, well. If I must surrender," the Cosian shrugged, clasping his hands together, "then might as well go out with a bang."

Ebbe was confused. Those words didn't match his supplicating gesture. Then, in growing horror, she realized the Nihil was holding a small transmitter, and it was flashing. A buzz sounded, followed by the clicking of two dozen ground scavs waking from their mechanical slumber behind him.

"Ride the Storm!" the Cosian spat, grinning as a wall of ugly droids, their glowing red eyes alive and menacing, began bearing down on Ebbe and C-06N.

STAR WARS

THE HIGH REPUBLIC

TALES FROM THE OCCLUSION ZONE

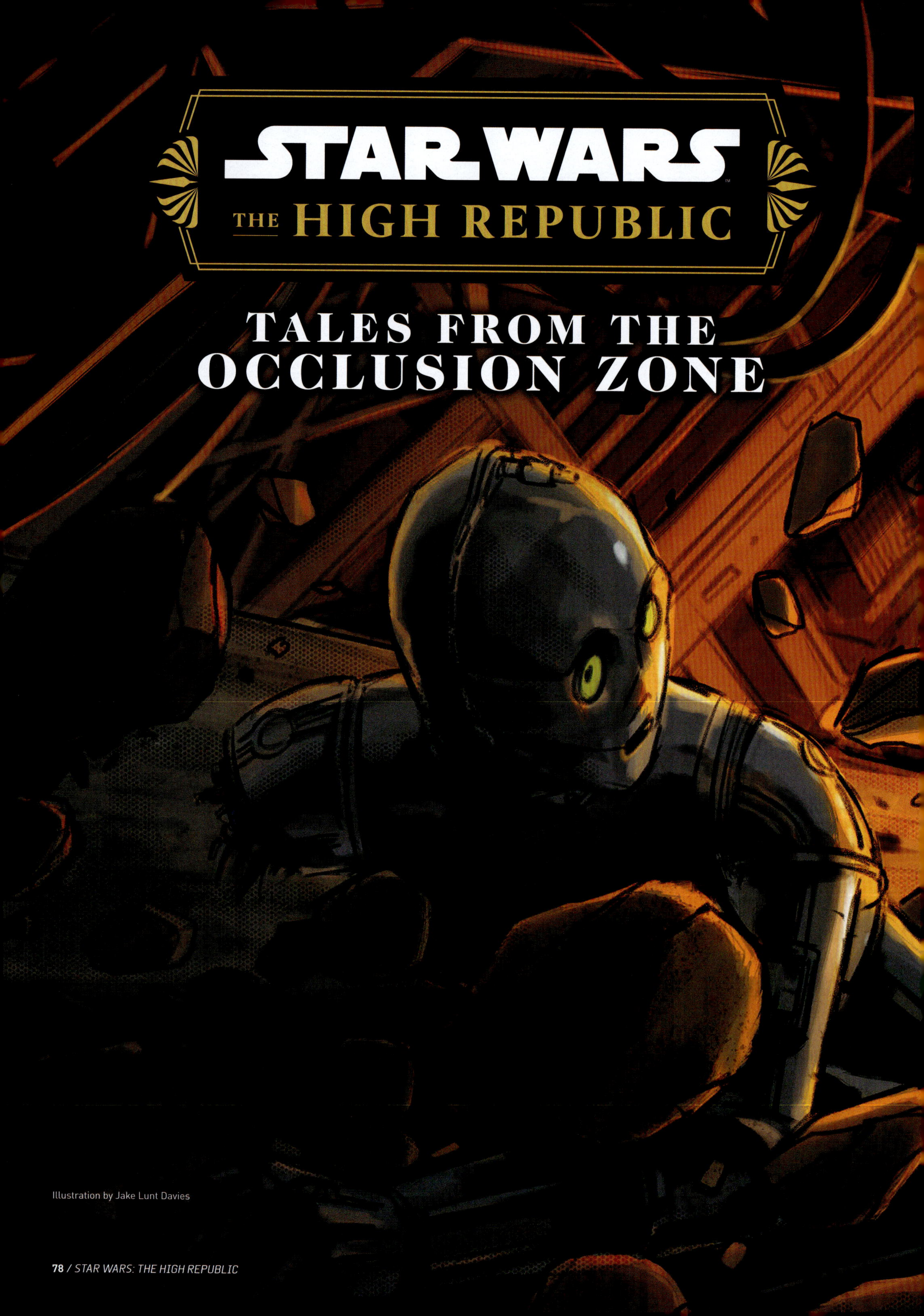

Illustration by Jake Lunt Davies

"The Will To Fight"

By Lydia Kang

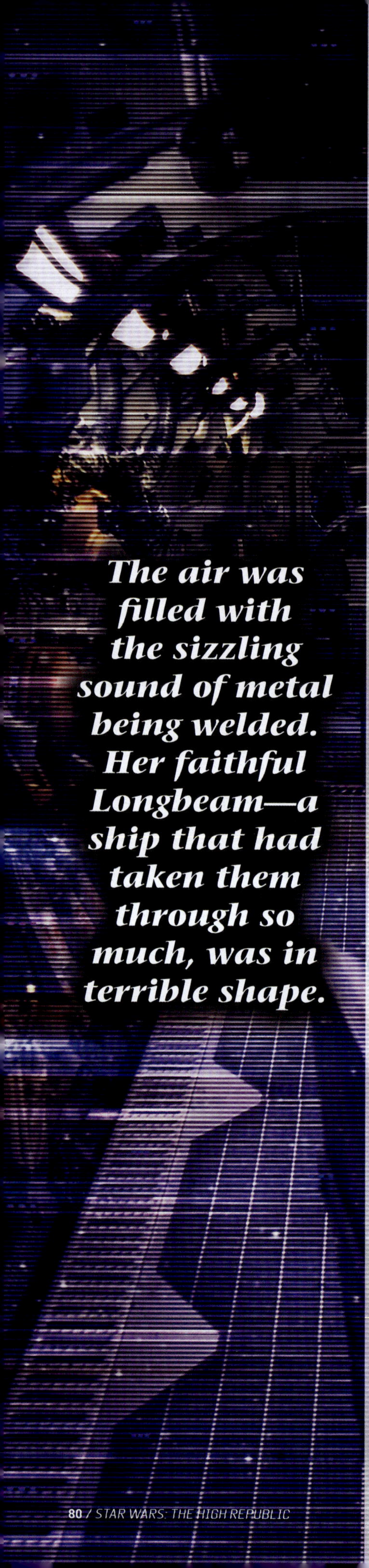

The air was filled with the sizzling sound of metal being welded. Her faithful Longbeam—a ship that had taken them through so much, was in terrible shape.

Previously, in a galaxy far, far away....

While Elping Tsoo and Visma Tarko fight a losing battle with ground scav droids overwhelming the Republic Defense Coalition, their comrade Ebbe Casset has infiltrated the source of the droids in a seemingly abandoned lommite plant. But Ebbe's victory becomes disaster as dozens of them attack—and it may turn the entire tide of the battle on Eriadu City.

Pikka Adren quietly sat in the cockpit of the *Aurie*, aboard the *Third Horizon*. One hand rested on her rounded belly, one on the yoke, as if one moment away from flying. She was safe, for now. But she didn't feel it.

The air was filled with the sizzling sound of metal being welded. Her faithful Longbeam—a ship that had taken them through so much, was in terrible shape. After finding her husband, she and Joss had battled as many Nihil ships as they could before being outnumbered. They'd barely survived to escape to Admiral Kronara's vessel. All this, after barely surviving the Occlusion Zone, as well as countless other battles.

Now there was a hole in the *Aurie*'s starboard side, her cannons malfunctioning, shields down... The crew of the *Third Horizon* was doing its best to repair the stricken ship as swiftly as possible, but they couldn't do it fast enough. The people on Eriadu—her friends—were fighting for their lives, and here she was, sitting around doing nothing.

Her belly ached a little, like she'd been lifting too many supply crates. The baby was kicking again. *Even this kid wants me to get up and do something,* she mused.

So Pikka listened to the comms and tried to follow the news of the battle, the deployment of troops, the loss of lives. After a few minutes, her belly ached again, this time more intensity. She winced in discomfort.

It couldn't be... a contraction? But no, she wasn't due for another two weeks. The prenatal program told her she would likely deliver late, not early. And false contractions were common.

She'd just turned the volume up on the comms chatter when a voice came straight through to the cockpit.

"Captain Adren? Are you there?"

"Yes?" Pikka answered.

"This is Ensign Avril in control. Someone on the ground in Eriadu City intercepted a message, but we're not sure what it means. Your name is in the communication."

"Play it," Pikka ordered.

It was mostly static. "Viz...ping?" More static. "Gah..." And then a snap of a harsh buzz, before, "Pikka! Joss!" The voice sounded desperate.

Pikka inhaled sharply. She'd know that voice anywhere.

"It's Ebbe," she whispered.

Her voice had a very particular clear quality to it, very much like her aunt's, Hedda Casset, who had perished as captain of the *Legacy Run* during its last fateful mission. It felt like a lifetime since the Great Disaster, since the Nihil had pummeled its way into Republic space. It had made Ebbe a fighter in the Republic Defense Coalition. And now she was in trouble.

"Where did the message come from?" Pikka demanded.

"We can locate the signal's origin but are unable to identify the source," Avril responded.

"I know the source. Send me the location."

Pikka was already flipping on switches, getting the *Aurie* ready. Her hull had been patched with a ferroceramic plate that would hopefully withstand reentry through the Eriadu atmosphere, and only one of the two ion cannons was working, but she was ready enough. Everything else could be rigged along the way, like they always did. This fight was their fight. It was their future.

"But Admiral Kronara has already deployed RDC ships to engage the Nihil. He has not authorized any deployments to the planet's surface until..."

"Tell Admiral Kronara to authorize engagement—

posthumously, if that's what it takes—but I'm blasting off. Through his hangar door, if I have to!" Pikka growled, wincing as pain blossomed in her abdomen. Not here. Not now. It was too soon.

Joss ran into the cockpit. "Why are you firing up the engines? She's not ready!"

"Ebbe's in trouble," Pikka managed to say through gritted teeth, trying not to let Joss see her discomfort. "We might be the only ones who can help."

All Pikka needed to reach Ebbe was one hour. Surely this kid could wait that long, right?

Ebbe froze.

Blaster in hand, she stared at the two dozen, spidery ground scavs coming alive before her. The red lights shone dully from their carapaces, and their spindly arms had been modified to fire upon her.

"Lieutenant Casset! What shall we do?" C-06N, the dusty protocol droid hissed at her side.

For a brief second, Ebbe wondered if droids, too, felt the specter of imminent death upon them.

"We're getting out of here, that's what." Firing as they withdrew towards the wall, blasts singing her hair as near-misses got way too close, Ebbe saw a conveyer belt exit through a hole in the wall.

"This way!" she yelled to C-06N.

They ran towards the opening, Ebbe whacking a power switch on. The conveyer belt hummed to life, dragging scattered lommite ore of various sizes. A shot glanced off C-06N's leg, making him tumble onto the belt, face down.

"My leg," C-06N cried out. Another bolt landed right on his shoulder, and his arm fell loose, tumbling to the floor. "My arm! Can't you shoot any better? I thought you were a *Lieutenant!*"

"Shut up, Sixen!" Ebbe yelled back. The belt was wide enough to hold them both as she scrambled onto to her belly. Her blaster fired nonstop, left, right, up, back, keeping the converging scav droids at bay. One droid leapt forward, almost a step away from Ebbe, prompting her to swing her arm in defense, her wrist ricocheting against a chunk of lommite the size of her head. Pain reverberated down her arm, but the worst of the blow was absorbed by—oh no—her wrist comm. She managed one last shot to the underside of the droid, which fell over, its red light going dark.

The belt pulled them into a dim room filled with ore processing machines in repose. She spoke into her wrist comm. A large crack crazed down its center.

"This is Lieutenant Casset. I've located the rest of the ground droids and need backup immediately."

There was no answer. "Visma! Elping?"

Nothing.

"Ghal?"

Nothing.

And then, as if a prayer to the stars themselves, knowing that her last view of the *Aurie* was of the ship spiraling away from an inevitable, fiery end, she rasped out one last request.

"Pikka! Joss! Anyone, please!"

Her comm crackled to life, before it went silent again. The conveyer belt was taking them into another room, into a lower level. Warm air puffed up and an orange glow lit up the end of the tube that led to the bowels of the building. Soon, they would see the furnace room ahead.

Oh no. Their conveyer belt was going to dump them straight into a smelter the size of a bantha.

"We're doomed," intoned the droid.

Halfway across Eriadu City, in what once was a thriving market square, Visma stood on the carcass of the scav droid. Three more surrounded her, ready to finish her off. There was no time to think. They fired upon her simultaneously, and she dove and rolled onto the ground. Two droids ended up shooting each other, fizzling in their death. The third kept firing, but was ►

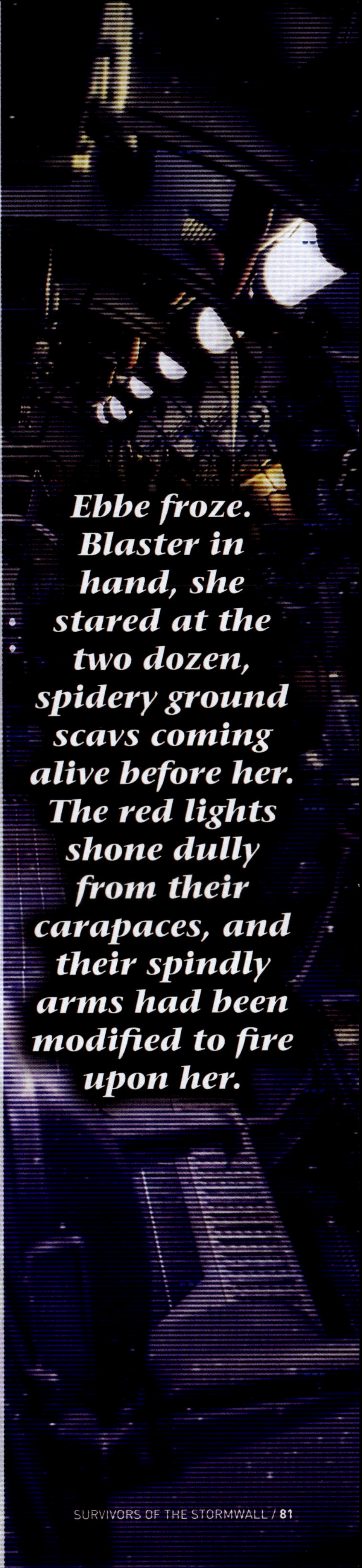

Ebbe froze. Blaster in hand, she stared at the two dozen, spidery ground scavs coming alive before her. The red lights shone dully from their carapaces, and their spindly arms had been modified to fire upon her.

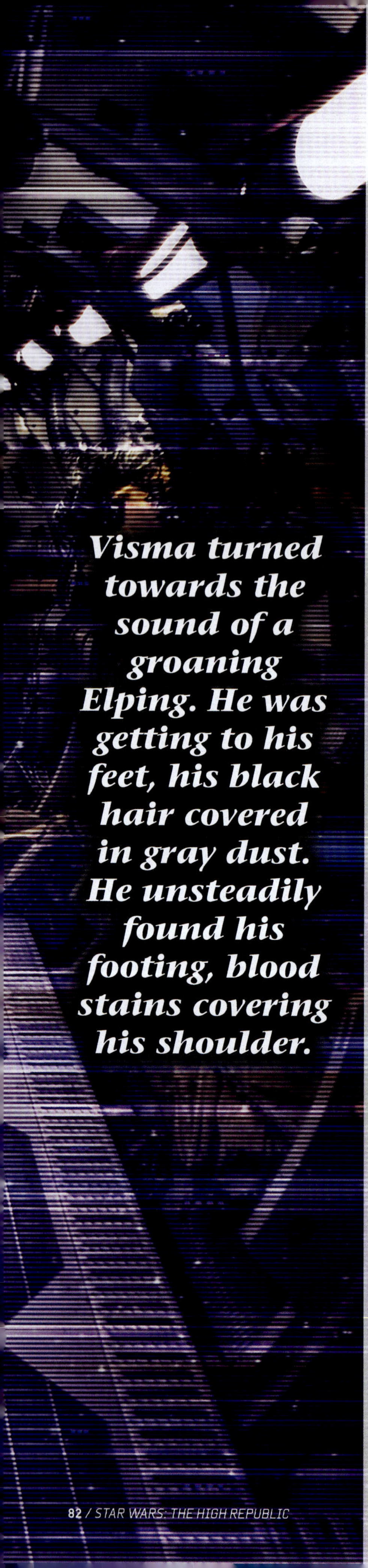

Visma turned towards the sound of a groaning Elping. He was getting to his feet, his black hair covered in gray dust. He unsteadily found his footing, blood stains covering his shoulder.

unable to get a clean shot as Visma ducked behind the pile of twisted transparisteel and rubble.

Her comm crackled.

"Visma!" It was Ebbe. A garbled word followed. Visma turned towards the sound of a groaning Elping. He was getting to his feet, his black hair covered in gray dust. He unsteadily found his footing, blood stains covering his shoulder. A medic had finally put on a temporary pressure dressing and his blaster-wounded limb was bound tightly against his chest.

She went to his side. "You have to get out of here. I'm going to find Ebbe and help her."

"I'm coming with you."

"You can barely stand!" Visma chided him. Elping's face, slightly pale, suddenly grew angry, fast as a switch. He looked so furious, she almost jolted back from his expression of rage. His good arm rose so quickly it was a blur, the sound of a blaster firing near her ear startling her.

She spun around to see a Nihil staggering backwards, his weapon flying from his hand, thanks to Elping's well-aimed shot.

"I can stand, and more," Elping said. "Let's go find Ebbe."

"And Sixen," Visma added. "He comes in handy, sometimes."

"I thought he was just a bag of bolts?" Elping chided, as they ducked low and ran as quickly as they could to find a transport, Visma following right behind him.

"He is. But he's *our* bag of bolts," Visma said.

The sound of incessant blaster fire told Elping and Visma that they were in the right place. Ghal Tarpfen and half a dozen RDC were spread out, firing at the scavs that seemed to be defending a defunct lommite plant on the outskirts of the city. Three of the droids were trying to attack and shoot from the eastern wall, while more seemed to be slowly emerging out of a south exit. The scavs here were bigger, bulkier, and well protected, and Ghal's scattered group was getting nowhere and losing ground.

But where was Ebbe?

Elping, firing with his one good arm, was occasionally pausing to catch his breath when he thought Visma wasn't looking. He wouldn't last much longer, injured as he was.

"Ebbe! Report!" Visma hissed into her comms, but there was no response. She ran towards a giant lommite transport being used for cover by RDC. A deep voice shouted nearby.

"Visma!"

Large yellow eyes stared back at her. Below them, a mouth tight in grim defiance.

"Ghal!" Visma exclaimed. "You okay?"

"I'm fine, but this—" the Mon Calamari gestured to the battlefield—"is terrible," she shouted, ducking as blaster fire rocked the transport. Rubble flew up and pelted them. "We don't have enough firepower to fend them off. But if we retreat, they'll enter the center of the city," Ghal said.

Another RDC officer shouted through the comms. "We have to retreat. We're outnumbered."

"We can't leave!" Visma hissed. "Ebbe is still in there!"

"Lieutenant Cassett is beyond help," the officer argued. "We can't all die for one person who might already be dead."

Visma looked over at Elping. His firing arm had fallen to his side, his face drained of color. The energy had left his eyes. Dread filled her. Was this how they would be defeated? After battling every hour of their lives, for months?

"We have to retreat," Visma spoke into her comm. From a distance, Elping shook his head. "We have no choice!" she yelled.

An explosion filled the air, and rubble rained down on them. Visma and Ghal ducked and shielded their faces with their arms. An enormous scav droid, by far the largest of the wretched machines they'd yet seen, stood before them in the clearing cloud of dust. Its red eye shone, scanning in all directions at once. It had three arms, weaponized with blasters, and even one small proton cannon. Each limb pointed at Ghal, Visma, and Elping.

It was over.

The rising heat from the smelter was unbearable, causing Ebbe's vision to blur.

"My circuits will melt!" C-06N cried out.

"Stop complaining!" Ebbe hollered.

The conveyer belt began to tilt downward, until lommite chunks of varying sizes began to bounce and sweep past the two. Several hit them, bruising Ebbe and clanking against the droid. Warm blood dripped off her cheek.

Whether the Cosian Nihil turned on the smelters, or the scav droids, she didn't know. But in a few seconds, they'd be taking a bath in molten lommite.

"Hang on!" Ebbe said, her fingers grabbing the ribs on the conveyer belt.

"With my *one* arm?" questioned C-06N. "It's not a complaint, but it is unlikely that we will survive—"

"Shut up!" Ebbe yelled.

She held onto the ribs with one hand, and pulled a grappling gun from her utility belt, aiming for a huge support beam above the smelter. In her jacket pocket, three small detonators were ready to go. Smelter and detonator might be an excellent combination, if she could only escape falling into the former.

"Is this really going to work?" C-06N cried, shying from the fierce heat, the glow making his silver body appear golden.

"It had better, or we're cooked," Ebbe said. "On the count of three, let go and grab hold of something! One, two...!"

C-06N shrieked.

Elping, Ghal, and Visma stared at each other. How could it have come to this?

A squat Nihil raised his rifle at the group behind the scav droids. "Drop your weapons," he said, his voice like metal scraping on stone. Elping dropped his blaster, his open palm sagging at his side. Visma swore to herself and did the same.

Ghal, instead, looked to the sky.

Visma and Elping's eyes followed hers. A shadow overtook them, blocking out the light from the coming sunset.

It was the *Aurie.*

Both Nihil and droids noticed it the same moment they did, raising their arms skyward to fire at the Longbeam. The *Aurie* circled back. It slowed almost to a hover near the battle grounds outside the factory. The scavs seemed to waver, as if irresistibly attracted by the ship. The Nihil yelled at them to maintain their positions, but they seemed immune to his shouts.

Oh, thought Visma. *Their old programming. They can't stand it, not peeling that ship to pieces. But would their new directives as ground scavs override their original purpose?*

"Hold your fire," Ghal ordered everyone on the fields.

The *Aurie* flew dangerously close, its starboard wings tilted towards the ground. The droids hesitated, and the pause in attacks from the RDC seemed to befuddle them. It was like they were waiting for something.

"Take cover!" yelled Ghal.

The *Aurie* fired its cannons at a grouping of ground scavs, obliterating two and sending two others tumbling hard against the wall of the building. The others seemed to wake up from a reverie, and immediately pounced off the ground, flying towards to the *Aurie* in a scattered, black cloud gathering like a storm around the ship. They scampered across the hull and immediately began to tear it apart at the seams. Visma quickly dispatched the Nihil, who was whirling in confusion.

"Joss! Pikka!" Visma screamed, as she raised her blaster to the air.

Just then, an enormous eruption seemed to shake the very ground. The north end of the lommite plant began to cave in on itself. The walls crumpled and smoke issued from within, before an explosion of bright orange fire blew upwards like a ▸

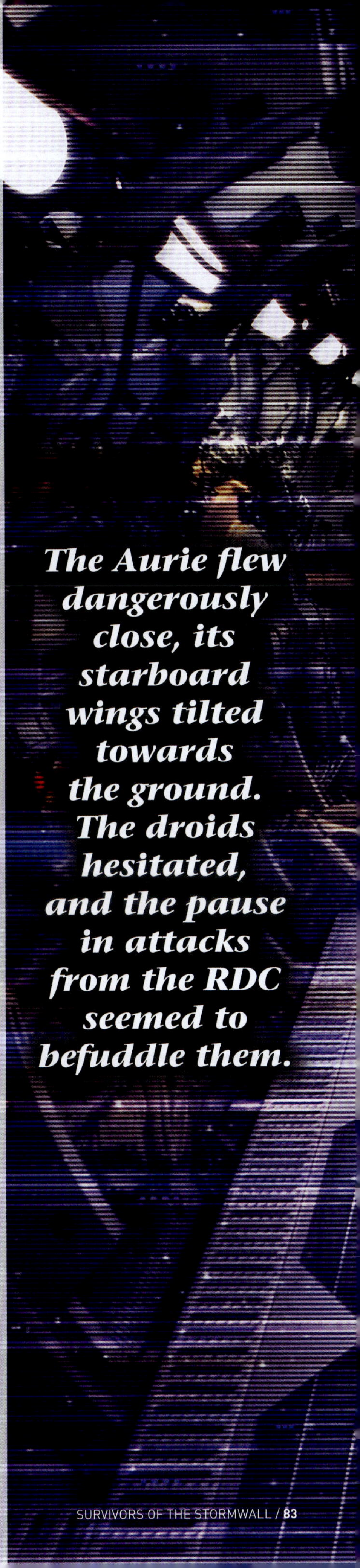

The Aurie flew dangerously close, its starboard wings tilted towards the ground. The droids hesitated, and the pause in attacks from the RDC seemed to befuddle them.

The droids swarmed around the already battle-scarred Longbeam, like ravenous parasites. The agent on the ground turned their firepower upon them as the Aurie rose into the air.

starburst. Half-built scav droids flew outwards, irreparably damaged by the explosion that seemed to come from the deepest level of the plant.

"What is going on?" Ghal said.

"It's Ebbe!"

From the edge of the collapsing fireball, a lone RDC agent was running full speed away with a silvery droid at her heels. They tumbled safely to the ground, watching the *Aurie* fly away, covered in scavs.

The droids swarmed around the already battle-scarred Longbeam, like ravenous parasites. The agent on the ground turned their firepower upon them as the *Aurie* rose into the air, spinning but unable to keep its wings even. As it turned nauseatingly, Visma saw a large hole on the starboard side with scavs crawling in to invade the innards of the ship. Smoke issued from the nose of the craft. It began to drop out of the sky.

Visma gasped, "They're going to crash!"

"Fire at the droids!" Ghal ordered. "Everything you've got!"

One by one, the chorus of a dozen blasters began decimating the scav numbers. But by the time they'd taken out nearly all of them, the Aurie was already in a death spiral heading north of the lommite plant.

Visma and Ghal met Ebbe at the edge of a fallow field, where they followed the smoke towards the ship's likely crash site. The impact as it hit the ground was deafening.

Visma shut her eyes for one moment.

What if Pikka and Joss didn't...

She shook her white hair and ran even faster to the wreckage. Inside, a booted foot kicked out the transparisteel from a gun emplacement and a dazed figure stumbled out.

"Joss!" Ebbe yelled. He waived off the hands offering to help him up.

"Pikka," he said, grunting pain. "*Go to her.* Now!"

The door to the cockpit was jammed closed. A giant crack of sky opened from above, where the carcass of a scav droid hung halfway inside. Ebbe shot at the locking mechanism of the door, but it didn't budge.

"Wait," Joss said. His tall frame nearly touched the ceiling of the Aurie. Arms bulging, he tore a vibroblade off the leg of the scav droid, the sound of twisting metal loud and horrible. In less than two minutes, he'd cut through enough of the door that they could wrench it open.

"Pikka!" Joss yelled, running to her side. She was still strapped into her pilot's chair. Her eyes were closed, and her arms hanging slack. Her breath was shallow, and a bruise was blossoming against her collarbones where the harnesses had dug into her body. Ghal touched her arm.

Pikka moaned, grimacing. Together, they gently laid her onto the wet floor of the cockpit. A dark red, bloody splotch stained her shirt, above her ballooning abdomen.

"She's wounded!" Joss yelled.

"The ship's computer," Pikka gasped, eyes still closed. "Plug me in."

"Plug you—what are you talking about? You've been shot," Ebbe said.

Sixen hovered behind them, muttering. "No projectiles! There are no projectiles here!" He waved his one arm. "The viewport is intact! Isn't it obvious?"

"Plug me in, now! Oh, stars—ugggghhhh," she yelled in pain, eyes tight with pain. "Sixen! Tell them!" Pikka said, gasping. She could barely breathe enough to speak.

Visma, the RDC personnel, and Ghal turned towards the silver droid. He raised his one dusty arm.

"Captain Adren hasn't been shot. She's in *labor*. She sustained a minor injury from the deceleration forces against her harness. She is asking to be assessed by the medical program loaded into the *Aurie* to assist with her delivery. Now!"

"Why didn't you say so?" Ghal said, her yellow eyes bulging.

"She can't talk, and no one listens to me!" C-06N said, exasperated. "Oh, and her birth waters have broken. Marvelous! You're standing in it."

"Love, the *Aurie* is completely down," Joss said. "We can't use the *Aurie*'s natal program."

"What are we going to do?" Visma said. "Ebbe?"

"Don't look at me!" Ebbe said, exasperated. "Can we get her to a medical tent across the city?"

Pikka gritted her teeth as another contraction came on swiftly.

"This is happening now, right here," Joss said. He looked at the group surrounding Pikka. "It's time."

"I haven't trained for this!" Visma said, raising her hands in alarm.

"I have!" exclaimed C-06N.

"*What?*" Ebbe said, eyes wide.

"We had Sixen upload emergency medical programming these last few weeks. Just in case," Joss said.

Visma's mouth dropped open.

"Everyone, stop talking!" C-06N said, waving his one arm. "I need all of you to leave this room except Captain Adren and Lieutenant Casset, to assist. Lieutenant Tarko, bring me the delivery kit from the medical bay." He seemed to puff out his dusty and blaster-singed chest. "And for once, everyone, do exactly as I tell you."

EPILOGUE

Elping leaned against the wreckage of the *Aurie*. His wound had started bleeding again, and Visma was treating it with a medpac. She pressed on the new dressing gently, but Elping winced nevertheless.

"There. It's all done," Visma said, looking at her handiwork.

"The bandage, or the battle?"

"Both," Visma said. "Scavs are all destroyed, and we have Eriadu back again."

"What happened to the Stormwall?" Elping said.

"It's down, though I don't know how or why. All I know is, Admiral Kronara and Jedi Master Keeve Trennis and her fleet did it. The RDC, the Eriaduans...we *all* got Eriadu back." She stood up and reached an arm out to help Elping stand. She put her arm around his waist to steady him.

"There was a time where you'd rather I fell than let me lean on you."

"No one emerges from a war alive and unchanged," Visma said quietly. "For better, and for worse," Elping said.

"Let's just think about the better part," Visma said, voice soft.

Two figures emerged from the other end of the *Aurie*. Ghal Tarpfen and Joss accompanied Pikka, lying on a hover gurney. A small bundle was wrapped up against her chest.

Elping and Visma smiled, meeting them.

"Say hello to our newest pilot," Pikka said. She smiled through her exhaustion. Joss had his arm around Pikka and stroked the satin cheek of the child.

"But not too close! You're all filthy!" C-06N said, waving his arm anxiously.

"What a little tadpole," Ghal said, yellow eyes blinking fondly.

Around them were littered chunks of destroyed scav near the wreckage of the *Aurie*. Fallen RDC were being attended to by medics. Beyond the lommite plant, smoke rose in coils from Eriadu City. More reports of the Nihil being defeated and scattered. The Battle of Eriadu was officially over. And yet, so many had been lost. So much destroyed.

"It's hard to believe something so beautiful could have come out of this," Ebbe said, glancing around.

"Hard to believe," Pikka said. "But it was worth it. Every battle, every fight, every breath. It's always worth fighting for a better tomorrow."

Joss leaned in, kissing his child's head, "Little Hedda."

Ebbe's lips quivered, and her eyes went glassy, "A classic choice."

To think, all of this had begun with the Great Disaster, and the loss of one of the most important people in her life, her aunt. Ebbe saw C-06N anxiously watching them all, a protector for a new generation. Visma and Elping leaning on each other. Ghal looking protectively over the Adrens. And the Adrens cradling their newborn, Hedda.

Within each one, a fierce flame of hope. And tomorrow, a new day.

What will they all do now? Ebbe wondered, and then she smiled.

They'll live.

THE END

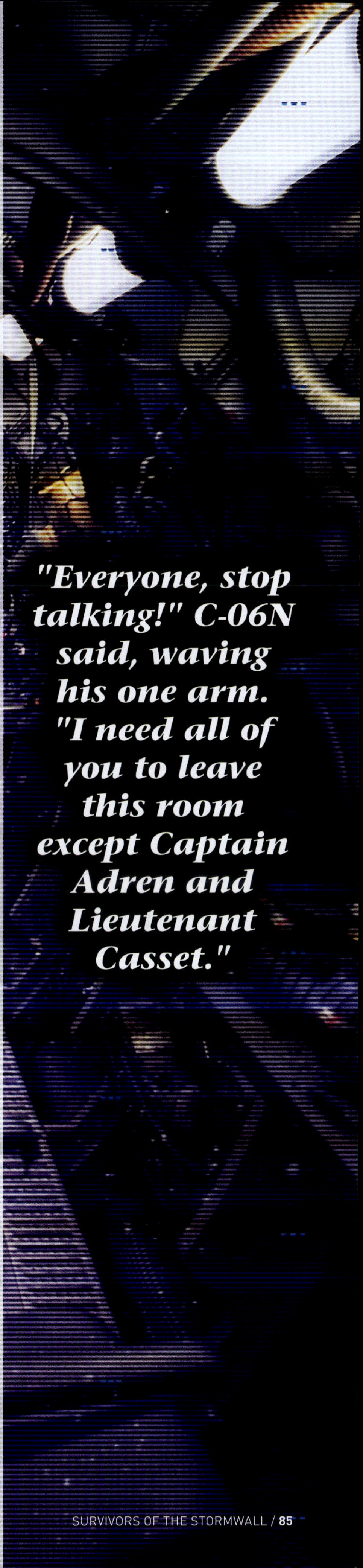

"Everyone, stop talking!" C-06N said, waving his one arm. "I need all of you to leave this room except Captain Adren and Lieutenant Casset."

CONCEPT ART

Star Wars creature designer artist Jake Lunt Davies' involvement with the franchise began with designing BB-8 and numerous creatures and droids for *The Force Awakens*. Over the past decade he has contributed designs to many other projects for Lucasfilm, including the Disney+ series *Andor* and 2027's upcoming movie release, *Star Wars: Starfighter*.

Star Wars Insider commissioned Davies to illustrate the nine short stories that comprise *Tales of the Occlusion Zone*, with a brief to envisage a scene from each tale as if he were creating a piece of concept art for a feature film. The process of crafting each composition resulted in several rough concepts for each final illustration, as presented on the following pages.

FRIEND OR FOE?

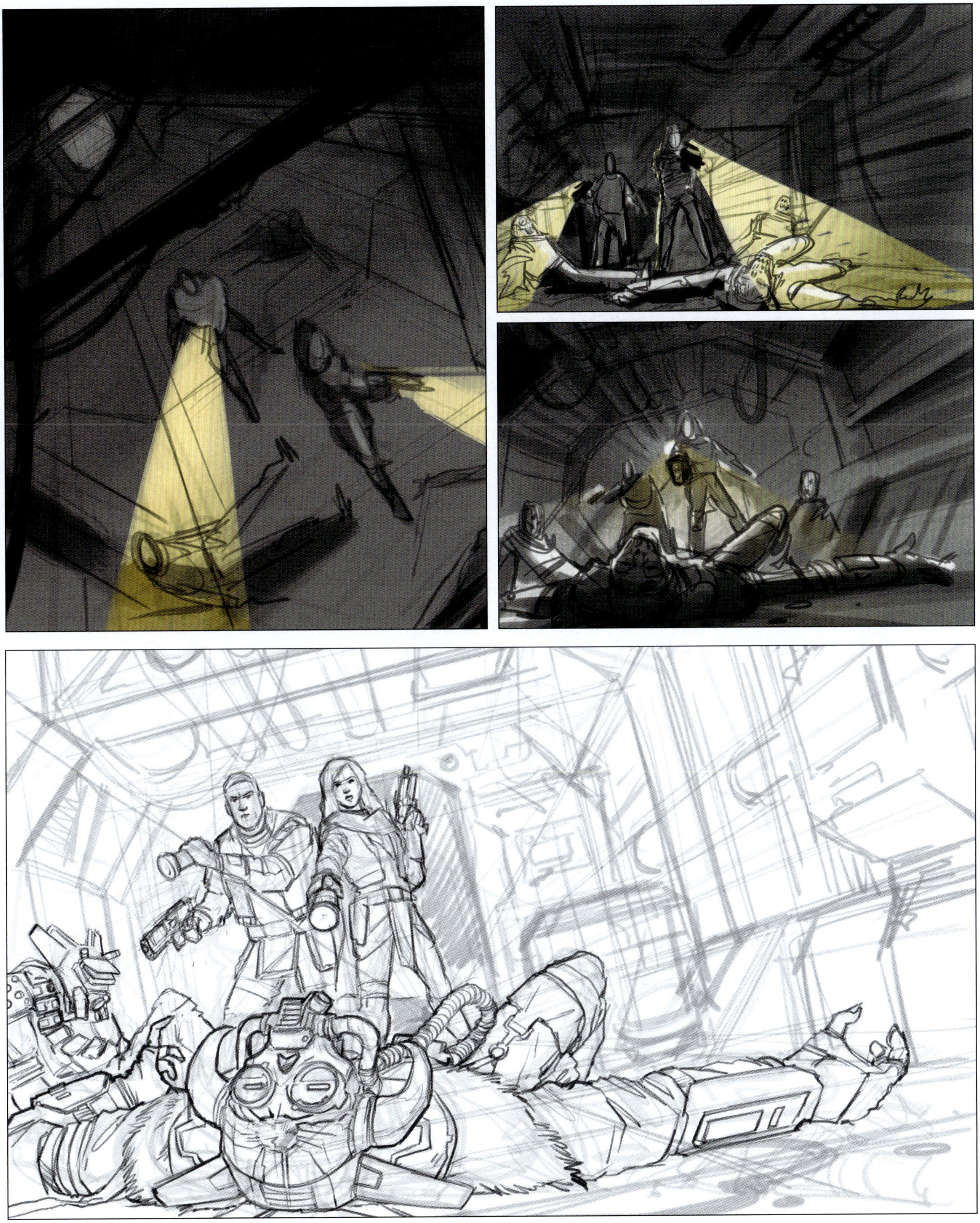

SURVIVORS

PATHOGEN

FAMILY TIES

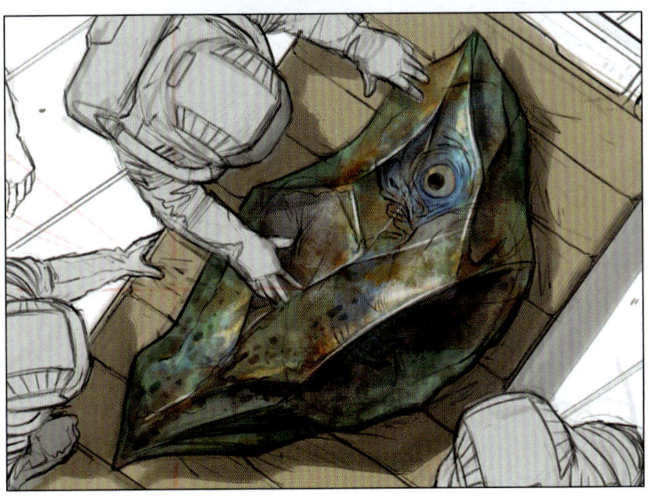

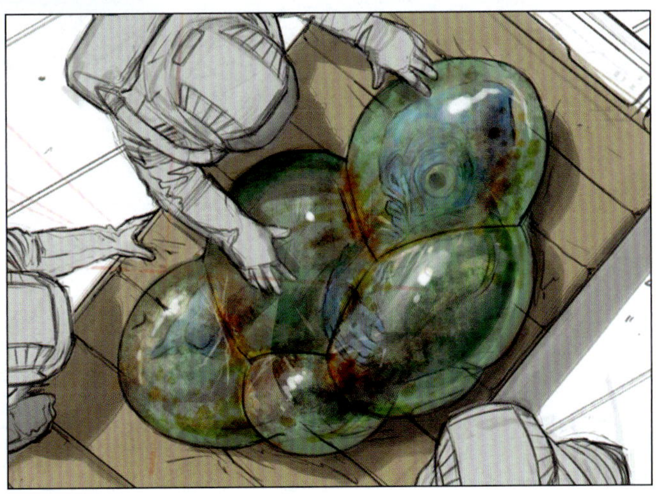

THE FATE OF ERIADU

SPARKS FLY

OUT WITH A BANG

THE WILL TO FIGHT

"We set out to create something new, but that was still very authentically *Star Wars.*"

Creative Director Michael Siglain, Lucasfilm Publishing

01

STAR WARS INSIDER

THE HIGH REPUBLIC

LONG LIVE LUMINOUS

The architects and authors behind *Star Wars: The High Republic* reflect on the publishing initiative's light, life, and legacy.

WORDS: CHELSEA ZUKOWSKI

"Those we love are never truly gone." It's a foundational phrase in *Star Wars* storytelling—from Obi-Wan Kenobi sharing the sentiment with a young, impressionable farm boy to Luke Skywalker using it to officiate Han Solo and Princess Leia's wedding. It suggests the compelling idea that the stories we cherish imprint themselves upon our hearts, leaving lasting, luminous legacies, thereby becoming immortal.

It's the same way that the writers and fans feel about *The High Republic*, an extension of the *Star Wars* timeline that spread across three phases of storytelling in books, comics, and other media—even reaching TV screens with *Star Wars: The Acolyte* and *Young Jedi Adventures*. This was a time filled with love and light despite being engulfed in some of the darkest moments in galactic history. Our love for this era, which has so far driven four years of storytelling, has ensured that the High Republic will never truly be over.

"It stemmed from the Obi-Wan Kenobi line in *Star Wars: A New Hope*, 'For over a thousand generations the Jedi Knights were the guardians of peace and justice in the Old Republic,'" says Michael Siglain, creative director at Lucasfilm Publishing, whose concept of a multi-publisher initiative grew into *The High Republic*. "We started making lists: What do we love about *Star Wars*? What do we want to see in *Star Wars?* What haven't we seen in *Star Wars*? But it all stemmed from what George Lucas created. We set out to create something new, but that was still very authentically *Star Wars*. And I'm happy to say that I feel we achieved that."

02

03

01 Project Luminous concept art by Phil Noto.

02 03 The Japanese edition of *Light of the Jedi* was published in two volumes.

04

04 The French language edition of *Light of the Jedi*.

Bold Beginnings

Star Wars: Light of the Jedi by Charles Soule launched *The High Republic* on January 5, 2021. During its entire run, the initiative spawned two dozen novels, several audio dramas, short story collections, manga volumes, reference books, and a ton of comics. The stories explored the Golden Age of the Jedi Order and what it meant to be a Jedi in a time of peace. It also planted the seeds of disharmony that would, centuries later, grow into a Jedi Order destroyed by politics, war, and manipulative darkness.

Project Luminous, as it was originally known, was the brainchild of Siglain. "I first pitched the concept in 2014," he says. At the time, Lucasfilm was gearing up for the sequel trilogy, so it wasn't until around the release of *Star Wars: The Rise of Skywalker* that he says the "stars aligned" for the ambitious project.

"The original goal was to create a multi-publisher crossover that would have a book and a format for every reader. The secondary goal was to create that shareability factor that is so inherent in *Star Wars*," Siglain explained. Another goal was to "create a little corner of the galaxy that publishing could call their own." ▸

LIGHT OF THE JEDI

"I think when people think about *The High Republic* down the road, they'll think about the Jedi," says Charles Soule. "We've seen so many stories in *Star Wars* set during an era when they were in decline, or essentially gone, or bravely trying to rebuild themselves from almost nothing. *The High Republic*, at its heart, is an attempt to show an Order, and a Republic, at their strongest point. We've been hearing about what the Jedi meant to the galaxy for a thousand generations—we wanted to show it, and I think we succeeded."

05 Starlight Beacon was a centerpiece of Phase I storytelling.

"We all entered the space with creativity at the forefront."
Daniel José Older

After approval from Lucasfilm President Kathleen Kennedy came the authors, who were key to identifying a specific era of the *Star Wars* timeline. Settling on an era centuries before the Skywalker saga allowed them "the right amount of creative freedom to do something truly new and original but still truly authentic," Siglain says.

The High Republic emerged as a sweet spot on the timeline—long enough before the prequels to not impact them but close enough to include a few long-lived, recognizable characters and connections. Through creative freedoms, organic storytelling, and story conferences at Skywalker Ranch, the premise and period evolved quickly, becoming more interconnected with every story.

"We didn't have the whole thing from the start, and there were a number of beats I didn't know would happen until I sat down to write *Trials of the Jedi*," says Charles Soule, who penned the first and the last novels in the initiative. "Plot and character beats could emerge from casual conversations over a drink, or a texted question, or at a high-level meeting," he adds. "We all talked to each other all the time, and we were all committed to working together and helping each other tell the stories we wanted to tell."

Soule, along with Claudia Gray, Justina Ireland, Daniel José Older, and Cavan Scott, were the original authors of *The High Republic*. They faced the daunting task of creating foundational story beats, themes, and characters. For Scott, the building blocks of *The High Republic* were laid in the second week of brainstorming—key elements like the Republic Fair and Starlight Beacon (briefly nicknamed the Light Star). "Some elements of the ending have changed in their setup, just because we allowed ourselves space for the storyline to evolve as we told it," Scott explains. "But it was pretty much there from that second week of planning. It's just the different ways to get there have changed a little bit."

For Older, one of the brightest parts of planning and creating the High Republic was the synergy between the authors. "Synergy does not mean that we all agreed

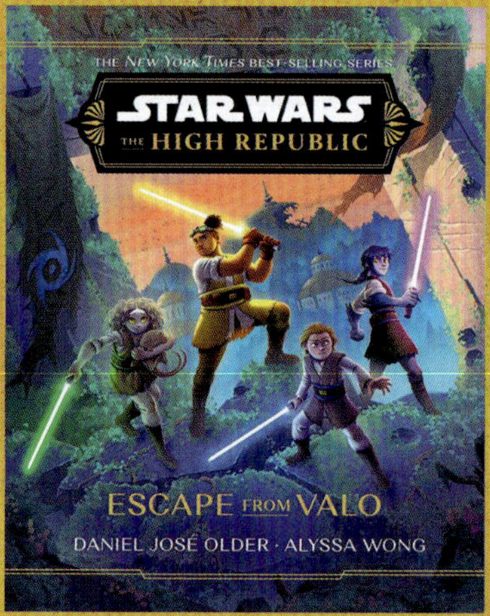

06 *Escape from Valo* cover art by Petur Antonsson.

07 The Valo Fair. Illustration by Petur Antonsson.

08 Left to right: Michael Siglain, James Waugh, Charles Soule, Cavan Scott, Daniel José Older, Justina Ireland, and Claudia Gray at Celebration 2022.

on everything, but that was the fun part. We brought so many different things to the table and then we bounced them off each other," says the writer behind *Midnight Horizon*, *Escape from Valo*, and all three phases of *The High Republic Adventures* comics. "We entered the space with creativity at the forefront." There was a "true spirit of collaboration" among the authors, who made the storytelling better by challenging and uplifting one another.

Once characters, elements, and story beats had been established, the original five authors asked themselves questions like: *Who do we need here? What's going to really make the story sing? How is the story in conversation with this other story through overlapping moments?* "I really loved those moments of synergy," Older says. "Where the stories are overlapping, and you get to see them from different points of view. It's all very *Star Wars* to me."

A New Fandom is Born

The High Republic was a hit from its launch, with the first two books—*Light of the Jedi* and *A Test of Courage*—hitting the number one and two spots on their respective *New York Times* best-seller lists. It was the height of the COVID-19 pandemic, and there were no book tours, signings, or conventions to promote the new stories.

"Online, there was a core group of people who were absolutely invested from day one," Scott says, who woke up on the release day of *The Rising Storm* to see fans already talking about it. "I'd never experienced it to that level before. And then it just grew from there."

With all the excitement and interactivity online during the first year, Older says it was "very clear by then that our fandom was something special and beyond anything I'd experienced. The creativity, the humor, philosophical thoughtfulness, and the sense of community. Fandom should be fun, and I think our fandom exemplifies that in every way," he says.

Star Wars Celebration 2022 in Anaheim proved to be a major change of gear.

"It was such a moving, overwhelming experience for me, for the authors, and I think that's the point where we really knew, wow, this is so much bigger than what we hoped it could be," Siglain confirms. With an auditorium packed with more than 4,000 High Republic fans, Siglain recalls, "It felt like Beatlemania."

"People were thrilled. *Beyond* thrilled," says Soule. "It was astonishing, and so much more than any of us expected. I'm smiling just thinking about it."

The response from the fans in Anaheim and then again at *Star Wars* Celebration in London the following year was a humbling experience for Scott. "It's that thing you can't quite believe, and you realize that these aren't our stories; these aren't our characters," he says. "As soon as we've told the story, they're out, it's part of the community and it will always be there." ▸

09 *A Test of Courage* illustration by Petur Antonsson.

Pulling a *Star Wars*

Phase I concluded with an epic cliffhanger involving catastrophic loss and a devastated galaxy. The main story wouldn't pick back up until fall 2023. With Phase II, *The High Republic* pulled a classic *Star Wars* move by diving further into the past.

"I remember when we were conceiving the whole thing and the notion of jumping back in time for Phase II came up. That was a very brave thing to do as storytellers," Older considers. "It could have completely blown up in our faces if we hadn't done our job in Phase I. But we were really excited. Phase II gave us the opportunity to make the world so much bigger and more expansive."

The second phase took readers back 150 years before the events of the first set of releases, to explore the origins of the Nihil and the Nameless through tales of hyperspace prospecting and frontier living at the edges of the known galaxy. There was also a Forever War between two planets and the chaotic Battle of Jedha that marred the Holy City.

Phase II also added five new authors: Zoraida Córdova, Tessa Gratton, Lydia Kang, George Mann, and Alyssa Wong.

"I was really excited to be able to work with everybody," says Córdova, who wrote *Convergence*. "And then finding out that Lydia, George, Tessa, and Alyssa were also joining the fray. It felt like when *The Avengers* got more teammates."

Though the main story had already been established by the five story architects, the new authors still enjoyed creative freedom in exploring the growing galaxy. Through Pathfinders, frontier Jedi, Force cults, tragic monsters, enemies-turned-lovers, charming charlatans, and mysterious Force-soaked planets, the Phase II stories expanded lore dating back into galactic history.

"I think Phase II holds a really special place in people's hearts because it is different; it's laying historical groundwork," *Cataclysm* author Lydia Kang says. "We got to do things that had never been done before."

George Mann, who penned *Quest for the Hidden City* and *Star Wars Insider*'s Phase II short stories, saw beauty and fun challenges in going back in time. "We had a lot of room to invent," he explains. "And what's great about doing a prequel is that you know where you have to end up, so you can pick the thematic elements that you want to seed in to build for later."

For Tessa Gratton, who co-wrote *Path of Deceit* with Justina Ireland and then *Quest for Planet X*, becoming a *Star Wars* author was nerve-wracking and exciting. "I've been a lifelong *Star Wars* fan but never thought I'd be writing professionally for Lucasfilm," they say. "I joined via Justina wanting to co-write *Path of Deceit* with me, and it was a perfect entry—monsters, cults, teenage angst, and kissing are some of the things I've always loved writing about in my own work."

Each of the Phase II authors returned for Phase III, which saw the action switch back to the Phase I period for an epic conclusion to the Jedi's yearslong fight with the Nihil, the Nameless, the Blight, and themselves.

10

10 *Convergence* cover art by Yihyoung Li.

11

11 *Cataclysm* cover art by Yihyoung Li.

12

12 *Quest for Planet X* cover art by Petur Antonsson.

THE ACOLYTE AND YOUNG JEDI ADVENTURES

"With both shows, it was really humbling for us to see characters that we created go beyond the page," says Mike Siglain. "It really does show that, like the book initiative, *Star Wars* is for everyone and there can be something for everyone. You can have a really exciting, fun, bright, hopeful, animated show for kids and you can have something that is really thoughtful and mysterious."

13

Córdova brought her penchant for heartwarming, monster-filled fiction for younger readers and gave us Churo the Hutt in *Beware the Nameless.* Gratton joined Ireland again for the action-packed thriller *Defy the Storm* and the achingly romantic *Temptation of the Force.* Kang told tales of citizens fighting back against the Nihil on the other side of the Stormwall in *Insider*'s "Tales from the Occlusion Zone." Mann gave the Jedi a *Star Wars: The Empire Strikes Back* moment in *The Eye of Darkness* and answered long-awaited questions in *Tears of the Nameless.*

"The big story beats of the whole project—from *Light of the Jedi* to *Trials of the Jedi*—were already basically plotted out before anyone wrote a word," Gratton says. "The original five authors created the whole arc and then welcomed the rest of us to help with elaboration and detail. Some things shifted around depending on the needs of the story, but for the most part the story we told was the story they always meant for us to tell."

13 *Beware the Namelss* art by Petur Antonsson.

14 *Defy the Storm* cover art by Corey Brickley.

15 *Tears of the Nameless* cover art by Corey Brickley.

"We got to do things that had never been done before."

Lydia Kang

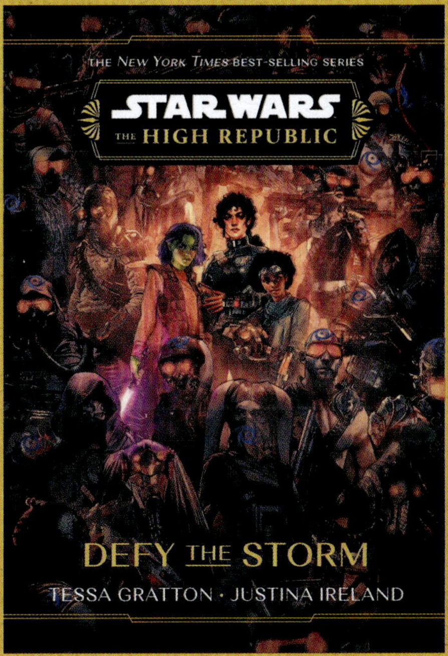

14

15

The End of the Beginning

"This has been a big part of my life, of the authors' lives, and no one is ready for it to end," Siglain says. "They've given so much to it for all these years, so I think they're ready to take a step back and exhale."

While the grand plan initially devised as Project Luminous has now been realized, Siglain is quick to assure fans that it was just the beginning for the storytelling era.

"What we're doing this summer is the end of this particular story, but it certainly is not the end of *The High Republic,*" he confirms. "This is just the end of the beginning. Hopefully that gives everyone a little bit of hope that yes, this may feel bittersweet, but we have plans."

"We love the characters we've created as much as anyone could—we're some of their biggest fans, and would love to see their adventures continue," Soule says. "But we all really wanted these last books to feel conclusive, like everyone reading them would get a true ending for the stories they've been enjoying."

Whatever comes next for the High Republic, the era has left an impression on its authors and fans. "Nothing every really goes away in *Star Wars*; it's very true what Luke said to Leia in *The Last Jedi,*" Scott concludes. "It's always going to be there, and we're already starting to see stories with things from the High Republic popping up. To see it become a part of the wider *Star Wars* tapestry is incredible."

Phase III: Trials of The Jedi

Star Wars Insider looks back at the third phase of Lucasfilm's *The High Republic* publishing initiative, with contributions from authors including Zoraida Córdova, Tessa Gratton, Lydia Kang, George Mann, Daniel José Older, Cavan Scott, Charles Soule and Alyssa Wong.

WORDS: CHELSEA ZUKOWSKI AND AREZOU AMIN

Wave 1

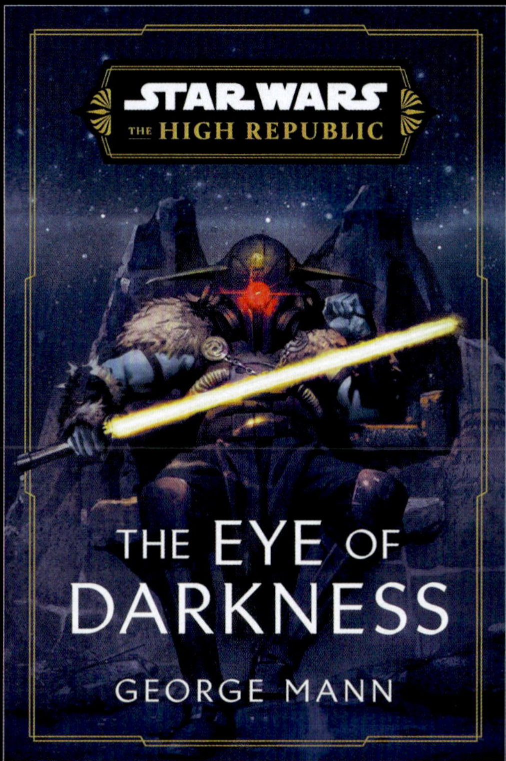

The Eye of Darkness

Writer: George Mann
Random House Worlds, Adult novel I
Avar Kriss is trapped behind the Stormwall, a barrier which places part of the Outer Rim under Nihil occupation. The Jedi work to dismantle the Stormwall, while also contending with Marchion Ro and his horde of Nameless creatures..

"We always knew it was going to be the book where the Jedi have lost," says George Mann. "It introduced a new status quo. Marchion Ro has won and the Stormwall is going up. I had lots of conversations with the team about where all our characters were going; talking about setting up a trajectory that was going to take us through to the end.

"There was this specific moment that unlocked the book for me, where Marchion Ro opens up to Ghira Starros and says 'Nobody realizes that by winning, I've lost, because I have to become what I tried to destroy,'" Mann continues. "What does that do to him, and what path does that put him on?"

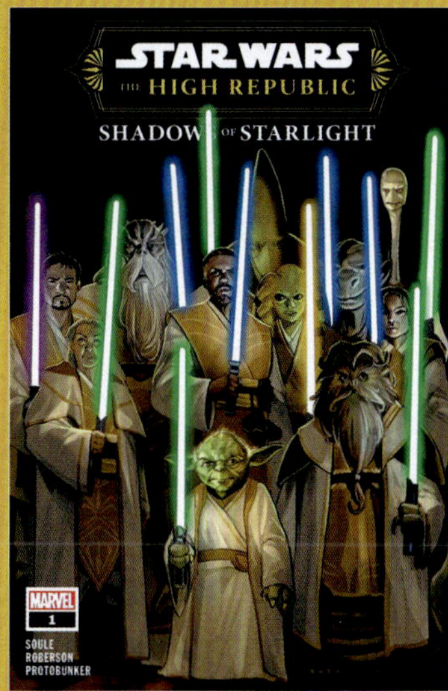

SHADOWS OF STARLIGHT

Writer: Charles Soule
Artists: Ibraim Roberson, Marika Cresta, Jethro Morales, David Messina
Cover Artist: Phil Noto
Marvel Comics, Four issue mini-series
Set during the "missing year" between Phase I and Phase III, following the destruction of Starlight Beacon, Yoda, Avar Kriss, Elzar Mann and Bell Zettifar plan their next moves in the face of Marchion Ro's victory.

"The Jedi aren't a monolith, despite how they might appear from the outside," says Charles Soule. "That was one of our big goals with the initiative—to create Jedi who were complete, fully-fleshed individuals with needs, desires, flaws, failings. People, in other words."

STAR WARS: THE HIGH REPUBLIC

Writer: Cavan Scott
Artists: Ario Anindito, Jim Towe, Marika Cresta, Laura Braga
Cover Artist: Phil Noto
Marvel Comics, 10 Issues
Collected in two trade paperbacks

"CHILDREN OF THE STORM" Issues 1-5
Jedi Master Keeve Trennis confronts both the Nihil and the Hutts, and comes face to face with former Tempest Runner Lourna Dee—whose allegiances are not what they once were—as well as her former master, Sskeer.

"THE HUNTED" Issues 6-10
Keeve Trennis, Sskeer, and Lourna Dee team up to stop Baron Boolan, Marchion Ro's Minister of Advancement, from kidnapping more subjects for his twisted experiments.

"Keeve and Sskeer's story has been my throughline for everything. I'm pretty much the only person who's written those characters all the way through, and it's something I never took for granted," says Cavan Scott. "There are things I wanted to say about what happens in a crisis and how people are forced to grow and take on roles that they're perhaps not ready for. What good and bad can come out of that situation. It was my polestar all the way through."

Escape from Valo

Writers: Daniel José Older, Alyssa Wong
Illustrator: Petur Antonsson
Disney • Lucasfilm Press, Middle Grade novel
Padawan Ram Jomaram teams up with three Jedi younglings who have been in hiding on Valo, to protect the Outer Rim planet and its inhabitants from the occupying Nihil.

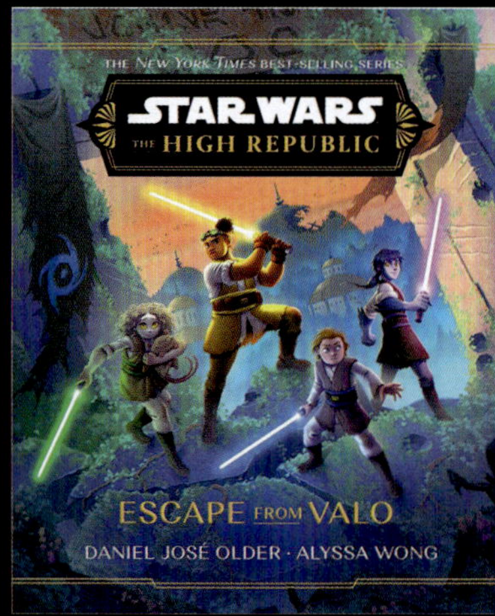

"Ram is a character close to my heart. I love him dearly," reflects Daniel José Older. "He's such a cool guy but he has no idea how cool he is. When we meet him, he's just trying to live his life. Someone pointed it out to me that Ram is almost like a reverse Luke Skywalker. Luke wanted to be fighting bad guys and taking on the Empire, whereas Ram just wants to live a quiet life in his small world, but the galaxy catches up to him."

Defy the Storm

Writers: Tessa Gratton, Justina Ireland
Disney • Lucasfilm Press, Young Adult novel
Vernestra Rwoh is dragged back into the heart of the fight against the Nihil, and joins some familiar faces to rescue her former Padawan, Imri, from the Occlusion Zone.

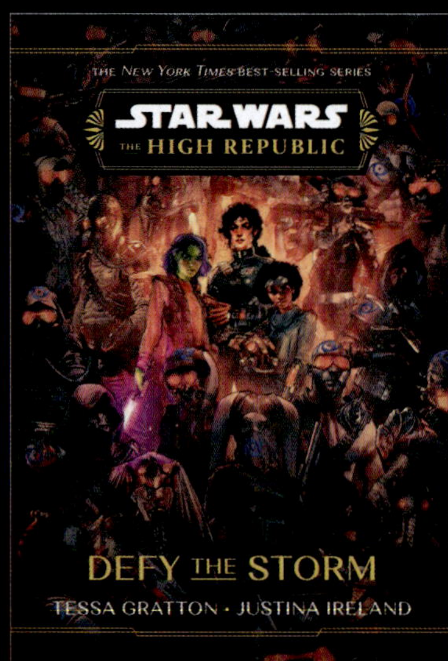

"I already knew the end game for the blight, so it was fun to figure out ways to tease what it is, what it could and would actually do, all while maintaining the mystery and pointing fingers in several wrong directions," explains Tessa Gratton. "Unlike the Nameless, who affect all Force users slightly differently, the blight is devastatingly the same. Instead of sharp fear, there's this overwhelming dread I wanted to bring to it. It's inexorable, even for Jedi."

STAR WARS: THE HIGH REPUBLIC ADVENTURES

Writer: Daniel José Older
Artists: Harvey Tolibao, Nick Brokenshire, Elisa Romboli, Toni Bruno, Caio Filipe, LeBeau Underwood
Cover Artists: Harvey Tolibao and Kevin Tolibao, Elisa Romboli
Dark Horse Comics, 20 issues
Collected in five trade paperbacks

VOLUME 1 Issues 1-5
Zeen Mrala and Jedi Knight Qort search for their friends who were lost in the crash of Starlight Beacon, including Zeen's love, Lula Talisola.

VOLUME 2 Issues 6-10
A reunited Zeen and Lula, along with their friends, brace for the arrival of the Stormwall on Eriadu, and prepare to fight the Nihil occupation.

VOLUME 3 Issues 11-13
Jedi Padawan Ram Jomaram and Jedi Knight Farzala Tarabal embark on a mission to Valo to rescue Padawan Gavi Takitaken and the Scarlet Skulls from the clutches of the Nihil.

VOLUME 4 Issues 14-16
Farzala, Lula, Zeen, Qort and their friends gather to defend the capital of Eriadu from the Warden, a Nihil commander bent on taking over the planet.

VOLUME 5 Issues 17-20
It's war, and the stakes are high as the Jedi freedom fighters and the Nihil invaders on Eriadu prepare for a final showdown.

CRASH LANDING

Writer: Daniel José Older
Artist: Rachele Aragno
Cover Artist: Rachele Aragno
Dark Horse Comics, One Shot
Collected in *The High Republic Adventures: Crash Zone*
On Corellia, Alys "Crash" Ongwa and her crew work tirelessly in their struggle to put an end to the Nihil occupation of her home planet.

SABER FOR HIRE

Writer: Cavan Scott
Artist: Rachael Stott
Cover Artist: Rachael Stott
Dark Horse Comics, four issue mini-series
Former Jedi Ty Yorrick finds work as a saber for hire until she discovers a Nihil plot to kidnap Force-attuned children, and must put a stop to it.

The High Republic: Tales from the Occlusion Zone

Author: Lydia Kang
Artist: Jake Lunt Davies
Titan Comics

"We wanted these stories to feature non-Jedi—the people who don't have the Force to help them figure their way out of things. We also wanted to go behind the lines of the Occlusion Zone and see what happens when you get stuck back there," Lydia Kang explains. "We threw a lot of terrible things at them; made things go from bad to worse to even worse then brought them out of the Occlusion Zone to Eriadu just when things were about to explode. We basically put those characters through the mill for nine stories."

"No Big Deal"
***Star Wars Insider* #222**
Joss and Pikka Adren are sent to intercept a Nihil vessel near the Stormwall broadcasting a distress signal.

"Friend or Foe?"
***Star Wars Insider* #223**
While on a rescue mission, The Adrens end up on the wrong side of the Stormwall.

"Survivors"
***Star Wars Insider* #224**
Stranded in the Occlusion Zone, Joss and Pikka find unexpected allies.

"Pathogen"
***Star Wars Insider* #225**
The Adrens and their new friends explore a Nihil prison ship in trouble.

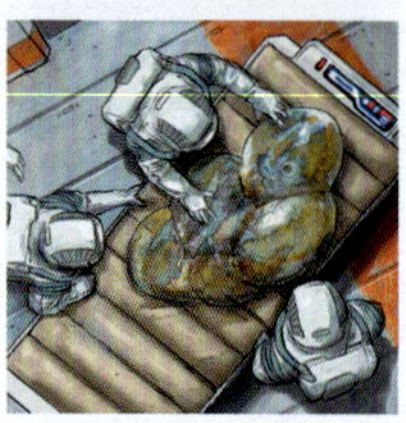

"Family Ties"
***Star Wars Insider* #226**
Joss and Pikka encounter an old acquaintance infected with the blight.

Wave 2

Temptation of the Force

Writer: Tessa Gratton
Random House Worlds,
Adult novel
Avar Kriss and Elzar Mann are finally reunited outside the Stormwall and embark on a new mission to try and stop the Nihil, while also finally facing their feelings for one another.

"When I was a kid I loved the space wizards," Tessa Gratton recalls. "I loved Luke and all the new Jedi in the Legends stories, but I was frustrated that Jedi were not supposed to love, because they weren't supposed to get attached to things. I knew that if I was awesome with the Force I'd be a terrible Jedi, because I wouldn't want to give up love (and kissing) or familial bonds. *Temptation* was my chance to passionately explain why I—and the Jedi of the High Republic era—shouldn't have to."

Beware the Nameless

Writer: Zoraida Córdova
Illustrator: Petur Antonsson
Disney • Lucasfilm Press,
Middle Grade novel
Three Jedi younglings and a senator's daughter stow away on a ship and wind up on a rescue mission where they encounter a young Hutt on a mission of his own.

"I wanted to show a different side of who the Hutts are," reveals Zoraida Córdova. "Churo is a tween Hutt who doesn't want to be in a cartel and just wants to study bugs and have friends. He's the most unlikely person to help save the day."

STAR WARS: THE HIGH REPUBLIC ADVENTURES PHASE III ANNUAL

Writers: Charles Soule, Rosemary Soule, Alyssa Wong, Zoraida Córdova, Cavan Scott, Justina Ireland
Artists: Andy Duggan, Liana Kangas, Juan Samu, Nick Brokenshire, Colin Craker
Cover Artists: Eduardo Francisco with Augusto Grillo
Dark Horse Comics, Annual
Collected in *The High Republic Adventures: Crash Zone*

A collection of short stories following Churo the Hutt, Driggit Parse, Vernestra Rwoh, Baron Boolan, and younglings Jon, Bree and Toko.

CRASH AND BURN

Writer: Daniel José Older
Artist: Nick Brokenshire,
Cover Artist: Rachele Aragno
Dark Horse Comics, One Shot
Collected in *The High Republic Adventures: Crash Zone*

Alys "Crash" Ongwa and her crew team up with the Nihil Krix Kamerat to take down Marchion Ro.

Tears of the Nameless

Writer: George Mann
Disney • Lucasfilm Press, Young Adult novel

When Jedi Knight Reath Silas and Padawan Amadeo Azzazzo are sent on a mission to find ways to stop the Nameless, they come face to face with the creatures once thought to be a myth—and learn the true meaning of fear.

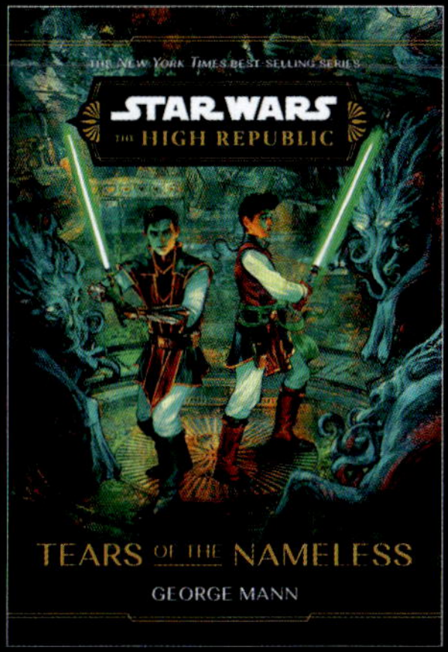

"There's a lot of swashbuckling and lightsaber fights in *Star Wars,* but we thought it was important to think about the personal effect that our story would have on the characters, especially on the younger ones," Mann says. "I've got older teenagers; I've seen how much pressure they put themselves under. Reath and Amadeo see themselves as Jedi. They know they have to be heroes. They have to be the best of the best. And if they don't, people they care about are going to die. What must that do to a teenager?"

THE WEDDING SPECTACULAR

Writer: Daniel José Older
Artists: Harvey Tolibao, Caio Filipe, Andy Duggan, Jo Mi-Gyeong, Toni Bruno, Megan Huang, Nick Brokenshire, Elisa Romboli
Cover Art: Cherriielle
Dark Horse Comics, One Shot
Collected in *The High Republic Adventures* Volume 3

Lula Talisola and Zeen Mrala finally join hands in marriage, despite battle looming on the horizon.

"Lula and Zeen's relationship was a story arc that I knew I wanted to get into from the beginning," says Older. "I wanted to explore what a positive version of a Jedi who has struggled with their faith or with the Order might look like. What if they have these struggles, but confront them directly instead of being burned by them or obsessed with them, or not allowed to deal with them? What happens if they get dealt with in a non-tragic way? I'm not inspired by tragedy, personally, in storytelling. I think it has its place for sure, but I felt this was an important moment, to end and to bring hope into the equation of love in this particular type of storytelling."

Seeds of Starlight

Writer: George Mann
Disney • Lucasfilm Press,
Audible Original novel
Padawan Cam Lindon and Jedi younglings Kildo and Tep Tep venture to Eiram, site of the Starlight Beacon crash, to investigate mysterious disappearances tied to the fallen space station.

Haunted Starlight

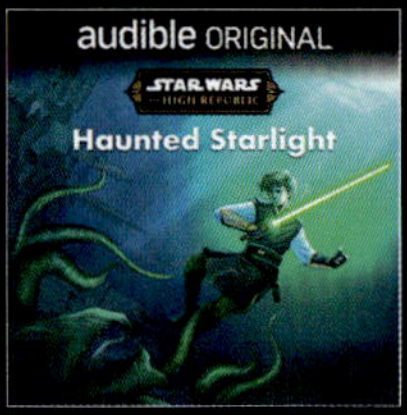

Writer: George Mann
Disney • Lucasfilm Press,
Audible Original novel
Padawan Cam Lindon and Jedi younglings Kildo and Tep Tep assist Jedi Master Eve Byre in thwarting an invasion on Eiram.

Tempest Breaker

Writer: Cavan Scott
Random House Worlds, Audio Original novel
Former Nihil Tempest Runner Lourna Dee teams up with the Jedi to track down Baron Boolan, and to seek out just what Marchion Ro is hiding beneath his offer to help the Republic.

ECHOES OF FEAR

Writer: George Mann
Artists: Vincenzo Federici, Vincenzo Riccardi, Juan Samu, Giorgia Sposito
Cover Art: Eduardo Mello with Valentina Taddeo
Dark Horse Comics,
Four issue mini-series

Reath Silas and Amadeo Azzazzo learn more about the mysterious Echo Stones that may be the key to defeating the Nameless.

"We spent books and books and books building the Nameless up as these horrific monsters; creatures born out of nightmare," George Mann says of the terrifying beasts. "It was about revealing what had happened to them and showing that they were victims, too."

The High Republic: Chronicles of Corellia

Author: Alyssa Wong
***Star Wars Insider*, Titan Comics**

"Heir Apparent"
***Star Wars Insider* #227**
Former Nihil Krix Kamerat and former Padawan Ruu form an uneasy alliance to secure coordinates to cross the Stormwall, using any means necessary to extract the data they need.

"Cracking the Mask"
***Star Wars Insider* #228**
Driggit Parse works to take down the Nihil from the inside by stealing a secret file of valuable schematics.

DISPATCHES FROM THE OCCLUSION ZONE

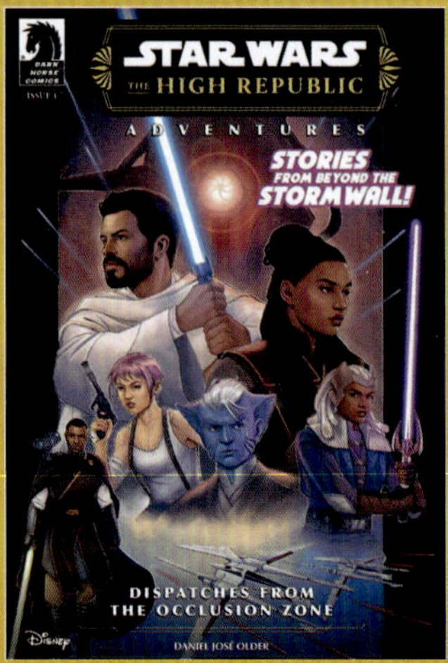

Writers: Daniel José Older, Alyssa Wong, Cavan Scott
Artists: Paris Alleyne, Valeria Favoccia, Lucas Marangon, Vincenzo Riccardi
Cover Artist: Jake Bartok
Dark Horse Comics,
Four issue mini-series

Jedi Knights Emerick Caphtor and Qort, rebel fighter Ruu, and saber for hire Ty Yorrick strike back against the Nihil from within the Occlusion Zone.

Wave 3

THE EDGE OF BALANCE VOL. 3

Writers: Daniel José Older, Shima Shinya
Artist: Mizuki Sakakibara
Viz Media

Jedi Knight Lily Tora-Asi defends the Jedi temple on Banchii against the Nihil, while her former master Arkoff uncovers the planet's secrets.

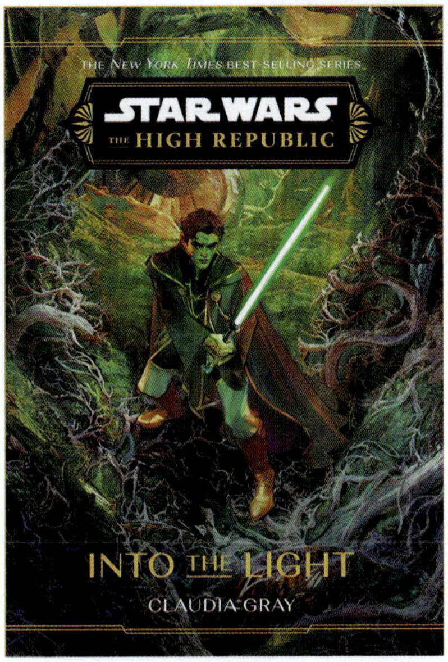

Into the Light

Writer: Claudia Gray
Disney • Lucasfilm Press, Young Adult novel
Reath Silas heads to Kashyyyk to try and stop the blight, which has taken root there, with the help of his former master Cohmac, and the fallen Jedi Azlin Rell.

A Valiant Vow

Writer: Justina Ireland
Illustrator: Petur Antonsson
Disney • Lucasfilm Press, Middle Grade novel
The blight spreads across Aricho, and scav droids are attacking anyone who approaches the planet, so Jedi Knights Imri Cantaros and Yacek Sparkburn and Jedi youngling Tep Tep, along with her friends Zenny Greylark and Churo the Hutt, rush in to help.

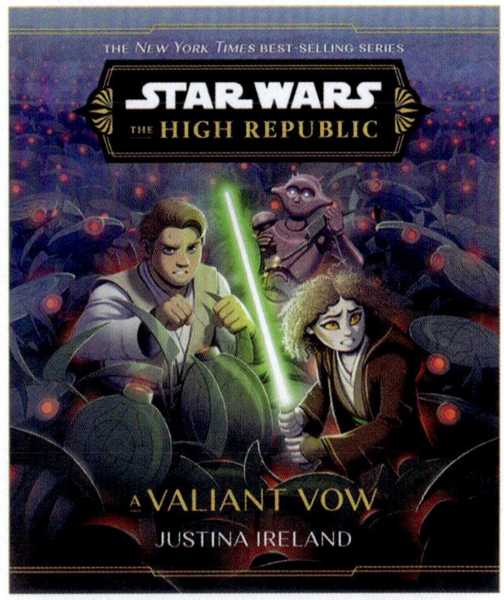

FEAR OF THE JEDI

Writer: Cavan Scott
Artist: Marika Cresta
Cover Artist: Phil Noto
Marvel Comics, 5 Issues

The Jedi face the Nihil over Naboo and Eriadu, led by Keeve Trennis, while Lourna Dee heads out on a mission for vengeance.

THE BATTLE OF ERIADU

Writer: Alyssa Wong
Artist: Elisa Romboli
Cover Artist: Jake Bartok
Dark Horse Comics,
One Shot, Collected in *The High Republic Adventures* Volume 4

Jedi Padawan Gavi Tavitaken finds himself on the opposite side of the Battle of Eriadu from his former best friend, the Nihil Driggit Parse.

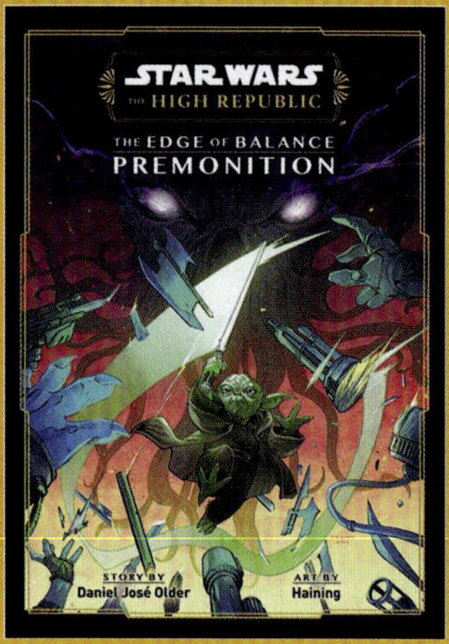

THE EDGE OF BALANCE: PREMONITION

Writer: Daniel José Older
Artist: Haining
Viz Media
After fighting to protect the Jedi Temple on Banchii, Yoda is lured into a trap by none other than leader of the Nihil, Marchion Ro.

THE EDGE OF BALANCE VOL. 4

Writers: Daniel José Older, Shima Shinya
Artist: Mizuki Sakakibara
Viz Media
Jedi Knight Lily Tora-Asi defends the Jedi Temple on Banchii from Baron Boolan with the help of Arkoff and Sav Malagán.

The High Republic: Tales from the Occlusion Zone

Author: Lydia Kang
Artist: Jake Lunt Davies
***Star Wars Insider*, Titan Comics**

"I'm not used to doing short stories in a serialized format, so there was a little bit of a learning curve to make sure that I was getting the stories right," admits Lydia Kang. "It was challenging, but I'm also proud of what we did with those characters and how they get through it. I had a lot of fun writing them."

"The Fate of Eriadu"
***Star Wars Insider* #229**
Joss and Pikka Adren return to an Eriadu under Nihil occupation.

"Sparks Fly"
***Star Wars Insider* #230**
Pikka searches for Joss while joining the fight as the Battle of Eriadu begins.

"Out With a Bang"
***Star Wars Insider* #231**
RDC officers Elping Tsoo and Visma Tarko fight back against the Nihil at the Battle of Eriadu.

"The Will to Fight"
***Star Wars Insider* #232**
Pikka and Josh Adren face more than a battle with scav droids.

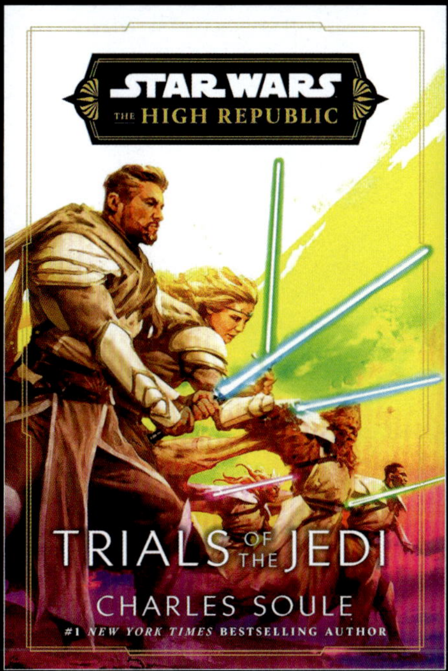

Trials of the Jedi

Writer: Charles Soule
Random House Worlds, Adult novel
Led by Avar Kriss and Elzar Mann, nine Jedi head to the Nameless homeworld to find a way to stop them once and for all while the blight ravages the galaxy and Marchion Ro lies in wait.

"When I was working on *Light Of The Jedi,* I was mostly focused on kicking this thing off rather than concluding it," says Charles Soule about his two novels that bookend the series. "But it seemed likely fairly early on, or at least possible, that I'd write the last book, so I started considering how it might work in the final beats. I had a pretty solid structure for the ending of the story as long ago as 2023, although it might have been earlier. When you're connecting with other authors' work the way we had to with *The High Republic,* you want to make sure you're planning ahead!"

THE BEACON

Writer: Cavan Scott
Artist: Marika Cresta
Cover Artist: Phil Noto
Marvel Comics, One Shot
Collected in *The High Republic: Fear of the Jedi*
The story comes to an end in this final volume which sees friends and allies from across *The High Republic* saga gather one last time.

"Everything I've written has been leading towards this final moment and those final pages with Keeve, which I think is one of the last things printed in this final phase," says Cavan Scott. "That's a big responsibility as well. Keeve might have one of the final things to say in *The High Republic* initiative."

STAR WARS
THE HIGH REPUBLIC

Chronological Reader's Guide

PHASE I: LIGHT OF THE JEDI

Light of the Jedi
Writer: Charles Soule
Publisher: Del Rey
Release date: Jan 5, 2021

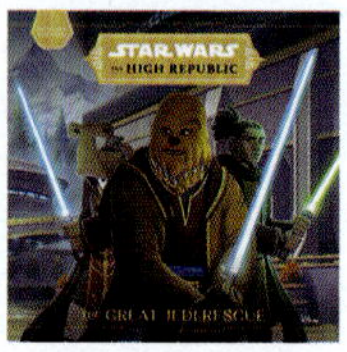

The Great Jedi Rescue
Writer: Cavan Scott
Publisher: Disney Lucasfilm Press
Release date: Jan 5, 2021
** Note that this story takes place concurrent with* Light of the Jedi.

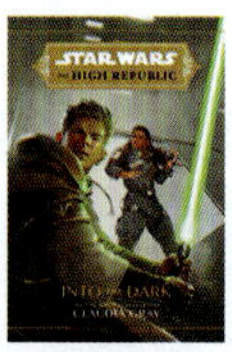

Into the Dark
Writer: Claudia Gray
Publisher: Disney Lucasfilm Press
Release date: Feb 2, 2021
**Note that this story takes place concurrent with* Light of the Jedi.

Star Wars: The High Republic Adventures (Ongoing Series)
Writer: Daniel José Older
Artist: Harvey Tolibao
Publisher: IDW Publishing
Release date: February 3, 2021

A Test of Courage
Writer: Justina Ireland
Publisher: Disney Lucasfilm Press
Release date: Jan 5, 2021

Star Wars: The High Republic (Ongoing Series)
Writer: Cavan Scott
Artist: Ario Anindito
Publisher: Marvel
Release date: Sep 7, 2021
**Note that while this story begins after the events of* A Test of Courage, *subsequent issues take place throughout* The High Republic.

The High Republic Adventures: The Monster of Temple Peak (Limited Series)
Writer: Cavan Scott
Artist: Rachel Stott
Publisher: IDW Publishing
Release date: Aug 11, 2021

The Edge of Balance, Vol. 1
Writers: Shima Shinya and Justina Ireland
Artist: Mizuki Sakakibara
Publisher: VIZ Media
Release date: Sep 7, 2021

The Rising Storm
Writer: Cavan Scott
Publisher: Del Rey
Release date: Jun 29, 2021

Showdown at the Fair
Writer: George Mann
Publisher: Disney Lucasfilm Press
Release date: Oct 5, 2021
**Note that this story takes place concurrent with* The Rising Storm.

Race to Crashpoint Tower
Writer: Daniel José Older
Publisher: Del Rey
Release date: Jun 29, 2021
**Note that this story takes place concurrent with* The Rising Storm.

Trail of Shadows (5-Issue Miniseries)
Writer: Daniel José Older
Artist: David Wachter
Publisher: Marvel
Release date: Oct 13, 2021

Out of the Shadows
Writer: Justina Ireland
Publisher: Disney Lucasfilm Press
Release date: Jul 27, 2021
**Note that this story takes place concurrent with* The Rising Storm.

Tempest Runner (Audiobook Original)
Writer: Cavan Scott
Publisher: Del Rey
Release date: Aug 31, 2021

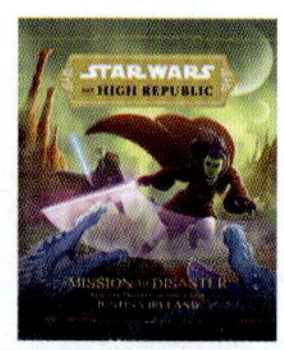

Mission to Disaster
Writer: Justina Ireland
Publisher: Disney Lucasfilm Press
Release date: Jan 4, 2022

The Fallen Star
Writer: Claudia Gray
Publisher: Del Rey
Release date: Jan 4, 2022

PHASE I

Midnight Horizon
Writer: Daniel José Older
Publisher: Disney Lucasfilm Press
Release date: Feb 2, 2022
**Note that this story takes place concurrent with* The Fallen Star.

The Battle for Starlight
Writer: George Mann
Publisher: Disney Lucasfilm Press
Release date: Feb 2, 2022

The Edge of Balance, Vol. 2
Writers: Shima Shinya and Daniel José Older
Artist: Mizuki Sakakibara
Publisher: VIZ Media
Release date: Feb 22, 2022

Eye of the Storm (2-Issue Miniseries)
Writer: Charles Soule
Artist: Guillermo Sanna
Publisher: Marvel
Release date: Jan 12, 2022

PHASE II: QUEST OF THE JEDI

Quest for the Hidden City
Writer: George Mann
Publisher: Disney Lucasfilm Press
Release date: Nov 1, 2022

Path of Deceit
Writer: Justina Ireland and Tessa Gratton
Publisher: Disney Lucasfilm Press
Release date: Oct 4, 2022

Convergence
Writer: Zoraida Córdova
Publisher: Del Rey
Release date: Nov 22, 2022

Star Wars: The High Republic Adventures (Ongoing Series)
Writer: Daniel José Older
Artist: Toni Bruno
Publisher: Dark Horse
Release date: Nov 30, 2022

Star Wars: The High Republic (Ongoing Series)
Writer: Cavan Scott
Artist: Ario Anindito
Publisher: Marvel
Release date: Oct 12, 2022

Star Wars: The High Republic - The Blade (Miniseries)
Writer: Charles Soule
Artist: Marco Castiello
Publisher: Marvel
Release date: Dec 28, 2022

The Battle of Jedha (Audio Drama)
Writers: George Mann
Publisher: Random House
Release date: Jan 3, 2023 (audio only);
Feb 14, 2023 (script)

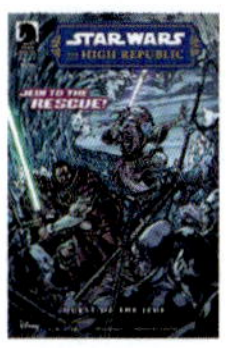

Quest of the Jedi
Writer: Claudia Gray
Artist: Fico Ossio
Publisher: Dark Horse
Release date: Mar 1, 2023

Quest for Planet X
Writer: Tessa Gratton
Publisher: Disney Lucasfilm Press
Release date: Apr 4, 2023

The Nameless Terror (Miniseries)
Writer: George Mann
Artist: Eduardo Mello and Ornella Savarese
Publisher: Dark Horse
Release date: Feb 22, 2023

Cataclysm
Writer: Lydia Kang
Publisher: Del Rey
Release date: Apr 4, 2023

Path of Vengeance
Writer: Cavan Scott
Publisher: Disney Lucasfilm Press
Release date: May 2, 2023

PHASE III: TRIALS OF THE JEDI

Tales of Light & Life

Writers: Zoraida Córdova, Tessa Gratton, Claudia Gray, Justina Ireland, Lydia Kang, George Mann, Daniel José Older, Cavan Scott, Charles Soule, and Alyssa Wong
Publisher: Disney Lucasfilm Press
Release Date: Sept 5, 2023

The High Republic — Shadows of Starlight (Miniseries)

Writer: Charles Soule
Artist: Ibraim Roberson
Publisher: Marvel
Release Date: Oct 4, 2023

Escape from Valo

Writers: Daniel José Older and Alyssa Wong
Publisher: Disney Lucasfilm Press
Release date: Jan 30, 2024

The Eye of Darkness

Writer: George Mann
Publisher: Random House Worlds
Release Date: Nov 14, 2023

The High Republic Adventures (2023) Ongoing Series)

Writer: Daniel José Older
Artist: Harvey Tolibao
Publisher: Dark Horse
Release Date: Dec 6, 2023

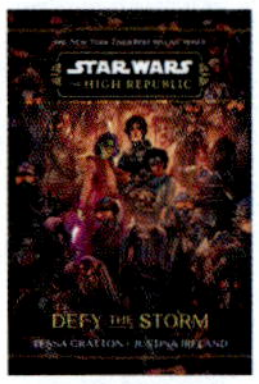

Defy the Storm

Writers: Tessa Gratton and Justina Ireland
Publisher: Disney Lucasfilm Press
Release Date: Mar 5, 2024

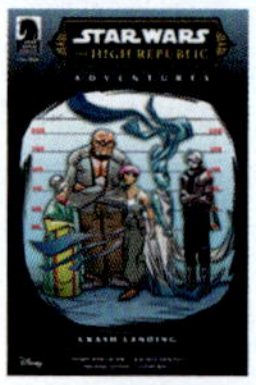

The High Republic Adventures — Crash Landing (One-Shot)

Writer: Daniel José Older
Artist: Rachele Aragno
Publisher: Dark Horse
Release Date: Mar 27, 2024

The High Republic Adventures — Saber for Hire (Mini-Series)

Writer: Cavan Scott
Artist: Rachael Stott
Publisher: Dark Horse
Release date: Apr 17, 2024

The High Republic (2023) (Ongoing Series)

Writer: Cavan Scott
Artist: Ario Anindito
Publisher: Marvel
Release date: Nov 8, 2023

Temptation of the Force

Writer: Tessa Gratton
Publisher: Random House Worlds
Release Date: Jun 11, 2024

Beware the Nameless

Writer: Zoraida Córdova
Publisher: Disney Lucasfilm Press
Release Date: Aug 27, 2024

Tears of the Nameless

Writer: George Mann
Publisher: Disney Lucasfilm Press
Release Date: Sept 24, 2024

Seeds of Starlight

Writer: George Mann
Publisher: Audible Originals
Release Date: Nov 14, 2024

The High Republic Adventures — Crash and Burn (One-Shot)

Writer: Daniel José Older
Artist: Nick Brokenshire
Publisher: Dark Horse
Release Date: Sept 4, 2024

The Edge of Balance, Vol. 3

Writers: Shima Shinya and Daniel José Older
Artist: Mizuki Sakakibara
Publisher: VIZ Media
Release date: Aug 13, 2024

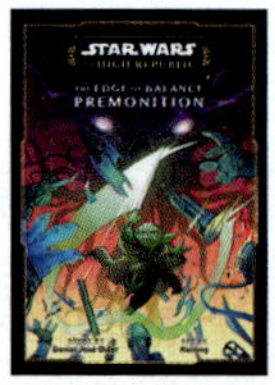

The Edge of Balance: Premonition

Writer: Daniel José Older
Artist: Haining
Publisher: VIZ Media
Release date: Apr 8, 2025

PHASE III: TRIALS OF THE JEDI

The Edge of Balance, Vol. 4

Writers: Shima Shinya and Daniel José Older
Artist: Mizuki Sakakibara
Publisher: Viz Media
Release Date: Apr 22, 2025

The High Republic Adventures — Echoes of Fear **(Mini-Series)**

Writer: George Mann
Artist: Vincenzo Federici
Publisher: Dark Horse
Release date: Sept 4, 2024

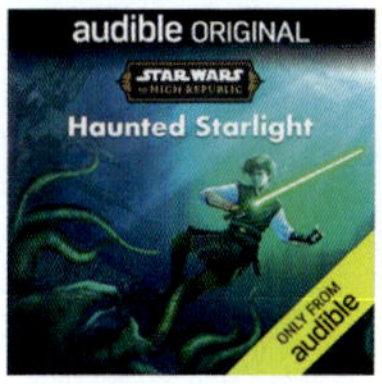

Haunted Starlight

Writer: George Mann
Publisher: Audible Originals
Release Date: Mar 6, 2025

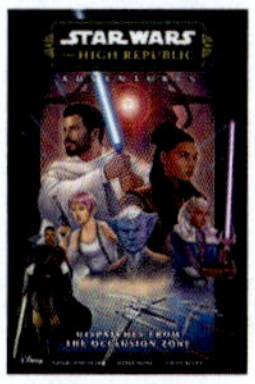

The High Republic Adventures — Dispatches from the Occlusion Zone **(Mini-Series)**

Writers: Daniel José Older, Alyssa Wong, and Cavan Scott
Artists: Paris Alleyne, Valeria "Lux" Favoccia, and Lucas Marangon
Publisher: Dark Horse
Release date: Oct 9, 2024

Tempest Breaker (Audiobook Original)

Writer: Cavan Scott
Publisher: Random House Worlds
Release date: Dec 3, 2024 (audio); May 13, 2025 (script)

The High Republic Adventures — The Wedding Spectacular

Writer: Daniel José Older
Artist: Harvey Tolibao
Publisher: Dark Horse
Release date: Dec 18, 2024

The High Republic Adventures Annual **(One-Shot)**

Writers: Justina Ireland, Alyssa Wong, Cavan Scott, Zoraida Córdova, Charles Soule, and Rosemary Soule
Artists: Liana Kangas, Nick Brokenshire, Andy Duggan, Lucas Marangon, and Colin Craker
Publisher: Dark Horse
Release date: Jan 29, 2025

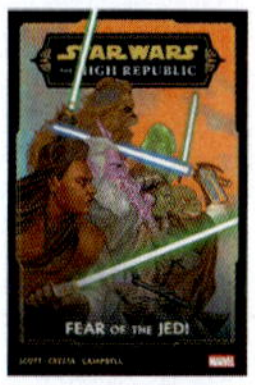

The High Republic — Fear of the Jedi **(Mini-Series)**

Writer: Cavan Scott
Artist: Marika Cresta
Publisher: Marvel
Release date: Feb 19, 2025

Into the Light

Writer: Claudia Gray
Publisher: Disney Lucasfilm Press
Release Date: Apr 1, 2025

The Battle of Eriadu

Writer: Alyssa Wong
Artist: Elisa Romboli
Publisher: Dark Horse
Release Date: Apr 30, 2025

A Valiant Vow

Writer: Justina Ireland
Publisher: Disney Lucasfilm Press
Release Date: May 6, 2025

Trials of the Jedi

Writer: Charles Soule
Publisher: Random House Worlds
Release Date: Jun 17, 2025

Star Wars: The High Republic - The Beacon

Writer: Cavan Scott
Publisher: Marvel
Release Date: Jul 30, 2025